HEMANT NAYAK

The Tools of the Ghost

First published by Endless Earth Publishing Mil 2023

Copyright © 2023 by Hemant Nayak

All rights reserved. No part of this publication may be reproduced, stored or transmitted in any form or by any means, electronic, mechanical, photocopying, recording, scanning, or otherwise without written permission from the publisher. It is illegal to copy this book, post it to a website, or distribute it by any other means without permission.

This novel is entirely a work of fiction. The names, characters and incidents portrayed in it are the work of the author's imagination. Any resemblance to actual persons, living or dead, events or localities is entirely coincidental.

First edition

This book was professionally typeset on Reedsy. Find out more at reedsy.com

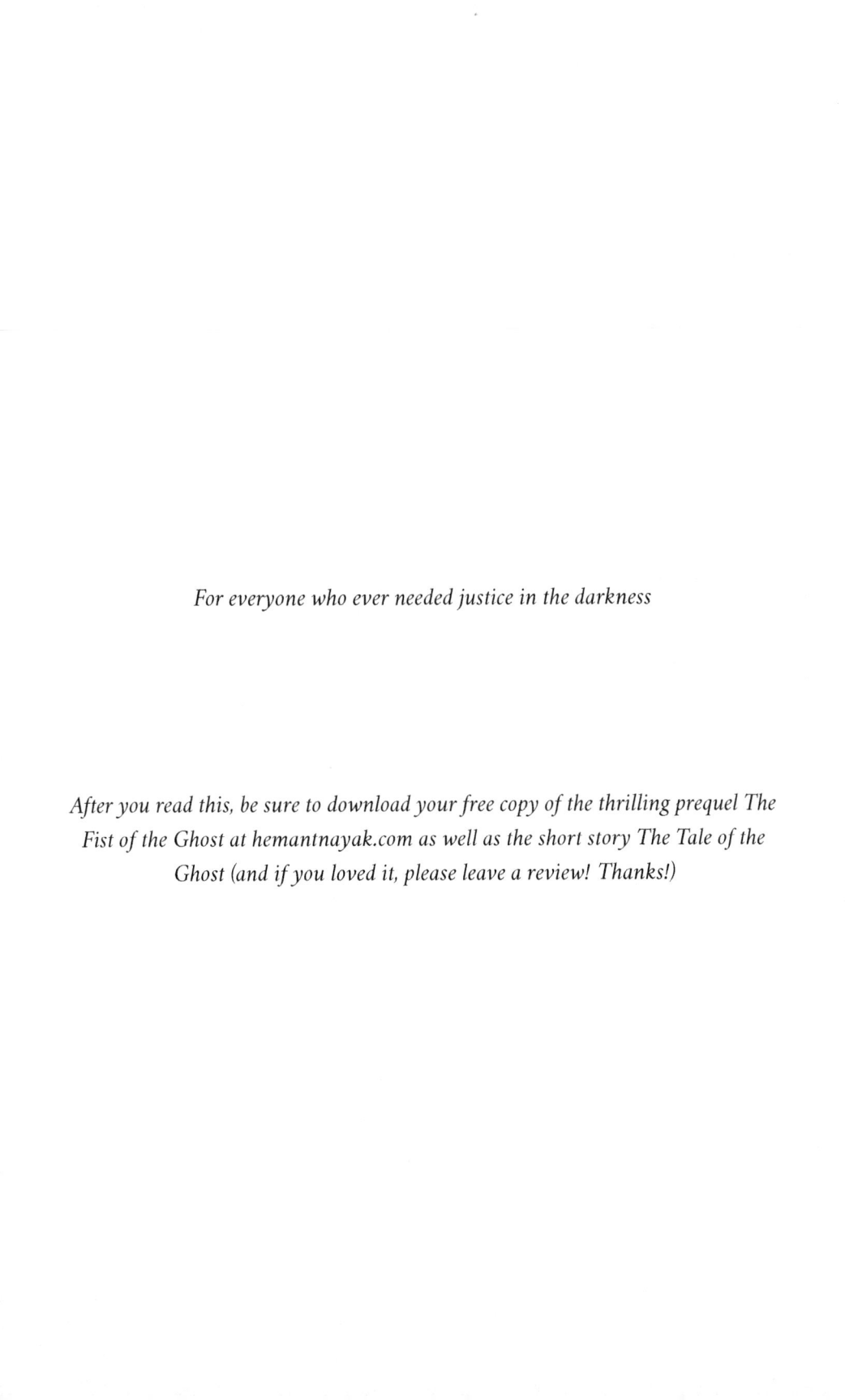

For everyone who ever needed justice in the darkness

After you read this, be sure to download your free copy of the thrilling prequel The Fist of the Ghost at hemantnayak.com as well as the short story The Tale of the Ghost (and if you loved it, please leave a review! Thanks!)

Contents

Chapter 1	1
Chapter 2	5
Chapter 3	15
Chapter 4	25
Chapter 5	29
Chapter 6	41
Chapter 7	53
Chapter 8	64
Chapter 9	73
Chapter 10	83
Chapter 11	98
Chapter 12	114
Chapter 13	123
Chapter 14	146
Chapter 15	154
Chapter 16	158
Chapter 17	169
Chapter 18	176
Chapter 19	185
Chapter 20	193
Chapter 21	204
Chapter 22	209
Chapter 23	212
Chapter 24	217
Chapter 25	234

Chapter 1

The Lord may forgive your sins, but the Dead remember, and the Tools of the Ghost are without number—excerpt from Psalm 151 of the Apocryphal Psalms of David

Warsaw, Poland, October 10, 1972

The monastery door shuddered.

Bishop Jako Krol clutched a foot-long wooden cross and whispered the final words of a desperate prayer. His eyes stayed fixed on a door that should have been invulnerable while candles along the wall sputtered with every blow. He'd employed every sacred protection he knew to defend this space.

Still, the door trembled.

"Holy Mary, Mother of God, pray for us sinners, now and at the hour of our death." Nine altar boys huddled around Krol, chanting in unison within the cramped space, heavy with the smell of incense and sweat.

"The Ghost won't break through, will he, Father?" Young Anatol stared at him, wide eyed, his voice an unsteady adolescent tenor. The boy was a strange one, prone to disturbing visions. Krol wondered if he was touched by madness or if, by some work of God, the boy possessed a window into a world unseen.

He waved a hand over the boy in blessing. "The Lord protects us, my son. There is no greater power. No demon from Hell shall harm us." Bishop Krol had struck a perfect deal. No demon or angel could touch him.

Anatol looked at him with limited belief when belief was the only thing that might save him, but he resumed his prayers and turned his eyes back to the door.

If only they were facing a demon from Hell, they would stand a far better chance.

With a groan of final defeat, the oak door gave way, hinges ripping from the wall. An iron bar split off the frame and spun high into the air, piercing the chapel's stained-glass portrayal of the crucifixion. A shower of color crashed around the doorway as the church's most treasured artwork rained upon them.

Krol crouched in terror, holding the cross. Next to him, a boy cried out as glass pierced his arm, and his white robe bloomed red. When the cascade finally ended, both Krol's hands were torn and there was blood on his lips, but he was alive. He tensed for what was to come.

A cold wind howled through the empty space as the Warsaw winter banished the thick pall of incense and smoke. Great crows swept in on the icy air, their wings spread wide. The birds took up perches in the chapel like judges in their own court.

There were eleven crows, the same number each time.

A tall figure, wearing a tattered gray coat, crashed through the mangled doorway, waving a ragged hat like a drunken scarecrow. His skin was lifeless silver, his eyes shining coal. Over his shoulder he dragged a bulging sack big enough for a corpse.

From beneath his robes, Krol drew a Luger pistol and fired eight times. The children cowered as the echoes of the shots died down. At this range, Krol could not miss.

Yet, the shadow in the doorway remained.

The figure waved his ruined hat before him, sweeping away the stink of gunpowder and incense. His boots crunched broken glass. He reached up to his face and drew a two-inch-long shard of leaded blue window from the center of his eye.

"Whosoever shall smite thee on thy right cheek, turn to him the other." The piece of offending glass fell to the floor with a clink as punctuation. "But why, I ask, when an eye for an eye seems so much more reasonable?" His voice was the harsh rasp of someone whose throat had been cut.

CHAPTER 1

Krol held the cross before him like a shield against the invader. God would protect him. God would forgive him. He had been so sure.

"Pray for us now at the hour of our death," the children continued their plea to God.

The boys' words bolstered Krol's faith. He squared his shoulders. "Leave this place, Outcast. I know who you are. The sin you committed is the only crime that can never be forgiven."

The figure ran a hand over his coat and ignored Krol. He looked up, addressing the crows. "A button. I've lost a button. You know how hard these are to replace?"

The world went silent except for the cold and ceaseless wind. A crow clacked its beak as if in disapproval of the delay. Krol measured the distance to the door. Perhaps he could make it.

"Here, sir." With a swift tug, the boy, Anatol, tore a button off his own robe. He tossed it high. The white disk spun in slow motion like a sacramental wafer until it disappeared in the apparition's hand.

The figure in the doorway turned the button over in his hand and said nothing. The awful silence extended until Krol thought his heart would beat out of his chest. Before Krol could will his legs to run, the figure raised his head.

"As hard as I try, I cannot remember the last time I received a gift. One wish, boy, for your button. Tell me, who here shall live?"

Anatol did not hesitate. He pointed at the injured child on the floor. "My brother, sir." He swallowed. "And the other boys as well."

Krol glared at the child. "Anatol?" But the boy turned away.

The figure stepped forward. "He did not name you, priest."

"Go back," Krol commanded, desperation creeping into his voice. "Do you understand what you have done? Not even Hell dared take you in. *You* are the root of all evil."

The figure in the doorway stilled, his dark eyes blazing. "I no longer pray for forgiveness, priest. I have no need for yours." He reached into his sack.

Krol's mind raced with dark visions, imagining the Ghost's hand closing around a horrible weapon of torture.

3

Wind screamed through the hole in the chapel where the stained-glass crucifixion no longer protected anyone from winter's blasts. The crows spiraled high, beating the gusts down upon Krol with outstretched wings.

Cold seeped into the priest's hands, found his heart, touched his soul. He dropped the wooden cross and it snapped with a crack. The candles wavered and went out.

Jako Krol remembered the psalms he had forgotten and screamed an endless scream. As the winds surrounded him, he recalled the warning the old priest had whispered through the confession booth after he absolved Krol's first murder.

"Forgiveness is no province of the Dead, and the Tools of the Ghost are without number."

Chapter 2

Present day, Seattle

Special Agent Kiran Patel slammed the phone down, then adjusted it to make sure it sat straight. That call had gone to shit fast. She sharpened two rather chewed-upon pencils and laid them perfectly parallel. Her long, thin fingers placed them gently like chess pieces on a board, just so, as if how the erasers lined up made a difference. Spartacus, the smelly beast of a dog sprawled across her kitchen floor, raised a huge black ear, and promptly resumed snoring.

All her life, Kiran had secretly hoped that straightening out the little things, placing them in lines, setting them in order, might help bring the chaos of the greater world into line as well. Like a magic spell, or voodoo doll, except with the intent of making things better instead of ruthlessly torturing someone. Of course, it hadn't worked.

In her second year with the FBI, nothing had fallen into place and certainly not the case she was working on now. Still, none of the evidence of her failure stopped the habits. The workings of her mind and heart followed their own plans and were hard to persuade with logic alone.

The logical thing to do would be to stay home and follow orders. She should kick back, maintain a sense of personal detachment, and wait to see how things turned out. Instead, she put on a jacket and checked the clock. A quarter to nine. She had thirty minutes to get to an abandoned church on Fifth and Pine, the one place in Seattle where she'd been forbidden to go. She looked in the mirror and sighed at a hair out of place and a slight tear in the sleeve of her powder-blue jacket. A less-torn jacket would have been nice, but the dog had chewed up her coat and it was pouring.

The call from the Director of Criminal Investigations had been unambiguous.

"Don't tell me I'm being unjust, Patel. Justice is a myth. How did you make it through Quantico? You've uncovered some leads, but you belong behind a desk. There's no room for forgiveness here. You and Anatol keep the hell out of this."

Belonged behind a desk? Kiran picked up one of the pencils and put it down before she started chewing. The Director was probably right. She wasn't sure she'd want someone with her level of anxiety on this case either. Still, she had every right to be there when they brought the kids out. If she hadn't found that church, they'd still be running in stupid circles. And by that she meant extremely tiny circles. True, Jefferson would glue her butt behind a desk if anyone found out, but she could go wherever the hell she wanted to if she was out for a stroll or shopping or doing whatever normal people did.

Before she left, she filled a bowl of water for the black shag beast she was dog-sitting for Anatol. The giant mutt thing was probably still digesting the coat she couldn't afford to replace. He made the whole place smell like damp dog, which made her mother hate to visit, which was the real reason she let Spartacus stay. She kicked the LSAT prep book toward the beast, hoping it would be chewed to pulp as fast as the MCAT book. The sticky note on the book's cover read "You can do it too, Cutie!" in her mother's annoyingly perfect cursive.

She aimed a finger at Spartacus who actually raised his enormous head. "Eat any more clothes and you're evicted. You'll be on the curb with your squeaky toys, waiting for the pound. Imagine yourself, all hairy and tough, surrounded by pink unicorn squeakers. You'll never live that down."

Spartacus flopped on his side and sighed like a thunderstorm, which was the exact level of attention most people paid to her ultimatums. Her partner, Anatol, claimed his joints ached and he needed a break from walking Spartacus, but Kiran suspected he was tired of Spartacus never listening to a word anyone said.

Kiran locked the door twice before going back in to adjust the brass Ganesha on the mantlepiece and confirm she'd turned off the oven for the fourth time. She threw on a bright orange scarf to make it clear she was only a common citizen out for coffee and grabbed the steel-rimmed glasses she'd left on the table. She took the stairs. Elevators could get stuck, which reminded Kiran of being buried alive, which made her palms sweat. Her watch read nine. *Fifteen minutes.* Now, she had to run.

Water soaked her pants as she sprinted through puddles, past brand-new buildings and giant construction cranes gone silent. The Seattle Kiran had known since she was a child had changed. The dingy town built around fishing and Pike Place Market had been seduced and seeded by an endless infusion of tech money. Shiny condos reflecting the clouds had erupted out of nowhere while she wasn't looking. Rents blew up with them. People who could no longer afford their own city either fled to the outskirts or to their vans underneath an overpass. The saucer-shaped Space Needle still dominated the horizon, but the old city, filled with the beat of ocean waves and sailors' stories, faded away a little each year with every look the other way. It reminded Kiran of how they'd built right on top of the previous Seattle in the early 19th century after fires and floods. When she had been in fourth grade, her teacher told her class that the old tunnels still ran under the city and that people were still buried down there who had never been found. Kiran had sat at her school desk imagining the spirits drifting through tunnels under her feet and shivered.

The long stretches of dark puddles Kiran jumped over reflected only streetlamps and night sky. At this hour, she'd usually be running past crowds of people still out, hitting the bars and restaurants on Capitol Hill. But the streets were deserted. Two months ago, eleven children had vanished on the same day in the most brazen coordinated kidnapping in US history. Eight from the Seattle area, three from Portland, which made the crime an interstate FBI matter and dropped it in her lap. Something worse than spirits was haunting Seattle and no one blamed the citizenry for hiding in their homes.

Thus far, four cops and two agents were dead: two found impaled in a grisly fashion, others missing limbs, and not a single child recovered. The investigation had turned up nothing about the twisted assholes who had orchestrated the crimes other than that they called themselves Death to Twelve, a name both cryptic and disturbing. The only major lead was a note sent specifically to Kiran's partner, written by one of the missing children, saying she wanted to come home and see her dog. The words on the bottom of that note had not been penned by a child. *When the 12th is taken, the King will once again sit on his throne.* The unsanctioned release of that letter had resulted in every parent in the city hiding away their children for fear of them becoming that twelfth child. If that wasn't creepy enough, the note was signed with the cult's name written in blood. Kiran didn't let herself think about whose blood they'd used. Why they'd singled out Anatol to receive their message was something she still thought about even now, as she splashed through the rain.

Three blocks from the church, she noted a van parked on an empty side street. Standard black twelve passenger Chevy, three scratches on the driver's door, brand new tires. Windows tinted too dark to make out any sign of life. That would be SWAT, running through their final check. A UPS driver smoking a cigarette while leaning against his truck was the only other person she passed. He looked like he could use an infusion of iron. She'd never seen people so pale outside this city. The driver scratched his face and smiled at Kiran which succeeded in creeping her out. She ran faster.

With six minutes left, Kiran turned the corner on Pine, stepped into a dark alley next to the Imperial Ramen Queen, and brushed the dripping hair out of her eyes. The rain had stopped as Seattle rains tended to do, leaving behind puddles and mist. She shifted next to a dumpster, maintaining a view of the street. On the other side of the block, the steeple of St. James towered over everything, dominating the street. The Gothic limestone structure looked out-of-place on a road full of small businesses. Before she ground her teeth away, she pulled out a piece of clove gum and started chewing. The smell of cigarette smoke and cheap cologne told her she wasn't alone.

Special agent Anatol Zagorski stepped out from behind the dumpster and put out his cigarette on the steel lid. Her partner had cut himself shaving, had a fresh coffee stain on his coat, and hadn't changed his socks since yesterday.

CHAPTER 2

Anatol shook his head as he handed Kiran a fresh pack of clove gum. "You look terrible. I told you to sleep, but do you listen? No." Almost three decades in the bureau had done nothing to diminish Anatol's Polish accent or sense of fatalism. Kiran had wondered at the bureau chief's motives when he'd paired them together. The combination of the youngest and most senior member was either for laughs or because they couldn't find anyone else willing to work with her.

Kiran jammed another piece of gum in her mouth and started winding a strand of hair behind her ear. "Sleep is hard with your giant dog snoring. And he ate my coat. I'm charging you for that." It was easy to blame Spartacus, but they both knew why she wasn't sleeping. Instead of counting sheep, the names of all those kids ran through her head half the night. Alternating emotions of depression and rage were terrible sedatives. Professional detachment was a trait Kiran did not possess.

"You have an anger problem," Anatol said.

"You sound like my therapist." She opened the fresh pack Anatol gave her. "And I told the world to stop pissing me off, but did the world listen? No. So I'm not the only one who doesn't listen." She started unwrapping pieces of gum. This was going to be a multi-pack night.

Anatol ran his fingers over the iron fishhook hanging from his silver necklace. The hook was big enough to catch a shark or some other giant denizen of the deep, and sharp enough too. A fishhook had always struck Kiran as an odd item of jewelry to wear against your skin, but she didn't question old men's fashion choices. The lines of a jet-black tattoo snaked down the back of Anatol's hand and disappeared into the cuff of his shirt. She had often wondered how drunk her partner must have been to visit a Polish tattoo parlor and pay them to brand him with that weird mark.

Anatol handed her two more packs. "Something's wrong here. I feel it. What do you see?"

Anatol didn't worry without reason.

"Now you want the angry person's opinion?" Kiran chewed and considered. Anatol was one of the few people who had faith in her hunches. "I passed SWAT on the way. They'll have a second van coming in from the opposite direction to cover the back. The street is quiet. No one else on duty unless you count the two plainclothes cops in the noodle shop, and they seemed pretty intent on eating."

Kiran straightened her glasses and ran her eyes over the church once more. "No shades drawn, and it's dark inside. Even the yard lights are off," she said. SWAT would have an easy time getting close to the building without the lighting. "No movement since I got here. No one on watch. None of the jerks even walking past a window. Three main points to hit the building, front entrance, back door, or through the storm cellar on the west side." She shivered at the thought of having to go in through the basement, which made her think of crypts and being buried alive. She wound her hair around a finger. "There are four crows perched on the front gate which is ajar—"

Anatol raised a hand. "Enough. We wait."

If Kiran was right, the kids were in that church. The priest had left town for some emergency, he hadn't held mass in weeks. She'd spoken to every parishioner she could track down and an actual nun. One of the churchgoers swore she heard children's voices when she tried to come by. Kiran's leads had set this entire raid in motion. She chewed harder. Eleven children. So many crushed families and a city afraid of the dark. What worried her most was that the kidnappers had made no demands for ransom, given no explanation for what they'd done. Two years of working in the bureau and the darkness of the human soul still surprised her. That was another secret she kept to herself. Robbing banks, stealing cars, even dramatic shootouts she understood on an instinctual level; greed was real, thieves were sneaky. But taking children? She woke from her fitful sleep every night and hoped that she had got it wrong, that it was all a bad dream, but no. Evil existed, and it had damn well arrived.

The door of the Ramen Queen screeched open on rusted hinges and two figures—the first tall, the second shorter and broad-shouldered—stepped into the alley. Kiran sighed. They didn't need the police to distract them, especially not these disasters.

Anatol cleared his throat. "Getting crowded in here, gentlemen. Don't get trigger happy."

CHAPTER 2

The first figure stepped closer and leaned against the wall. "Your lack of faith wounds me, Anatol. Natural charm and good looks are the only weapons I need. What up, Kiran?"

Greg Reese was a Black transplant from Detroit, a head taller than Anatol, and if Kiran forced herself to admit it, as good looking as he claimed in his black leather jacket and jeans. Even his close-trimmed beard looked sharp. Unfortunately, he was overly aware of that fact and had the bearing of a king amongst commoners. His partner, Enrique Gonzales, grew up in Mexico and was half Zapotec. Gonzales managed to mesh a wooden bead necklace and a long sleeve maroon shirt and make it all work. His wild hair and rough and tumble look made him appear more like an outdoor adventure hero than a Seattle cop. The two detectives had been on this case since the beginning. As far as she could see, they'd made no contribution whatsoever to anything.

Kiran mock-shielded her eyes. "I'm currently being blinded by blazing charisma is what's up, Reese. Maybe you could find another alley to deploy your deadly charm weapon? We're trying to work."

Reese made no move to vacate. "Work? For real? Gonzo was just asking me over a bowl of noodles. 'Why are the feds here?' And I said, 'Gonzo, only the best of the best would notice that. Let's go see what the Polish spy master and the Rookie are up to.'" Here he gave Kiran's torn puffy blue jacket a once over. "Now this is most definitely a SWAT operation. It seems to me that you both are fish far outside your stream."

Anatol cleared his throat. "The best detectives haven't done shit on this case and the best detectives better shut the hell up so we can hear." He raised a hand, displaying a black walkie talkie. "SWAT let me in on their coms link."

Kiran decided once again that she loved her partner more than anyone.

Reese narrowed his eyes. "The best are always underappreciated."

"Everyone knows Gonzales is the handsome one," Kiran said. She wasn't lying. She was a fan of the rugged look.

Gonzales fingered his wooden beads and manifested a smile so brief she thought she'd imagined it. "Word," he said in the softest of voices.

Anatol glared at them then checked his watch. "Two minutes." He turned on the radio and the murmur of SWAT going over the last details of the plan came over.

"Go," the radio crackled then went silent.

A gray van came into view one minute later, turned the corner, and drove behind the church.

"At least there won't be anyone shooting at us for once," Reese said.

"Correcto." Gonzales' bad knee clicked as he leaned against a wall.

Kiran sighed and did her best to ignore the SPD detectives. The two men struck her as better suited to Shakespearean tragic acting than police work. She counted ten more seconds, running her orange scarf between her fingers, before she gave in to her anxiety. The other van should have been here by now. She spit out her gum and started on two new pieces.

"Something's wrong," she said. Three blocks should have taken no more than a minute. The UPS driver reappeared in her mind, tipping back the last of his beer, casting a hungry look in her direction. She bit her tongue and swallowed the gum. Shit. Her brain shifted into a different gear she was all too familiar with. That driver wasn't carrying packages.

She grabbed Anatol's arm. "Tell them to abort. The cult hit the other team. They know they're coming." She should have questioned that driver.

Anatol looked her in the eyes and said nothing. Then he clicked the radio. "Chen, we think the other team may be in trouble. You've got reason to abort."

Static crackled across the com and Kiran was seized by the certainty that SWAT was already in deep trouble.

Chen's voice proved her wrong. "What the hell are you talking about, Anatol? We've received no word from Bravo team of any problem."

The radio crackled again before she could try to explain.

"This is Bravo team. We're in position." The voice came across calm and prepared, making Kiran look like a complete idiot.

Chen's sigh of relief carried over the radio. "I told you to stay off the damn com, Anatol. We don't need more of your partner's distractions. If she's wrong about this church, I'm going to kick both your asses personally."

"We still have no eyes on B team," Anatol said.

Something went tight in Kiran's chest, and she found it hard to swallow. She could have kissed her partner at that moment. Anatol might say she looked

CHAPTER 2

terrible, might tell her she was late, disorganized, too unsure of herself. But he, at least, didn't doubt her. It was odd that one of the greatest friendships she'd found was with a grouch who never seemed thrilled to have her as his partner. In a department that questioned her right to exist, his trust had sustained her.

The radio hummed with static. "This is Bravo team. We're on the west side of the building." The voice was hazy but confident and made Anatol's belief in her look foolish.

"That's enough, Anatol." Chen's voice sounded over the radio. "Bravo is in place. It's a go." Kiran imagined the SWAT team leader rolling his eyes.

A thud of a door being knocked in echoed over the radio and every nerve in Kiran's body sparked. A long silence followed during which the windows of the church glared down at her, dark and foreboding, like the eyes of a monster. SWAT would rush in, control the area, and find the children. She longed for nothing more than to hear SWAT shouting, "Down, get down!" and the voices of safe kids, but silence was all that came over the radio.

Two minutes crept by before she was sure.

"It's too quiet, Anatol. They were impersonating B team. SWAT is walking straight into it." The gears in her head turned again. The church yard swam before her eyes.

Reese gave her a look that said, *You're weirder than I thought*, before shifting his gaze back to the church. "That's insane." Kiran almost punched him.

"Quiet," Anatol said. "Talk, Kiran."

Kiran hesitated. Anatol knew how she thought, the strange way her mind worked, and accepted her. She hated to explain in front of Reese or Gonzales. She hated speaking in public as much as someone prying off her fingernails. But there was no time.

"They knew SWAT was coming and took out half of them before they got here." The image of the oversize UPS van filled her mind. She imagined it sliding across Pine Street, imagined cultists jumping out as the rear doors swung wide. Her heart raced. "They'll have blocked off the main roads to delay help arriving. I bet they have an escape route underneath the church. They'll either blow the whole building or gas them. SWAT may already be dead."

Gonzales lifted an extremely doubtful eyebrow.

"Find your own alley, Enrique," Kiran said. "I take back the handsome thing."

Reese poked his head out the alley and looked down the street. "It's a lot paranoid, Gonzo, but it's a graveyard out here. Too quiet."

Kiran held her breath as her guts twisted. She felt the world shift, felt her whole body tense a moment before the church bells rang.

CLANG... KA-CLANG. The bells tolled like they were being struck with a sledgehammer. An upstairs window shattered, sending glass fragments spraying across the street.

Someone screamed.

"Backup—we need help in here!" Chen shouted over the radio before it went dead.

Kiran's thoughts spun. Why were there no shots fired? Why wasn't SWAT fighting back? "No one else will get there in time." Sometimes, she just knew. "No one else can help."

Anatol reached inside his trench coat and stepped out of the alley. "Stay here, Kiran. Send help when it arrives."

"Death wish." Gonzales pulled out his radio and started calling for backup before shaking it and trying it again. "Mierda. Just static."

"They don't pay us enough for crazy sacrifices," Reese shouted. "Don't be stupid, Anatol. We'll get back up here in time."

Kiran started after her partner. "I wish you were right, Reese. But you're not." She drew her gun and ran toward the sound of a man screaming. Her stomach felt like it was going to drop to her feet. Her mother was probably right: she should have kept the MCAT book.

Chapter 3

The first page of Kiran's fifth grade diary read as follows: "Please God, don't let me become the world's greatest criminal." She'd glanced up at her little brass statue of the Hindu god, Ganesha, while she penciled that line and tried to look as virtuous as possible.

Kiran made sure to keep the secret of the strange way her mind worked. It tended to ruin casual friendships when people learned you saw things naturally from a criminal perspective, imagined how every security system could be beaten, every locked picked. Most kids hadn't studied how to hotwire a car by her age. They surely hadn't practiced on their family station wagon.

Four years after college graduation, Kiran was painfully aware that the only thing that had prevented her from fulfilling her nefarious destiny was fiction. After thousands of childhood hours hiding in a closet with a flashlight, armed with whatever she could steal from her father's book collection, Kiran had grown too attached to the hunt for the murderer to assume the other side. Her criminal instincts had been thwarted.

Anatol knew how her mind worked. She suspected he'd known from the very first time he'd looked at her and agreed to take her under his wing. She had always been sure of Anatol.

Now, rushing after him toward the church, she was suddenly quite unsure of him. She was quite unsure of a great many things. The air grew heavy as she ran, like the clouds above were about to unleash a true thunderstorm far removed from the city's usual drizzle. Great pools of rainwater appeared in her path, reflecting the moonlight and wide stretches of shifting sky. She was struck by the thought that if she splashed into one of these puddles, she might never emerge. Everything seemed off, like they were running into another world they had best avoid.

Her partner stopped and took cover behind the church's neon lawn sign. She crouched beside him. A glance behind confirmed that Reese and Gonzales were still in the alleyway, shouting into their dead radios.

Anatol looked at her and frowned. "You never listen." He drew an enormous gun from his coat, half wood, half filigreed brass, that looked like an oversize eighteenth century dueling pistol. She'd never seen anything like it. He took a deep breath. "I need you to understand that I was a coward, Kiran. I was too afraid to summon the Ghost again."

It was the strangest thing she'd ever heard him say and she had no idea what it might mean. "What have you been smoking and where did you get that weird gun?" He was starting to make her even more nervous than her baseline. Anatol wasn't allowed to be afraid or start losing his mind. She was the one with the license to worry.

Anatol glared at her again. "Listen for once and stay put. Wait for backup. Your gun is not going to help." He dashed toward the church's front entrance with a speed she hadn't known he still possessed.

"Oh yeah, I'll stay." She sprinted behind him, her mind spinning. Something else was going on here. What was in that church?

When the world went slow, Kiran's mind was like thick syrup. If she was bored, she might twirl a strand of hair for an hour and chew a pen to death. But when things went fast, her neurons were quicksilver.

She caught Anatol halfway across the lawn, grabbed the back of his coat, and slid down with him into the wet grass behind a gigantic oak.

Anatol was breathing hard. He leaned against the tree's trunk and pointed to his grass-stained pants. "You almost got yourself shot."

That wasn't even worth an eye roll. "You wouldn't shoot me if the world depended on it."

He put a hand to his face and squeezed his eyebrows together. "It might."

"Whatever. I'll get you some new pants. But we can't charge in the front. They'll be waiting."

Anatol raised an eyebrow. "Cellar entrance? Through the crypts?"

CHAPTER 3

"Are you trying to make this worse?" She spit out the old gum and popped in what remained of the pack. Even the word crypts started her hands sweating. "Back door. We just need a distraction." SWAT always left one member behind to run coms. They might know what had gone wrong. If she was right, and the cult was going to blow the whole building, she and Anatol had very little time to get whatever was left of SWAT out of there.

She aimed her gun at the front door and pulled the trigger. Absolutely nothing happened. Three more pulls. Three more dead clicks and her sense of reality slipping grew. There was nothing wrong with her weapon; she'd checked it five times.

"I told you. Your gun won't work." Anatol aimed his freaky pistol and fired, almost deafening her. The front door shook. She needed to ask him about that later.

They ran around the perimeter, staying close to the trees, headed for the SWAT van. Outside the van they found the coms man, sprawled with a knife in his chest, his eyes staring at nothing. Kiran fought a sudden wave of nausea.

"This side is no better," Anatol said.

Kiran judged the distance to the back door. At least from here they were hidden from view by a few trees.

"We need a bigger distraction. Make sure no one puts a knife in my back." Kiran rifled through the poor coms guy's pants and fished out the keys. The van's engine turned over with one crank. She spun the van ninety degrees, wedged a nightstick onto the accelerator, and jumped out.

The van rumbled across the grass, picking up speed.

"That's bigger," Anatol said.

Kiran pointed. "Shoot out the alcove windows. We go in there."

The van hit the back door of the church like a battering ram, airbags exploding. Shouts erupted from inside. Anatol fired just as the van crashed, taking out a long window on the alcove's east side. The two of them sprinted for the opening.

Kiran stepped into darkness and smoke. Through the church's leaded windows, the van blazed in the night. Her breath puffed out in whisps before her in air that was impossibly cold. At least three bodies lay on the floor. And

17

near the back door, a group of people, turning ever so slowly toward them, their pale faces reflecting the flames. These were the damned cultists they'd been after.

One of the cultists shouted something she couldn't make out and raised what looked like a spear as Anatol leveled his gun. The spear flew and Kiran dove.

She landed on a cold stone floor amidst a mess of tumbled pews. The blast of Anatol's answering shot echoed through the church. Kiran raised her head in time to see Anatol drop to one knee and fire again. Another cultist with a spear stood for a moment, his body rotating with the force of the shot, before tipping back to crash amongst the pews.

"Patel, help me."

Kiran turned and caught her breath. Five feet away, Chen lay in a pool of blood. The SWAT team leader's eyes were full of desperation, his hand pressed to his thigh. Kiran's heart tried to beat its way out of her chest as she crawled toward him. The long knife someone had stabbed him with lay next to him. He'd lost a terrible amount of blood.

"Hang in there, Chen," she tried to sound reassuring, but the break in her voice gave her away.

She tore off her orange scarf and wrapped it around Chen's thigh, tightening it like a tourniquet, praying no one would skewer her while she worked. She gave a final twist and her scarf turned dark brown with Chen's blood, but the hemorrhage stopped.

Chen took a full breath and trembled. "You were right. B team never arrived."

She placed the knife in Chen's hand. "Send me a Starbucks card when you get out of the hospital."

Chen drew a combat knife from his vest. "Trade you. Find the kids, Patel."

"Deal, but you're not allowed to die." Kiran squeezed Chen's arm hard and tried to force down her rising panic. "You... you owe me expensive coffee." She stopped stammering and took Chen's knife. It couldn't be less useful than her gun.

Smoke billowed above the floor. More of these crazy people with spears

CHAPTER 3

could be hiding anywhere. Before she got up, she heard a bootstep far too close. Chen pointed to his right.

Kiran shoved the pew with her shoulder, knocking it forward. She kept pushing and was rewarded with a grunt and the sound of someone falling hard. She came up and found herself lucky. The man creeping up on her had struck his head against a pew and wasn't getting up any time soon. Kiran tightened her grip on the knife and gave thanks she hadn't had to use it. She'd signed up for the FBI, not to be a goddamn ninja.

Anatol stepped out of the smoke, and she grabbed his arm. Her partner was hiding something. "Why is this a gothic martial arts disaster? And why the hell is your antique gun the only one working?"

"You shouldn't have followed me." Anatol completely ignored her question and pointed to a body of another SWAT member. Kiran's stomach rolled; the man was missing an arm.

At that moment, the dinner her mother had left in the fridge exited her stomach and hit the floor. Before she could finish retching, the front door swung open, and two hooded cultists stepped through. One leveled a goddamned crossbow at them, too fast for Anatol to raise his gun, too fast for her to move. She knew it was aimed straight at her heart. Kiran's last thought was that her mother was going to be so pissed when she came to her funeral.

A moment before the cultist could fire, Reese dove through the door and hit him with a flying tackle. The SPD detective grabbed the other cultist on his way down and managed to take them both with him. The tangle of men crashed into the pews with a crack of wood and snap of bone.

Reese threw two punches before Anatol could get a shot off. He got to his feet and looked around. "What the hell are these people doing with spears and bows and shit?"

Kiran turned to her partner. "I wish someone would tell me that."

Reese straightened his black leather jacket "Where the hell is SWAT?"

Before anyone could answer, Reese fell to the floor. One of the cultists had kicked him in the leg. The cultist raised the crossbow, took aim at Reese, then shifted to the figure charging through the door.

Gonzales barged in with a cultist hanging onto his back, apparently trying

THE TOOLS OF THE GHOST

to strangle him. He flipped the man over his shoulder, straight into the one with the crossbow, then picked up an entire pew. He slammed the pew down on the cultists like the wrath of God, stumbled into a bench and ended up flat on his back.

"¡Ay, Dios mío!" Gonzales grabbed his knee.

Kiran gave a silent thanks. The SPD detectives weren't elegant, but the cultists stayed down. She scanned the rest of the floor. For the moment, the place was quiet.

Reese slid an arm under his partner and heaved him off the floor. "Damn. Nothing works around here. Radios, guns, nothing. It's like the Middle Ages." He hobbled forward with Gonzales. They stopped when they reached Chen, still clutching the tourniquet.

"Well, shit," Reese stated the obvious.

Kiran flinched at a crash on the floor above them and a from somewhere up there, a scream.

"Help. We need help, now." A central staircase of wide spiraling stone lead to the church's upper level.

Anatol grabbed Reese's arm. "Get these two out. Get help."

Reese took another look at Chen and nodded. He lifted the SWAT commander with one arm, slung him over a shoulder, and still managed to support Gonzales who was a living wall of muscle. Gonzales was trying to help Reese with Chen while mumbling something, but he could barely stand. Reese dragged them both out of there.

Kiran snatched up the fallen cultist's crossbow and scrambled behind Anatol, trying her best to scan the darkness for threats. She'd never fired a crossbow, but it had a trigger. Hopefully, it was point and pull. Director Jefferson's words, telling her she belonged behind a desk, came back to her as sweat dripped down her back. A desk job was looking really good right now.

They climbed stairs slick with what Kiran hoped wasn't blood, past statues of what she assumed were saints, looking down at them with disapproving eyes. The flight ended in front of a dark red door that should have already been knocked down by SWAT but was decidedly shut. She pressed herself against the wall to the right. Anatol took left.

CHAPTER 3

Someone shouted on the other side of the door. The voice sounded more like the growl of a beast than a human.

Anatol clutched his necklace and a weight of great age appeared on his face. "Who protects the children when the monster is on the other side of the door?" Her partner slipped into Polish, and Kiran could no longer understand him. She was struck by the feeling that Anatol had slipped someplace far away, and she was in danger of never getting him back.

"What is happening?" Her question went unanswered, and her sense of panic screamed up a notch. Seeing Anatol afraid managed to activate every neuron in her fight or flight response. Now was not the time for a panic attack but she was leaning heavily toward flight.

A pained scream shattered her paralysis.

Kiran slammed her shoulder against the door which blessedly gave way. She slid inside, throwing the door wide and rolling right. Anatol, thankfully, rolled left just behind.

Shit. Broken bodies were everywhere, strewn over railings, half-way through windows, tossed across the floor.

On a raised platform twenty feet across the room, stood a creature out of a church nightmare. An enormous man, far larger than any man should be, bearded and hunched with cords of muscle, was clutching an extremely unfortunate SWAT team member. A sickly yellow light bathed the giant's feet. He was shaking the man the way a dog shakes a rat.

The monster turned and met Kiran's gaze. He dropped the SWAT member like a discarded toy and appraised her.

Her rising anger beat down her all-consuming terror. She aimed dead center and pulled the crossbow's trigger. "Suck this."

The monster moved in a blur then raised an arm in a twisted salute. In his fist, he held the bolt she'd just fired. He squeezed his hand and it snapped.

Anatol screamed in Polish and fired his pistol, scoring center mass. The giant staggered back but didn't fall, despite the golf ball-size hole decorating his sternum. The brute simply bared his teeth in response. Anatol continued his Polish tirade and fired twice more.

The giant leaped forward, covering the distance between them in an instant,

21

then froze as Anatol raised his arm.

Anatol's black tattoo shone in the dim light. "Go back to whatever Hell you came from," he said, "before I make you face him again."

The giant's laugh chilled the sweat off Kiran's skin. "Anatol, you knew I was here yet were too afraid to call him. You felt me on the other side of that door yet were too afraid to pass through." He tapped the side of his hairy head. "You know what will happen if you use the mark to enter my mind. You are right to be afraid."

She couldn't believe Anatol knew this bastard. She let the crossbow fall and drew Chen's knife. If guns weren't working, maybe steel would.

Before she could move or Anatol could take another breath, the brute lunged, knocked his gun aside, and seized him by the neck. He heaved Anatol off the ground with one hand and bared his yellow teeth. The giant spun about the room with her partner, knocking over furniture, as he shook the life out of him.

Kiran charged in a panic, every step far too slow, fearing she was already too late.

The giant brought his face within inches of Anatol's. "After all these years, you disappoint me." His words were like speech without vocal cords. "You could have saved me. Could have forgiven me like any good child should have."

Anatol spat in the giant's face. "Forgiven you, Krol? You always belonged in Hell."

Krol lifted Anatol higher. "Still thinking like an altar boy, scared that the door might break down." He slammed him against the wall with a dull thud of flesh striking stone. Anatol's body went limp, and Kiran's mind went hot with flames.

Sirens screamed outside the church as Kiran buried the knife in Krol's back and twisted.

The giant turned his head ever so slowly and looked down on her with searing eyes, searching her soul, appraising her worth. Evidently, she did not measure up. He swatted her like a fly, not worthy of attention. The casual blow knocked every bit of air out of her. She slammed against the ground

CHAPTER 3

and rolled.

Boots struck the floor below. Either backup had finally arrived, or more damned cultists were coming to finish them off.

Krol turned back to her partner. "You should have called him, Anatol. He's late for the party. You will pay for that mistake."

Anatol raised his head. "I don't know how you've returned, but I promise you won't be coming back again."

"Promises, promises." Krol flung Anatol across the room.

Kiran's breath caught in her throat as her partner's body arced high, almost reaching the vaulted ceiling, then plummeted, crashing into a pile of stacked steel chairs.

Krol didn't bother to glance in her direction. At the sound of boots hitting the stairs, he bounded straight through a stained-glass window and disappeared into the night.

Kiran picked herself off the floor and limped to Anatol, ignoring the screaming pain in her ribs. She placed two fingers against his neck. Blood ran freely down his forehead, but his pulse was there, faint, ever so faint. She lowered her face to listen for breathing and warm air brushed her cheek.

She cradled his head in her hands. "I am going to kill you if you die on me."

Anatol opened his eyes. "Would it hurt more to die twice?"

"You don't want to find out. You stay alive, or else." Her heart hurt fiercely. She had no idea what she was saying.

Anatol took a ragged breath and his hand closed on her forearm. "It falls on you now, Kiran. I'm sorry." His eyes shut again, but his grip on her arm only tightened.

Kiran blinked as the tattoo on Anatol's forearm began to snake down his wrist. She panicked and tried to pull away as it slid over her hand, but she couldn't break free. Black ink crawled onto her like a living thing, burning its way into her skin. The pain stretched up her arm, pumped through her heart, seared into her bones until her muscles spasmed and she screamed. The black mark swirled over her forearm like grasping tentacles, tangling together in a whirl about her inner elbow that coalesced into the shape of a fisherman's hook. The mark pulsed a final time as if satisfied, then went still.

The pain subsided as Anatol's hand dropped to the ground. What was left of her energy drained out of her. She felt herself falling.

The door flew open, and a squad of men with guns instead of spears charged through. She summoned the last of her strength and found her voice. "Agent down! I need help." She held her partner tight, and tears filled her eyes. She couldn't lose him. Couldn't lose any more family.

Chapter 4

Kiran had always imagined she was born the daughter of a witch and a mysterious inventor and had secretly been adopted. That would explain both why she was nothing like her siblings and the cryptic birthmark on her right forearm in the shape of a rabbit's head.

Despite this attractive and convenient solution, it appeared that she was quite properly born in a Seattle hospital and that her supposed parents were the only ones she'd ever had. When she was eight, she made sure to check the photos, and there she was swaddled in a blanket with the correct date written on top. And there was, of course, the birth certificate which read Swedish First Hill, Seattle, but that could have been a fake.

By the time she was ten, Kiran understood where her strangeness came from: her father was the most unusual person she was ever going to meet. It wasn't his mismatched socks, or the fact that he woke up at two p.m. and stayed awake puttering all night until he made her breakfast at six and then collapsed on the sofa soon after. It was more in the way he saw the world.

Her father laced his fingers together and stared off into space. "Seven drops of water, shining on a copper penny, lying in the middle of the road—does that mean anything to you, Kiran?"

Kiran wrapped her hands around the hot mug of coffee he'd made which he'd started serving her at age five. "I don't think seven drops of water could fit on a penny, Baba."

He rubbed the center of his forehead with his thumb. "Don't talk rubbish. They're trying to tell us something, something about another place. I saw that penny in a dream. I knew that if I were brave enough to turn it over and risk the road, I would be in another world." He reached into his pocket and drew out coins which he threw onto the table before them. Three nickels, a dime, and great quantity of pennies rolled about the table, several bouncing onto her plate of food. Her father stared at them, his gaze far off. "Another world lies on the other side of each of those coins, if only we could see." He rubbed the corner of his eye in the way he did only when he was most spent. "It is the duty of every father to reveal those worlds, wait no, I mean to protect their children from them. To protect them at all costs." He fell asleep on the kitchen table soon after and Kiran put a blanket over his shoulders.

At the age of twenty-four, her father had become a chess grandmaster, which had been his primary qualification for marrying her mother. He was famous for his unconventional style with a focus on relentless mad attacks. When the game became more systematic and predictable, geared toward beating computers instead of imaginative play, he grew bored and stopped competing. But he would still play chess with Kiran every morning while she ate hot dosas, an Indian sort of pancake made with rice and lentils, and coffee he prepared, before he collapsed on the sofa and began snoring. During these games when he was only half-awake, he would ask her questions.

"Did you know that Hinduism teaches that we shall be reborn in different forms, an ant, a bee, a snake, algae, until one day we understand the meaning of life and need never be born again? Do you know what that makes the world?"

She chewed the delicious paper-thin dosa and considered, "A place where we shouldn't step on animals?"

"It makes the world a puzzle, Kiran. The greatest mystery you can imagine, and we were born to unravel it."

"What if the world wants to keep itself hidden, Baba?"

He smashed his fist on the breakfast table, sending chess pieces tumbling and her coffee sloshing to the floor. This attack on the table did not surprise her as much as some might think. She got up to find a mop as an enormous smile lit her father's exhausted face.

"Then you attack, Kiran. You attack with every piece you have in a way that no world would expect until every secret is revealed."

CHAPTER 4

One day he began a chess game by asking her which was the most important piece, the easiest of questions. She pointed to the king, then the queen, but he shook his head, no each time.

Then he raised a pawn. "Neglected, sacrificed, forgotten, but the pawn is you, it is me, it is the lost child, abandoned in the dark. Chess books will tell you that within every pawn lies the power to be a queen, but what they don't understand is that every pawn is already the queen of its own story. Within their structure, their pattern, lies the secret of the game. Someone else will always look after the king. All those fools, following the rules, running blind. Never abandon the pawns, Kiran."

She would sit alone in her room, long after her mother insisted that she be in bed, running her fingers back and forth over the silky part of the pillowcase, while she solved the puzzles her father had left her: chess problems, riddles, math tricks, always a challenge before their next breakfast match. Her mind would turn as she slept in a race to find the solution, before he raised his eyebrows, wondering if he'd stumped her.

One day, she felt something rectangular and hard under her pillow. She slid out a heavy hardcover of *The Collected Stories of Sherlock Holmes*. The note from her father read, "No rubbish here." She spent the night running her fingers over the thick shag rug in her closet, reading. She was hooked.

Her brother and sister had of course taken after their mother and been perfect and organized in every way. Dr. Sonya Patel, her older sister, earned a PhD in bioscience, and Dr. Prashant Patel, her older brother, an actual neurosurgeon, were shining examples of all she could have accomplished. Worse, they were both sickeningly generous with sage advice. The Patel home's walls were decorated with her brother's and sister's endless awards and diplomas, newspaper clippings, and huge photos of them holding trophies. Normal families would have put up landscape paintings.

Her mother always said, "I could have married an MIT engineer but instead I chose the romantic chess master. Life is about choices, Kiran. Don't make my mistakes."

But the ideal family life ended when cracks started seeping into her father's mind. She noticed it first in his chess. Though still brilliant, his moves became erratic, like nothing he would have done before.

"The goal has changed, Kiran." His attacks became even more inspired and unpredictable—he might sacrifice everything to capture a knight and be satisfied that just one of his pawns survived when he'd clearly lost everything.

In the end, he lost himself. They called the police, the FBI, the neighborhood watch. He never even showed up on local surveillance cameras. Her mother insisted that he had abandoned them. That he was too smart to ever be found. That he had castled his king and was hiding away in some impregnable fortress where he had no responsibilities. It was an irredeemable offense in her eyes. Her mother declared she would never forgive him, said that Kiran should never forgive him either.

But Kiran believed otherwise. She'd packed a notebook, a flashlight, and a backpack full of peanut butter on whole wheat and set out to find him. Half the police force turned out to search for the missing twelve-year-old. She'd wandered alone and lost, scared out of her mind. Part of her prayed for someone to find her, while the rest of her demanded she keep searching.

For three days they failed to locate her as her mother raged. On the fourth night they discovered her sitting in an alley, dirty and confused, scribbling in her notebook. She'd tried to run away from the officers; swore she was getting close to finding him. They'd had to hospitalize her overnight to give her IV fluids and run blood tests. The picture of her rescue in the papers showed a girl with tangled hair and a notebook under her arm, threatening the police with a very big stick clutched in one hand. She'd explained that a woman under a bridge somewhere had given her the tree branch, had promised it would help her.

The police gave up looking for her father a week later and Kiran never forgave them. She could have done better, could have brought him home, if only she'd tried harder, been smarter.

Her father hadn't run away, hadn't abandoned them. He couldn't have, she was sure. He'd flipped the penny and gone to battle on a distant chess board. He'd left her a note in her closet, tucked into her copy of Sherlock Holmes which they found at the bottom of her backpack: 'Attack. Don't think rubbish. Castling early is a coward's move.'

Chapter 5

The morning after the church disaster, Kiran filled a Styrofoam cup with bad coffee in the hospital waiting area. She'd already arranged the sugars in order and lined up the Splenda packets. The little habits that had started after her father disappeared only got worse with stress. After rotating the coffee pots so they faced the same direction, she took a sip and managed to scald her tongue before sitting down. Under her sleeve, the tattoo that had invaded her arm still burned. Scrubbing and scraping at the mark for almost an hour this morning had accomplished nothing. The damn thing was like an occupying force that had taken up residence and was holding its ground. She tugged the sleeve as far down as it would go, feeling violated and terrified at the same time. Anatol would know how to get rid of it, he had to know. He would get out of here and they would figure it out. She sent a silent prayer to Ganesha to let it be true.

For the tenth time, she ran over the events of last night and worried she was losing her mind. She couldn't discount that possibility, but Anatol was definitely in the ICU. If he was here, the impossible things she thought she'd seen might really have happened. She drank more coffee.

Every attempt she'd made to see her partner had been rebuffed by hospital staff. She wasn't family, wasn't a doctor as her mother often reminded her, wasn't anybody important. And she suspected Director Jefferson had instructed hospital staff to keep out the Indian FBI agent, no matter who she claimed to be.

Her mother sat next to her, vigorously stirring her own coffee because Kiran happened to be the one agent in the Seattle field office who grew up in the city and had a host of overbearing family.

Her mother scowled. "There's no real milk here. This powdered creamer is bullshit." She considered Anatol a member of the family and had insisted on being there no matter what Kiran said.

"It's all bullshit to you, Mom. If they had a real cow in here with fresh hot milk, you'd complain it was the wrong breed." She'd lost patience with her mother about six years ago, at least.

"Don't start with me." Her mother gave her the one eye squinting look.

Kiran looked into her own coffee. "Right, that would be unpasteurized milk, and we'd all get rabies or brucellosis or whatever." She waved a hand in the direction of her brother, the doctor, who would know the appropriate medical term for the disaster that would befall them because of raw cow milk. He was conveniently collapsed in a nearby chair. She sighed. Her mother didn't lose fights and she noticed everything. Kiran had tried to comb her hair to hide the fresh bruise on her jaw from when she'd hit the floor, but her mother had seen it right away. Luckily, she couldn't see the bruise across her chest where Krol's hand had connected.

Her brother didn't answer and continued to look worried. Anatol had been to her mother's house a dozen times and had met them all. He loved her mother's Indian cooking and never minded listening to her ramble on for as long as she liked. Her entire family loved the old man. It was a horrible hospital family reunion, waiting for news and expecting any moment some doctor to come out and tell them Anatol was dead.

Special Agent Henry Le arrived instead and slipped into a chair. Le was one of the senior Seattle field agents and the right hand of the Director of Criminal Investigations. He was cool and calm one hundred percent of the time, unless her mother was present. "He's awake and breathing without a machine."

A terrible weight on Kiran's chest lifted just enough so she could speak, "So, he's going to be alright?"

"I didn't say that." Le wouldn't meet her eyes. "He doesn't look good."

Her mother cut in before Kiran could ask another question. "You were supposed to keep her safe, Henry. You promised me you would keep her out

CHAPTER 5

of the fights and nonsense."

Kiran choked on hot coffee. "You're kidding, right, Henry?" Her mother invited over half the agents she worked with. Le was never one to refuse a meal.

Le looked sheepish. "Well, I tried to..."

Her mother looked like she might bite someone. "You've eaten in my house, Henry. You were supposed to make sure. Not just *try*." Even Le backed down in face of her mother's wrath.

"Look, Mom. Henry didn't do anything."

Her mother smashed her coffee cup in the trash. "He was supposed to do something." It was impossible to get more than one sentence in edgewise when her mother got started. "Kiran, you aren't Sherlock Holmes bringing justice to the world. Do you want me here in this lobby wringing my hands because my daughter is dying? Or should I be waiting outside a psychiatric ward once you've driven yourself mad like your father did?" Her mother wiped her eyes. "You're not cut out for this. Stop acting like some Bollywood actor in a cop movie."

Kiran couldn't believe she was having this discussion in a hospital waiting area. She spoke without meeting her mother's eyes. "Amma, you'll get your advanced degrees and I'll be wearing a sari and you'll finally be happy one day, okay?"

"They won't be my diplomas, Kiran. They'll be yours, and we will all be proud of you."

Le stood up. "He's asking for you, Kiran. I don't know how much longer he'll be awake."

Kiran bolted up and spilled the last of her coffee on the floor.

Her mother didn't even look up.

Le held the stairwell door open. He leaned down and lowered his voice. "The boss is outside his room, and she's pissed. No one's blaming you, Kiran, but they were close."

Kiran bit her lip and nodded. Jefferson had told her to stay out of it. Anatol was her fault.

Amalia Jefferson was sitting outside the ICU room's door leafing through a sheaf of papers. At forty-three, Jefferson was the youngest head of the FBI's Criminal Investigation Unit in history, an African American veteran with long braided hair and a strikingly beautiful face who managed to command discipline with her eyes and with unquestioned competence. Over the years she'd lost none of the physique that had made her a college track champion. When Kiran joined the bureau, she'd fantasized that Jefferson would be a secret ally. It had not worked out that way.

The look Jefferson gave her held no sympathy whatsoever. Kiran opened her mouth to try to explain but she cut her off.

"I told both you fools to stay clear. And don't think I was just trying to keep a rookie safe. It isn't always about you, Patel. I was trying to keep a decorated agent six months from retirement alive and you go and screw it up because you think you're too smart for anyone."

"I never would have… I didn't mean to…" Kiran stammered. The weight of everything pressed upon her. If she had just listened to all the people in the bureau who'd discouraged her and quit while she was ahead, Anatol wouldn't be here. Kiran fought back the tears. She couldn't cry in front of Jefferson.

Jefferson didn't let up. "You didn't think. I told you that you belong behind a desk, and I meant it. I should take your gun and badge, but I promised that Polish fool to not kick you to the curb." Jefferson raised her finger. "You're good at arguing, but you stink at listening, so shut up and pay attention because I'm only going to say this once."

Kiran clenched her jaw.

Jefferson took a deep breath. "I worked alongside Anatol when I started out. He took me under his wing, tried to teach me. He told me things I didn't believe possible, things I had to keep quiet, but he always turned out to be right. I owe him my life three times over, and the one thing he begs me for is to not get rid of you." Jefferson swallowed and the veins stood out on her neck. "I always thought I would be next, that I would have to shoulder the burden." Jefferson looked at Kiran's arm, at the black mark disappearing up her sleeve. "But he said no, it wasn't going to be me, that I had a different role to play. Like some goddamn Polish prophet, him and his nonsense."

Kiran wasn't sure what Jefferson was talking about, but it was clear she was

CHAPTER 5

hurting. Interrupting her now was not a good idea.

"You are going to go in there and listen to him with everything you've got and stay quiet. These may be the last words he has the strength to say. The doctors don't understand why he's still alive. His kidneys are gone, he's got blood on his brain…" Jefferson's voice broke midsentence. "His spinal cord is severed at the waist."

Jefferson became a blur as tears filled Kiran's vision. No one had told her how bad it was. Her body shook and there was nothing she could do. Jefferson's hand on her shoulder was the last thing she expected.

"I know you love him like I love him. That's the only reason I could put up with your bullshit. And because you love him, you're going to listen, cuz he's saving it all to tell you what he must. You're going to stay quiet and soak it in and nod, aren't you?"

Kiran nodded.

"After you talk to him, before you do anything else, you come out here and see me, alright?" Jefferson fixed her with a stare that wouldn't let go.

Kiran nodded again, not able to process any of this. Jefferson pushed her through the door, and she saw her partner for the first time since the church disaster.

Anatol lay at the center of a mess of tubes and wires and drips. His body was covered in bandages and sutures, but his eyes opened, bright as always, when she walked in.

"You're late," he said.

"I had to walk your dog before he peed on my floor." She tried to smile through the cloud of tears. She went to Anatol's side and wound her fingers through his, making sure not to touch the IV in the back of his hand. Her deep brown skin was a stark contrast with his far-too-pale white. "You look stylish," she lied.

"I thought Jefferson was going to shout you to death out there. So damn loud even when she tries to whisper."

Kiran couldn't keep up the act any longer. "I'm sorry, Anatol. I should have kept us away from there, kept you away from that thing."

Anatol waved his fingers at her. "How's my dog?"

33

"He ate my LSAT book." Spartacus had also allowed her to cry into his thick fur. He'd actually licked her once.

She sat in the chair next to the bed.

Anatol shook his head. "Jefferson tells me that three of the SWAT officers survived that mess because of our little rescue mission. We didn't give Krol enough time to shake their unconscious bodies to death." A long coughing fit seized Anatol. When it finally released him, he trembled from the neck down, but his legs never moved. "They found enough explosives in the church to take out half the block. You were right, they were going to blow the building. We never gave them a chance."

She held up a hand for him to stop. "Go slow. You don't look like you're ready for Olympic speeches yet."

"Enough small talk. I don't have time for that shit. Promise me you'll take care of my dog?"

Kiran opened her mouth to protest but he cut her off with a look. She nodded. "I'll watch Spartacus until you get out of here but—"

"Jefferson told you to listen. I know that's almost a physical impossibility for you but try. Open the drawer by the side of the bed."

Inside the drawer, she found Anatol's black necklace with the iron fishhook. The strange gun he'd used against the monster, half iron half brass, took up most of the drawer. A brown envelope lay beneath it. It was all stuff she wanted as much as a blow to the head. Taking that necklace would mean he wasn't going to wear it anymore.

She started to protest, "There's no way—"

"Do you want those kids back?" Anatol cut her off. "You damn well do, Kiran. It's personal for you. Like when you were lost, looking for your father, hoping against hope. You know what it's like out there, alone, with a hole in your heart, hoping for someone to come." He waved a hand at the drawer. "All yours now. I don't have the strength to explain everything, whatever you don't understand now, you'd better read in that letter." He winced as he drew in a breath. "You know what you saw in that church, don't you?"

"Some kind of overgrown body builder freak you used to lift weights with? Some crook you'd met before who wasn't very fond of you?" Part of her

CHAPTER 5

desperately wished Anatol would say she was right.

Anatol wheezed a sigh. "Don't bullshit me, Patel. Did your gun work? Did you expect a bunch of half-starved cultists with spears could stop SWAT? What do you think this is?" With a supreme effort Anatol leaned forward and pulled up the sleeve of Kiran's shirt, revealing the black tattoo snaking halfway up her arm. "The mark traveled from me to you because it needs to live on. If you want to know what it is, what is really happening out there, if you want to save those children before it's too late, tell me what you saw. Tell me and I'll know if you really have the mind I'm staking everything on."

Kiran closed her eyes and saw the giant bounding across the floor, ignoring the gaping wound in its chest. Saw it heave Anatol into the air and shake him like a ragdoll. She remembered her father's strange words about flipping over a coin and finding another world. Kiran opened her eyes and stared at the tattoo, black as a starless sky. She met Anatol's gaze.

"I saw something, felt something, not from this world. Something guns couldn't kill. Something evil." And it had left her shaking inside ever since.

Anatol let go of her and collapsed back into his pillows. "Damn right he's evil. Straight out of Hell, if I'm right."

He took several long breaths before he spoke again, "Your mind works, your eyes see the truth, your heart cares. I wasn't wrong. The barrier between worlds is thin, Kiran. There are many realms, many worlds of the spirit. At times creatures from other sides slip through and their magic imposes its own rules." He rubbed at his forehead in sudden pain. "We are not going to bring those kids home the usual way. There are times when guns don't work. Times when we need help."

Kiran tried to interrupt him, tried to get him to pace himself, but Anatol glared at her and continued.

"Fifty years ago, I was a boy in Poland. That thing that tried to kill me last night was once my priest, Jako Krol, a genius and a murderer. He committed horrible crimes, crimes against children, and no one could stop him. He'd made some deal with the devil, and he was too damn smart to catch. But I was with him when he died, with him when the creature summoned to destroy him arrived. It was the most terrifying moment of my life. There's no way I can explain how Krol's back, but this cult stinks of him." Anatol coughed and spit out a clot of blood. He grabbed her hand when she turned in panic to call the doctor.

"Thirty years ago, I was like you are now, bullheaded and ignorant. I joined the Warsaw police force at the worst possible time. A madman was loose, and we couldn't stop him. Agents were getting shot and the clues didn't make sense. We tried everything, pulled in every backup, never slept trying to find the bastard but he was too smart, too quick to kill and disappear. The city was in shambles. People were locking themselves in their homes. One day, an old man found me at my desk with my head in my hands. He explained that the killer was a creature from a spirit world we would never be able to defeat on our own. He said he had looked for me across the continent, that he was far too old to face him again. Then he took my hand, and that tattoo went from him to me. He told me it was time to summon the Ghost."

"What do you mean? Like the Holy Ghost from the Bible?"

Anatol's face contorted in pain. "Heaven forbid. What game would God be playing with us if that were true? There is nothing at all holy about this ghost. He is the Unholy Ghost if there ever was one."

"Anatol, this takes crazy to a whole new level." She wished she believed that, but something about his words rang uncomfortably true.

"The mark will change you if you draw on its power, if you let it inside you. I was never sure how far I could use its magic and stay sane." He reached out and laid a finger on the black lines running over Kiran's arm. "That mark wasn't made by God. It was made by his angels with the help of the forces of Hell. Together, they sought to bind the Ghost. No one will ever know under whose orders they were working, but what they created has changed history."

Kiran thought she saw the black lines pulse on her arm. She pulled away from Anatol and grasped one hand with the other to stop it from trembling.

Anatol didn't seem to notice. "Kiran, you see things others cannot, just like I saw as a child. The mark will magnify that sight beyond anything you thought possible. You will see magic, smell it, long before anyone else. If you look deeply, you will glimpse other worlds, see into people's hearts, delve into their minds. Do not look too deeply or you will be lost. Do not let the

CHAPTER 5

mark change who you are and take control of you."

"Look, we'll set the crime lab on that scene. They'll figure it out. You need to save your energy."

"You Hindus believe in so many gods, in rakshasas, in all kinds of demons. This shouldn't be hard. I was born Catholic, though my faith in all that has been cast aside. I don't know who will forgive me when I die. It took me time to believe in the Ghost. Time to understand that there are things more terrible than the demons of Hell. Time you don't have. The worst of all those things is bound by a pact, is tied to us by that chain and hook I wore around my neck. The man who found me brought it with him from the old country. From him to me, from me to you as it has been for ages. You'll have to summon him or there'll be no end to this."

A shudder ran across Anatol's face as he recited from memory. "When the heroes have fled and all that remains is fear, you must pay the price and call him back, for though the weapons of Hell be vast, the Tools of the Ghost are without number." Anatol leaned forward. "Kiran, Krol is a nightmare. He's a super genius who's come back with the power of a demon, but make no mistake, the monster you must summon to defeat him will be infinitely worse. And you are the only soul in this world who can call him. You must be sure you can control him. Lose control and you will unleash a terror upon the world."

"Anatol, shut up now and rest." He was exhausting himself and freaking her out with all this talk of magic. Something was closing around her with every sentence he spoke, and she hated it. She stood up and started to arrange the flowers. The doctors might have to give him a sedative and maybe give her one too.

Anatol reached across and knocked the flower vase onto the floor with a crash. "Rest is the last thing I need. Time is short for me. Time is short for those kids. There are rules, rules you must remember." Anatol's voice was growing weak, but desperation made each word clear. "First, never promise the Ghost anything. Anything you agree to will bind you until the end of time."

Kiran bent to pick up the shattered vase pieces and collect the flowers scattered across the floor. "Never promise who?"

"You'll need two others to form the trinity. You can't do it alone. If you choose poorly, everything will be lost. The strength of your wills together will bind him. Jefferson will help you find the best people. Trust her in all things. Choose only from the people she selects. Third, never remove the necklace no matter what the Ghost says. If you do, he will tear your heart out with his bare hands and that won't be the worst of it. You will have loosed him upon the world to wreak whatever terrible vengeance he desires."

She got to her feet. "I'm going to call the doctors. You need some serious drugs."

Anatol seized her arm with unexpected strength. "Do you know why I chose you, Kiran? Chose you to be my last partner?"

"I hear it every day, affirmative action, two in one, a woman and a minority in the same go."

"No, that's why it was easy to do the paperwork, but I'm not asking why the department chose you. I'm asking why I picked a sarcastic anxiety-ridden kid to be my partner. You've chewed up every damn pencil I ever had."

"You chose me because I was smarter than anyone else you ever worked with. And you wanted someone to take care of your dog."

"I chose you because you have Heart. Soul. Spirit. You have the trinity within you. I believe you have what it takes to control the Ghost. But what I believe won't matter in the end. You must believe in yourself. You have to make a terrible decision. Have to decide if you are willing to take the risk to summon the monster. If you are willing to be the one responsible for it all."

"I was wrong about the sedatives. They're giving you too much morphine." The last thing she wanted was to be the one responsible for some supernatural murderer. She felt a panic attack coming on.

Anatol leaned close. "You have something, Kiran. I don't mean your drive to solve any damn problem you set yourself to. Not even the twisted way your mind works. I mean you, the real you."

Her voice broke as her heart cracked open. "You're choosing now to finally give me a compliment?"

Anatol ignored her. "You care that those kids are lost." He took a ragged

CHAPTER 5

breath. "Now if you ever cared about me, put that necklace on and keep it on if you hope to stay alive."

"I don't understand, Anatol. Why the hell didn't you explain before?"

"Would you have believed me if you hadn't seen it yourself? Believed that there are creatures from other realms that could come into our world? Well, there are, and the Ghost is the worst of them. Not even Hell would take the Ghost. They were too damn afraid of him." He squeezed her hand until it hurt. "Heaven and Hell bound him together, forced him into the pact, forged the links of the chain you will wear, but they could never change him. He is a monster, a betrayer. Don't listen to his lies. He'll tell you he's a spirit, a fallen god; none of that is true. The Ghost was a man some time, somewhere, in a past life, but I could never discover who he was. If I could have learned the truth, I could have understood him, controlled him fully." Anatol's eyes clouded over, and he looked off into a distant place before he spoke again, "What crime was so terrible that not even Hell would let him in?"

Anatol struggled to catch his breath. "Did you keep the wand you had when you were a kid in that newspaper photo?"

Kiran felt like he'd slapped her. The memory of holding a thorny stick before her as police officers reached out for her flooded back like it was yesterday. She had been so afraid of being caught, afraid of giving up the search, afraid of it all being her fault. "That was just some old tree branch I found, under a bridge. What does it matter?" She had no idea why her voice cracked.

"You're going to wish you had kept that." Anatol went into a coughing fit that wouldn't stop. Kiran clutched his hand as if she could squeeze life back into him as every monitor in the room started to alarm. The door to the room flew open and a flood of white coats rushed in, turning up oxygen, pushing her aside, calling for more help, until with one final spasm Anatol fell back and was still.

She felt something inside her die, then Jefferson was at her side pulling her away.

In one hand Kiran clutched Anatol's black necklace, in the other the brown envelope and gun. She didn't take her eyes off Anatol's face as they pushed a tube down his throat, but Jefferson dragged her outside, away from the old man she'd grown to love like the father she'd lost long ago.

"Did he tell you? Did you understand?"

Kiran nodded though half of her thought she'd gone mad.

Jefferson took Kiran's face in her hands, made Kiran look her in the eyes. "You don't have to do it. We can solve this without a monster from beyond. If you bring that thing in and fail to control it, we're all dead." Jefferson planted herself in front of Kiran and held out her hand. "It's not worth the risk, Kiran. Forget what he said. Give me the necklace."

Jefferson held out her hand and it was the most tempting thing in the world. She could turn over the chain and never think about all this madness again.

"Everyone back. Clear!" someone shouted from the room.

Kiran pushed away Jefferson's arm. Turning down the hallway she ran, her vision clouded, not sure what the hell she could do to get away from death and magic.

Chapter 6

Kiran didn't open the envelope until after she had watched Anatol's casket lowered into the ground, had cried as much as her body demanded, and convinced herself not to tear his letter up. Half the bureau had showed at the funeral and a good part of the SPD as well. She'd slipped away while the priest who'd never known Anatol was still droning on about how meaningful her partner's life was. Anatol despised priests.

The one person she'd been glad to see at the funeral was Chen. The SWAT team leader was out of the hospital and walking with barely a limp. He'd handed her a small box in which she'd found a new orange scarf about a thousand times more expensive than her old one. Underneath she'd discovered a Starbucks card and a note, thanking her and apologizing for bleeding all over her previous scarf. The new scarf had already proven invaluable for crying into.

She lay her blue jacket on the still-wet grass and leaned against an unmarked gravestone in a secluded part of the cemetery. The noon sky was a dismal shade of gray. The iron fishhook on Anatol's necklace burned against her chest like Antarctic ice. She hesitated before opening the envelope. She'd already promised Jefferson she wasn't going to follow its directions.

Jefferson and Le had cornered her at the funeral and made clear her options. They'd put together a joint task force and assembled the best people they could find. In exchange for Kiran not summoning a creature who might kill them all, they'd promised her a spot on the elite team. It would cement her career as a detective and made more sense than relying on superstition and madness. She wouldn't have to lead any crazy trinity Anatol had in mind.

Her leading anything seemed like a bad idea anyways. She'd given in to their logic and agreed to meet with the Chief of Police at SPD headquarters. She just needed to read Anatol's last words.

The wrinkled paper she pulled out of the envelope was a rambling mess marred by coffee-stains and a cigarette burn. She straightened her glasses and smoothed out the paper.

Kiran, I've tried much of my life to find out who the Ghost was. I believed that if I could uncover his origins, I could understand him, control his madness, make him less dangerous. But my search has been a failure. I've learned almost nothing about his past. I can only beg you to never forget the rules that bind him.

A trinity of souls is needed to control him, but the bearer of the mark must become his true master. Jefferson has promised she will put together the best people she can find for you to choose from. Select two you have faith in, who you would trust with your life in the direst of times. The two who helped me are long dead and I feared what might happen if I dared summon the monster without them.

Pierce your skin with the hook over the mark and say the words when the time is right. Do not send him back until his task is complete. He cannot be called again for a full year. The old man who gave me the chain implored me not to call unless there was no other way.

Do not believe for a moment that he cares about you or cares about anything. I have never found a shred of good within him. He carries with him a great sack which contains whatever he requires. His form must not be his original body, but I have always believed his eyes, the blackest pits of fury, to be the seat of his true self. Remember this above all else, if you remove the necklace for any reason, he will rip you to pieces before you take your next breath.

I am sorry. Your burden should have been mine, but I have grown old and cautious. I feared he would be beyond my control, and I would unleash a horror into this world. Don't let fear control you as I have, or you and the children will pay the price. Have faith in yourself because faith is the only thing that will save you. May whatever gods you worship guard and protect you from the most unholy of ghosts. Your friend in life and death, Anatol

PS—Spartacus loves those cookies with the peanut butter between them, but don't give him too many or he gets constipated.

CHAPTER 6

Kiran turned the stained piece of paper over and shook the envelope out, searching for some other note that explained all this insanity in more detail. A particularly large cigarette burn marred the writing next to the bit about piercing her skin. She was sure she was missing the key instructions. Something that spelled out what words she was supposed to say, or how she was supposed to draw her own blood, or if she should sacrifice a chicken or draw a pentagram on the floor or something. But of course, there was nothing. Anatol never paid attention to details, or he would have remembered how much she hated the idea of needles. Even the thought of drawing her own blood made her nauseous. She rested her head in her hands and closed her eyes.

None of it would matter. Hopefully, she could hide the necklace away and never have to think about summoning whatever monster waited on the other side.

* * *

At eight that evening, Kiran walked into a nearly empty SPD station in sore need of renovation. The fluorescent lighting was from the nineties, the floor was cracked linoleum, even the air smelled stale.

The officer who buzzed her in looked up briefly when Kiran displayed her FBI badge, then returned to reading her novel. Kiran stepped onto a main floor covered with cluttered desks and remarkably lacking in human beings. The department should have been buzzing with energy, full of officers following up on leads, and news reports pouring in, but they'd shut the place down for this meeting. Only two officers sat at their desks, far at the back of the room. Somehow, Kiran wasn't surprised to find out who remained.

Reese looked exhausted. His black leather jacket was thrown over the back of his chair, he hadn't shaved, and his boots were scuffed. He aimed a crumpled piece of paper and launched it in an arc that missed the garbage can by a foot. He balled up another sheet, missed again, then shook his head.

"Damn. You're supposed to be one with the target, you know, all Zen, but I can't be one with a lousy garbage can."

Gonzales' hair was wilder than ever. He had his leg up on a chair and a copy of *The Seattle Times* stretched before him. "Word," he said.

"What kind of a word do you mean?" Kiran asked. "I mean are we talking a verb, an adjective, maybe past participle? You're leaving it wide open, Gonzales." Kiran's nerves couldn't take a lot more. She didn't feel like interpreting Gonzales' barely audible monosyllables. In fairness to Gonzales, she didn't even remember what a past participle was.

Gonzales stayed quiet, looking wounded, and Kiran felt terrible. Picking on Gonzales was like poking a giant teddy bear.

"The two of you get hurt much back there?" she asked.

Reese sat up. "Nah, we're straight. And don't pick on Gonzo. You're better than that, K. He was just saying we are all destined for greater things than being one with garbage cans."

At that Gonzales nodded and raised his pinky in some kind of weird salute. If she hung out with these two any longer, she'd lose it.

"They're waiting for you in the back," Reese said. "Told us to send you along and then get the hell out. Your brilliant assault on that church not only almost got us killed, it got us kicked off the case. Chief said between two officers and two radios we should have gotten help there sooner. Next week we're back on the stolen car beat. They've brought in some crazy special forces spy types who know what they're doing. Allah be praised for pulling us out of the line of fire."

Gonzales sighed and folded his newspaper.

Kiran couldn't help but notice that the headline across the paper read, "Police Department Fails Again. Kids Stay Missing." The city's confidence in law enforcement was going nowhere but down.

Reese grabbed his coat and headed for the door. Gonzales slid the paper under his arm and followed. Their shoulders were slumped. They looked beaten. Kiran saw them for the first time in a different light. The two of them must be the most junior detectives in a department not known for its diversity. Pinning the failure on them was crappy business as usual. None of

CHAPTER 6

the glory, all of blame. She bit her lip. At least this way they wouldn't end up like the SWAT team. They'd both almost died in that church. This was a job for a much higher level of professionals.

"I'll head back." She started down the hallway toward a flight of stairs and tried to think through Anatol's last words.

"Other way," Reese yelled. "That way leads to the roof."

"Got it." Kiran went the other way. Anatol had told her Jefferson would pick the best people. That part she believed. Jefferson would have pulled in the most competent team anyone could find. If Kiran could convince them of the nature of their enemy, they could put together a strategy to take Krol down. Now that they knew what they were up against, they should have a chance. But even now, explaining it to herself, she didn't fully believe it. How could you fight that kind of monster even if you knew what was coming?

The sound of raised voices made the direction clear. She reached the open door at the end of the hallway labeled Dennis Short—CHIEF OF POLICE, and stopped short. Director Jefferson's voice rose above the others.

"You *are* going to accept her on the team because I said you will."

"Surest way to wreck a team is to put a rookie on it. Way I heard it, her partner bought a coffin, and she came out without a scratch. I'd bet my ass she was hiding under a pew the whole time in that church." The speaker had a harsh voice Kiran didn't recognize, but she was one hundred percent sure she really didn't want to get to know them.

The next speaker had a decidedly Irish accent. "If she gets killed in the first five minutes, it'll solve that problem."

Kiran made herself stop pulling at her hair and took a slow breath. Stepping into a room full of this many people, people she didn't know, was almost as bad as stepping into the church with all the cultists while it was on fire. Having to talk would be worse. Her palms were already sweaty. She was not going to shake anyone's hand.

Silence flooded the room as she pushed open the door. Kiran made out Jefferson holding a piece of paper in her hand with a blue crayon illustration in a style she unfortunately recognized. Le, the only other FBI agent in the room, was rubbing his temple. The chief of police sat at his desk, leaning on folded arms, and there were six others she didn't recognize, five men and a woman. The six strangers looked ready to deploy to a warzone. She had no doubt these were the members of Jefferson's elite team.

Kiran took a deep breath. "I already managed not to get killed in the first five minutes." A flicker of blue light crossed her vision and for a moment she felt like she might pass out. The room was an oven. "So that's not going to solve your problem." She put her hand on a chair and fought to hide the wave of dizziness.

"Patel," Jefferson began.

Kiran closed her eyes before speaking, "You're holding a piece of paper with a drawing of a dog and a heart in blue crayon. There's something written in red ink on the bottom which I'm hoping is not blood. What's the message?" The moment of dizziness passed, and the room came back into focus. Far too many sets of eyes were focused on her face.

Jefferson handed the paper to Kiran. "We've only had it for an hour, but crime lab's taken samples. It's the Jimenez girl, and I'm afraid it *is* blood, but not the child's." Her director turned a hard eye to one of the mercenary types leaning against a wall.

The drawing was signed in crayon *Andrea.* Andrea Jimenez, age six, snatched from her backyard while her father was inside fixing mac and cheese for lunch. Kiran had interviewed the devastated family herself. A wave of nausea swept over her as the image of the family photo album came back to her with all the smiling faces and the camping trips. Andrea's mother had held the album as her hands trembled.

Below the blue crayon was a riddle scrawled in scarlet. *'The King comes for the vengeance of Heaven and Hell. Nothing in this world, mortal or eternal, shall hinder him until his task is complete. The Twelfth will soon be taken from your hands.'*

Kiran held the paper up to the fluorescent lights and let her eyes go out of focus. Anatol insisted that Krol was a genius. What was he up to? Was he calling himself a king? What task was he trying to complete? The black mark under Kiran's sleeve throbbed with sudden intensity, and her nostrils filled with the smell of burning wood and incense. She tasted old blood and

CHAPTER 6

somehow, she knew. Krol had held this paper in his hands. Had sent it to draw them in.

"It's not what it appears." she told Jefferson, ignoring the rest of the room who wanted her out of here.

"How can you know that?" Jefferson asked.

Le answered before Kiran could make something up, "Whoever sent that note wants to taunt us, wants us to know that they are coming for another child, wants us afraid."

"It's more than that. He wants to draw us out," Kiran said. It was a partly a guess, but the imprint she'd found couldn't be coincidence.

"Draw us out?" One of the mercenaries had an Israeli accent. The man next to him looked to be his twin. "How does that note lead us anywhere? Your director said the crime lab didn't find a single print. The DNA matched no one."

Kiran handed the paper back to Jefferson and tried to banish the image of Krol shaking the life out of Anatol. She unclenched her jaw and forced the words out. "The handwriting almost presses through the paper. There's a faint imprint left behind from something they placed the paper on. Looks like it says Seattle Quality Meats to me. Half the letters are missing."

Le took the letter and held it up to the light. "I don't know, Kiran. It's damn faint, but I can make out maybe four letters. Shit. Crime lab only had it for ten minutes, but they should go back to school."

Chief Short slammed his fist on his desk. "That's a major warehouse. We have them."

The room erupted in a host of people shouting about how and when they should move on the warehouse, how much time they had to scout it out, and whether they should surround it now before the children could be transferred to another location.

"It won't work," Kiran said. "You can't just raid it."

One of the twins snorted. "If they're there, we'll have them out by morning. My brother and I have planned more infiltrations than we care to remember."

"We've time to set up sniper positions and get cameras in." A man with a decidedly Southern accent spoke for the first time. He was leaning against a wall holding his chin. "Won't make the dumb mistakes SWAT did."

Chief Short nodded in agreement. "I can have the entire block surrounded in half an hour. You can move your teams in through the ring."

A host of ideas followed as Chief Short unfolded a city map on his desk and outlined the area where the warehouse was located. Only Kiran and a red-haired woman in a black jacket sitting in a chair were silent. Finally, Jefferson got control of the room.

"Patel, you don't have to be part of this action if you don't want to. You've accomplished more in five minutes than the damned crime lab." She looked Kiran in the eyes. "From what you've seen of them already, what do you think is the best approach?"

"You're wasting what little time we have, Director." The Irish jerk who had wished her dead broke in before Kiran could think of a smart answer. "We don't need more cooks for this pot. You've got the best assault team in the business right here."

"An overconfident and likely dead team is what you have." Kiran ran a hand through her hair while she continued. She was out of gum and that totally sucked. "Anatol said that everyone who went after Krol in the past ended up dead. I went back and found his case file from the seventies. Eight members of the Polish police were found dismembered. Anatol said Krol was a genius. Krol wouldn't have left a note that leads us to his hideout without a reason."

The red-headed woman lifted a hand, silencing two others who were about to voice their opinions. "Patel, I don't know you, but you don't strike me as insane. A little odd, maybe, but not psychotic. I was willing to give your partner the benefit of the doubt, he suffered a head injury, but not you. You don't seriously believe this man we're after is Jako Krol? A priest who would be eighty-five years old by now if he were alive? A man who had his head bashed in 1972?"

Kiran met the woman's eyes and wished she hadn't. They were ice blue, rational, and harder than diamonds. These were the eyes of a person who was very sure of herself. Eyes that exuded a confidence Kiran pretty much never had.

"What I saw back in that church, demolished a SWAT team—" Kiran began.

CHAPTER 6

"A divided team, unprepared to take on an assault of fanatics," the woman interrupted.

"It was more than that." Kiran picked up the crayon written note once more and stared at it. "Whoever that man was, he wasn't entirely human. He was bigger, faster than anything I've ever seen. Anatol was sure it was Krol." Of course, she sounded like a complete kook. Why did the truth have to make her sound like a liar?

The woman looked Kiran up and down before speaking, "There were reports that the entire church was filled with smoke. They must have used a hallucinogenic, probably ketamine, which altered your perceptions, slowed your reactions, made you all easy targets. I appreciate the honesty of your account. Someone less reliable might have left the supernatural part out for fear of sounding batshit crazy. Now, at least, we know we'll need gas masks."

Jefferson let out a sigh. "Patel, meet Dr. Judith Garner, CIA Psychoanalytics and one of their best field agents. She's done her own analysis of this cult. She believes its leader is a former techie who has a vengeance complex. What she's saying makes sense."

Kiran nodded despite herself. And what the dumb FBI rookie is saying is batshit crazy, right. She knew Garner made sense, knew that everything that had happened to her inside that church could be explained as an LSD-fueled trip, but she knew what she had seen.

Her eyes found the three black tendrils of the tattoo twining out from the sleeve of her right arm. She had never visited a tattoo parlor in her life. Anatol had not sounded insane when he told her about the Ghost. Anatol had insisted she trust Jefferson to pick the best people. She couldn't let this team walk into a trap. If they failed, what would happen to the children?

Kiran forced herself to step closer to Jefferson. "You know what Anatol believed. He promised you would help when the time came. That I should trust you to pick the right people. If Anatol was right, the monster that killed him is going to rip this team to pieces. What do you really believe, Director?"

Jefferson's face hardened. "I believe you agreed to be part of this team and to leave Anatol's ideas behind. Even he acknowledged they were dangerous. More dangerous than whatever we're fighting. I believe you should know when to leave well enough alone, Patel. I don't need a junior agent questioning my authority. The kids don't have time for that."

Dr. Garner stood up and gave a sickening smile. "We've appreciated your thoughts, Agent Patel. They've been invaluable. I look forward to more of your analysis at a later date."

More assholes who appreciated her input? Kiran made a fist. "There's not going to be a later date. This is the one lead we have, and you are going to throw it away with a frontal assault. Krol wants you there."

"We will account for the fact that he may be robotically enhanced and use chemical weapons," Garner added. She turned to Jefferson. "Director, I believe your agent has contributed enough. I think she deserves a week of rest."

Jefferson narrowed her eyes at Kiran. "Take a walk, Patel. We'll talk tomorrow. You can be part of the debrief. Get some sleep. God knows you need it."

Kiran dropped Andrea's desperate drawing on the desk, spun on her heel, and walked out, banging her shoulder on the doorframe in the process. She slammed the door behind her which must have seemed beyond childish, and strode down the hallway, still shaking.

Kiran passed the main floor and was grateful to see that Gonzales and Reese were gone. She needed to be alone. The black ink on her arm was hot, the air in this whole damn place was unbearably hot, and her temper matched. She couldn't shake the image of Anatol in her arms, bleeding on the church floor. She found herself taking the stairs that led to the roof. Her mind was a fog. She needed fresh air.

She took the stairs two at a time up three flights to a steel door marked EXIT. She had to put her shoulder to it twice before it unstuck and spilled her out onto the asphalt-covered roof. The door crashed closed behind her with a squeal of rust on rust.

The Seattle night was strangely devoid of clouds. Stars and a new moon shone down on her. The roof was littered with empty beer cans, dented waste baskets, and a rusted water tower covered in pigeon nests. She drank in the cool air and ran her forearm across her brow.

CHAPTER 6

She had a crappy view of the city from here despite the clear sky. The roof was low, and the surrounding buildings hemmed the station in, but she could still make out the top of the Space Needle blinking green above the rest of the jumble.

Somewhere out there, Krol was hiding those kids. They must be beyond terrified, doubting whether anyone was ever coming for them. She forced aside the thoughts of what Krol might be doing to them. That way lay despair. She had tortured herself enough with those thoughts alone at night in her apartment. Instead, she pulled up the sleeve of her shirt and studied the pattern that had crept onto her arm like an alien scrambling for a new host.

The mark proved she wasn't suffering some lingering effect of ketamine upon a susceptible mind. She ran a finger over the pattern of black lines that had invaded her skin. They spun together like the arms of a many-limbed monster to end in a whirl about her inner elbow that coalesced into the shape of a fisherman's hook.

Pierce your skin with the hook over the mark and say the words when the time is right.

He had told her to have faith in herself when no one else did because faith was the only thing that would save her. If it were all nonsense and nothing more than hallucination, a way for her mind to process the stress of losing her partner, then it would make no difference if she tried. All she would lose was a drop of blood. She swallowed hard. But if it were real and Anatol was right, she would be calling into this world a nightmare far worse than Krol. A nightmare she had to control or who knew how many people it might kill? And if she failed to call it and Krol was more than a dream, then the team below would all be slaughtered, and along with them any chance at bringing the children back.

He'd said she had to have faith in herself when no one else did, but all she felt was doubt. How could she ever control a monster when she felt so out of control herself? She could never lead a team to take down Krol. They didn't even want her as a tag-along.

She felt the iron hook dangling from the necklace and noticed again how terribly sharp it was. She lifted her arm and the black lines shone in the moonlight. Nausea hit her like a punch to the gut. She was not going to fail those children. Before she could throw up, she pierced her skin with the pendant over the mark of the fishhook. She let the necklace fall back against her chest and grabbed the wall.

A scarlet drop of blood welled up from her arm and the black lines began to shine and burn. Clouds slid over the moon. The night closed around her like a net, like a question waiting to be answered, like a spell waiting for the words.

Speak the words Anatol had said, but what words? What had he muttered to himself when he was in the hospital? What had he said in the church? Kiran racked her brain as the clouds rolled across the moon and she felt the moment passing, felt whatever chance the world had at redemption slipping away. The words came to her in a rush, she wasn't sure if they were quite the ones Anatol had said, but wherever they came from, they rang true.

"When the heroes have fled and all that remains is fear, you must pay the price and call him back, for though the hordes of Hell be vast, the Tools of the Ghost are without number." She whispered the desperate prayer into the darkness.

And the darkness answered.

Chapter 7

A long, agonized scream tore through the night. Kiran drew back against the brick wall as the heavens flashed red.

She lifted a hand to shield her eyes as a ball of flame hurtled across the sky toward the space needle. It looked like a shooting star, burning bright as it broke through the atmosphere. She held her breath as she tracked its descent. If it kept on its path, it was going to destroy Seattle's most famous landmark.

Too late, she realized the meteor was turning, growing ever larger. It was headed straight for the station, like a fiery angel of death, and she was about to go out the way of the dinosaurs. She grabbed for the door to the stairwell but found it stuck fast as if the damned metal had fused to the doorframe and rusted in place. The scream of the meteor grew deafening, drowning out all thought, warping the air around her. She turned back in time to see the flaming ball hit the roof, bounce, strike the water tower, and spin in her direction.

Kiran threw herself to the ground as the world around her flew apart. Bits of debris pelted her hands as she covered her head and a wash of heat blasted over her. She lifted her head as a gout of flame shot up from a hole in the roof where the meteor had evidently landed. It had ripped through a brick wall and tore a hole in the roof the size of a swimming pool. The roof was ablaze.

She'd escaped the impact and now was going to die in a fire. Before she could get to her feet and throw herself at the door again, a creak of rusted iron caught her attention. She turned to see the water tower teeter on its last legs and crash down across the roof. Clouds of steam billowed up as hissing water met flame and surged in her direction.

THE TOOLS OF THE GHOST

Kiran rolled away from the onslaught of water and the expanding tear in the roof. She scrambled to the edge of the building and put her back to the low brick wall as hot water splashed over her arms and legs.

She froze at the sound of a scream.

It was a low guttural wail from within the cloud of steam that made Kiran clench her teeth. That was the cry of a person who'd been burned beyond death, who could know no salvation. Someone had followed her up those stairs. Whoever had come after her had been very unlucky.

Kiran picked herself up and made her way toward the ruined stairway. She was soaked through, her hair plastered against her face. The right side of her chest felt like she might have cracked a rib when she hit the ground, but she forced herself to keep moving. It could be Jefferson or Le hurt in there.

She stopped as a squad of ragged crows hopped out of the steam. The wet birds flapped soaked feathers, shedding droplets as they croaked complaints. Then, apparently dry enough, they flapped their wings and took flight. Kiran turned away as feathers brushed against her cheeks in a rush of air. When she looked again, the birds were high above, circling in the sky.

"Out, foul pigeons. Out. Nothing to see here except murder and blood," a voice that chilled her roared from inside the fading steam cloud. It was a cruel voice, utterly devoid of mercy. She was seized with the sudden certainty that it was the voice of a killer, the voice of death itself.

Her thoughts spun into high gear. That sure as hell wasn't Jefferson. None of the crew from below had followed her. Whatever magic Anatol had given her had worked. A fiend from the sky was hiding in that cloud of steam. She drew her gun and waited.

Out of the cloud of hot mist emerged an enormous gray bag covered in buckles and zippers and pockets of all sizes. The bag jangled and clattered as it swung back and forth like a monster from a child's nightmare, driving away the steam before it as if it had a life of its own.

Kiran scrambled to get out of the way as the bag almost knocked her over. Then with a final shake the enormous sack rose into the air and disappeared as a terrible figure walked out of the steam.

Six and a half feet tall, with silver skin and teeth that gleamed gray, the

CHAPTER 7

creature stomped toward her like a fiendish scarecrow from a realm of despair. But that was not what made her catch her breath. It was the eyes, darker than dead stars, that froze her blood. They were eyes that could watch a universe die and never shed a tear.

The figure adjusted the giant gray sack over its shoulder, then aimed a kick at the lone crow who had yet to get airborne. "Get out, Simon. Flap your feathers with the other mindless followers. Join your poultry brothers. I promise, this time I'm going to slaughter whoever called me. I swear by your moldy wings, I am going to rip off their arms," the figure rasped its threat as Kiran flattened herself against the wall.

A fresh cloud of steam hissed up around the apparition, obscuring him from view. The steam tickled Kiran's nose and she fought not to make a sound. She heard a zipper opening and imagined the monster pulling a foul weapon from that bag. A look over the edge of the roof told her she wasn't getting out that way. Whatever this thing was, it had her trapped.

The steam cleared once more. Kiran watched as the figure reached into the bag and drew out a long, ragged coat with one white button. He shook the coat out before thrusting his hands through the sleeves, grunting and mumbling to himself the whole time. For a second time he reached inside the bag and this time pulled out a wide brimmed hat, beyond ruined with holes and patches. He beat the air with the wreck of a hat, banishing the last of the steam before he planted it on his bald head. Then he closed the bag with a loud zip and threw it over his shoulder.

He peered across the roof. "Where are you? I will remove your entrails and read you your ill fortune. I will tear out your tongues for trying to bind me again." The figure blundered into several old garbage cans and sent them flying over the edge of the roof. He banged his fist against the remains of the rusted water tower. "There is nowhere three fools can hide on this roof." He careened forward, crushing beer bottles, falling to his knees before pulling himself up again and screaming into the night.

Kiran sneezed louder than she ever had. She'd been trying her best to hold it in but failed spectacularly.

The figure spun. He took three steps, leaped over the rent in the roof, and lurched toward her.

Her first bullet struck him in the leg, and he stumbled. Her second hit him in the shoulder and turned him ever so slightly. The third hit him dead center in the sternum as he leaped and had no effect whatsoever. He landed in front of her and knocked the gun away with one hand. With his other, he reached for her throat.

Anatol's necklace went cold as an ancient glacier against her chest.

His hand froze inches away from her skin. His black eyes went wide. "It cannot be." The figure drew back and rose to his full height before lunging at her again, both hands wide, stopping just short of strangling her. Then he backpedaled and lifted the entire bag like a battering ram, aimed at her head.

Kiran snatched her gun from the ground and scrambled to her feet. She threw up a hand in the universal signal for stop, and the creature hesitated before hurling the bag at her skull.

She stood there, trembling, and wet, and realized what this monster must be. This was the dead soul Anatol said she must summon. This killer trying to strangle her was the weapon she had to control.

"You're the Ghost monster thing?" was all she managed.

The Ghost raised an eyebrow. He didn't lower his bag.

Kiran pulled at her sleeve and the wet cloth ripped to her elbow. The sinuous tattoo gleamed in the moonlight. "I called you here. I'm the bearer or the tattoo wearer." She took a step back without thinking. "Not on purpose. It crawled up my arm, and I can't get rid of the damn thing." She pulled out the black necklace. "I've got the giant fishhook necklace." The terror of it all was gumming up her mouth. She felt her opportunity to save the kids slipping away. She was so screwing this up.

The Ghost leaned forward, narrowing his eyes. "You are a woman."

"I'm taking that as a compliment." She slipped the necklace back under her shirt and tried to keep the tremble out of her voice. "But it's me."

The Ghost took a step towards her, and she fought not to move, fought not to raise her gun. He continued until he towered over her, close enough for her to reach out and touch him.

The tattered hat brushed across her forearm as the Ghost examined the

CHAPTER 7

mark. "A woman." He locked eyes with her. She stared into the abyss of his face and shuddered.

"Still." She wondered if she should have said 'Word' like Gonzales but decided she couldn't pull that off as effectively.

His expression morphed into absolute disdain. "No woman has ever borne the mark, no woman has ever worn the chain, no woman has ever called me."

"I broke the glass ceiling."

The Ghost examined the sky. "What ceiling?"

She wiped the wet hair out of her face. "You are the Ghost, right? I got the right one?" Her mind was racing with every possibility from the gun at her side, to making a run for it and jumping through the hole in the roof, but she rejected them all. She had to get this right.

The figure bared his teeth which she took for a yes.

"There are children who've been taken by some kind of demon. We have to—"

The Ghost tilted his head. "Have to? I have to do nothing. Nothing you command, woman. Where are the others? Where are the Cup and the Sword? Where are the scoundrels from the Book of Giants? Where are they hiding?" He spun around and strode across the rooftop, kicking twisted iron and old garbage cans.

Kiran had no idea who he was looking for. Anatol had never mentioned a cup or sword or anything about a Book of Giants, but Anatol wasn't one to pay attention to the small stuff.

The Ghost returned and held out a fist. "Where are they? I sense nothing but the mark. Where is the remainder of the trinity?"

Kiran floundered. Shit. She was supposed to have picked two people from the super spies Jefferson had assembled before summoning this thing. Anatol had said it would be the most important decision she ever made, but honestly, she didn't see much to differentiate any of the killers below.

"Downstairs," she said. "I mean, the candidates are. I haven't picked them out yet, but they're just below us."

With every word she spoke the Ghost drew closer. "You have not chosen them yet? They are not sworn to die, burned in oil, should they abandon you?

They have not been tested against the Bull of Heaven?" His face spread in a twisted grin. "Then you have no control over me at all, woman." He raised his fists to the sky. "I AM FREE. All these endless years, and I am finally set loose because of a fool."

Anatol's warning came to her, and her heart dropped a hundred feet deep into the ground. She was about to unleash a creature on this world more dangerous than anything. She had screwed up royally.

"Listen," she said, "children are going to die if we don't do something."

"And I don't care." The Ghost dropped his bag on the roof and threw himself down upon it, resting his head back on it like a huge pillow. "There is always a monster who needs killing and sad victims who need saving. Let them be eaten alive this time. Let the demons be summoned from the portals of Hell and enjoy themselves for once. You can't make me stop them. You can't make me eat a ham sandwich."

Anatol's necklace still pressed cold against her chest, an ice burn that kept her thoughts from clouding. She had messed things up, but Dr. Judith CIA whatever-her-name-was, had been wrong. Kiran hadn't been drugged and she wasn't insane. Krol was from Hell or some other place, just as Anatol had said, and lounging in front of her was a weapon to fight him with. If she could find a way to control it.

She holstered her gun and tied her wet hair back. The Ghost hadn't gone off on a killing rampage in the city yet. He'd covered his face with his hat and looked to be taking a nap. His chest rose and fell as he breathed air like any other mortal creature. Her bullets hadn't hurt him, nor had falling from the sky in a burning ball, crashing with enough force to tear the roof apart. If the tools he carried in his bag were weapons without number, she needed him on her side, or those children had no chance. Nothing mattered except those kids. *If in doubt, attack*, her father had always said.

"You cannot leave unless I send you back, can you? Anatol said that you would stay until you were done, or I sent you back."

The Ghost grunted without moving his hat. "You understand so little. Did the previous bearer tell you nothing of the rules?" He eased his hat over his eyes and regarded her. "It is true. I cannot leave this world on my own, but

CHAPTER 7

why would I want to? I can take in a play. Eat at a diner. Kill people. Things I've wanted to do for ages."

"You don't care at all about the children who were taken?" Kiran felt herself losing control of this argument as her anger built. This creature had no heart at all.

"Less than I do about turnips, and turnips irritate me."

"Krol will kill them," she screamed.

"I am the Ghost. A slave, a weapon, a tool of the Fates. I care for no one."

"Damn you back to Hell, whoever you are."

The Ghost laughed. "They wouldn't let me in the club down there. They were afraid of me." He suddenly snatched the hat off his face and propped himself on his elbows. "Who did you name? Did you say Krol?" He fell back, laughing. "How fitting. Some relative of the Krol I killed before has taken his place? The Fates are indeed twisted."

Kiran snatched at any glimmer of interest. "Not some relative. It's the same man. The one you killed has come back as a monster. He murdered Anatol. Snapped his spine and killed him." Kiran's voice broke. "And I am going to make sure he doesn't get away with it. I am going to make sure he pays and never forgets." She did her best to control the tremble. "Anatol gave me the mark. He was my partner."

The Ghost waved a hand in front of his face. "You forgot the 'I don't care' part." But he fingered the white button on his coat as if lost in thought. "Krol." The Ghost removed his hat and ran a hand over his bare silver skull. "Krol annoyed me. He shouldn't be back. No one I send away has a right to come back."

"Then you failed to actually kill him. He got away."

The Ghost looked at her with an utterly bored expression. "Brains spilled across the floor is an extremely reliable sign of an early death."

A crow croaked above and caught the Ghost's attention. "I told you to get lost, stupid bird. There's nothing to feast upon yet." He dragged himself to his feet and hefted his bag over his shoulder. He started to pace the roof. He stopped in front of Kiran again and looked her over long and hard.

A crow cawed once more.

The Ghost raised a fist to the circling crows high above. "I DID NOT FAIL, THOMAS. YOU WERE THERE. SHUT UP, JOHN. I HAVE BROKEN NO PACTS WITH YOU BIRDS."

A chorus of crow protest erupted from above.

Evidently, he had named his crows. Kiran forced herself to stay still as the Ghost shouted at the birds.

The Ghost waved an arm at the sky. "Except for the one time. Alright, I know, I know, I haven't forgotten. One mistake, and you can't ever let it go, can you? But, whatever you birds claim, I spread Krol across the stones like a dead priest pancake. This is not a second failure."

"Not dead enough," Kiran dared. "It's always in the details. Like checking for a heartbeat or going to the gravesite and digging him up and making sure he's not in there. I bet you skipped all that."

The Ghost glared with a force that could crack stone. "They accuse me of breaking faith, of not finishing my task, of betraying them again." He closed his eyes as if considering, then opened them wide. "I hear anger in your voice, woman. Do you seek vengeance? Do you desire to see Krol cast before you in exceedingly small pieces? To hear his last screams and then remind him why he is screaming?"

Kiran said nothing, but she couldn't stop herself from making a fist. Part of her wanted Krol to go through all of that. Part of her wanted him to go through far worse.

The Ghost smiled a smile she did not like at all. "That I can work with. Perhaps we are not so different." He adjusted the bag over his shoulder. "Krol should stay dead. Very dead. I will not tolerate him mocking me. What do you offer, woman? What do you offer me to kill him again and lay him out before you?"

She had no idea what she could offer a being who had crashed like a meteor into the roof, but she couldn't give up this chance. "What does a ghost want?" she asked.

The Ghost's brow furrowed. He closed his liquid black eyes. "You begin with the hardest of questions."

His eyes fell open and he met Kiran's gaze. "I want pecan pie from the

CHAPTER 7

cheapest of diners, sad whiskey straight from the bottle, the last dregs of coffee poured from the pot, bacon burned beyond recognition. I want to soak in water hot enough to remove skin, to find the face of the woman I've long forgotten, to sleep for a thousand years on sheets that don't scratch. I want to be forgiven for things that can never be forgotten and drown memory for all time. But first I want to kill Krol, because he irritates me like a flea on my back. And I want to choose who comes along for the ride. You said the candidates stand below us. Allow me to select the two who will complete the trinity and with them we will grind Krol's bones to flour and I will eat him as my bread. Allow me to choose and I will be your weapon."

"If I let you pick from those below right now, will you agree to free the children and bring them home safe?" In truth, she had no idea which of Jefferson's candidates would be best suited to babysit this monster. As long as the kids were saved it made no difference.

The Ghost shook his head no. "You have misunderstood who I am, woman. I am no one's savior. No one's redemption. I am not here to protect you or to ensure anyone's survival." He rose to his full height and looked through her, to a place where only he could see. "I am the bludgeon, the wrecker, the ball at the end of the chain. I am the tormentor, the knife in the dark, the monster under the boogey man's bed. I am no fallen angel. I am the Ghost, and I rescue no one. Aim me at your enemy, and I will kill. Point me at Krol, and he will find nothing in this world or any other that can protect him. But saving children and keeping them alive, that is no concern of mine; that is your job and yours alone."

Kiran remembered to breathe. Anatol had warned her that the Ghost was nothing more than a killer, a terrible weapon chained to a purpose, but she had not ever fully understood. She needed to be smarter. She needed more from this killer than the promise to be a weapon.

"Lousy coffee and pie won't be hard but asking to pick both of them is a lot," she said.

She'd seen the gleam in the Ghost's eyes when he spoke Krol's name. He wanted vengeance, maybe not as much as Kiran did, but he wanted it and she needed to milk that. "And that's a lot of other things you're asking for. I need you to promise to be more than a loose cannon. You need to follow my orders. All of them." She feared she might be pushing him too far. That he might just throw himself back on the ground and not listen to any more she had to say.

"You have no experience in any of this. I am the spear that will pierce the heart of Krol. You are a child."

She nodded. "Maybe a child at heart, sure. But you will promise to follow my commands to the letter until Krol is dead and your mission here is complete. Promise that and you can pick whomever you like, as long as it's one of the people below."

The Ghost's eyes narrowed. "Caveat. If you ever have an inkling as to what you are doing, I will follow your commands. Until then I will do whatever is needed to crush Krol's skull once again. I will choose the Cup and the Sword from whatever unfortunate fools you've dragged together below." He turned away for a moment, then spun back. "And I still want the pecan pie and all the rest. Otherwise, I will close my eyes and sleep here until you tire of me."

Kiran had a sudden doubt, an itch at the back of her neck. How would he weasel out of this? What was he after? "Why do you call them the Cup and the Sword?"

The Ghost threw up his hands. "Did Anatol tell you nothing? Either he was a complete fool or …." The Ghost hesitated as if he was not sure of his own deduction.

"Or what?"

"Or he had too much faith in you." The Ghost shrugged and his ragged coat shifted over his shoulders. "Either way, Anatol is dead. His body rots away and becomes dust. His deficiencies no longer matter." He held up one gray finger. "But nothing can happen without this agreement. Is our deal struck in blood and time, or do your lost children die with Krol's hands around their necks?"

Kiran already hated this jerk, but she had to make the deal work. Anatol had warned her to beware of any bargain with the Ghost, insisted the Ghost would hold her to it for all time. But time was just what she and the children didn't have. She was coming for those kids, she was coming to pay Krol back,

CHAPTER 7

even if she had to bring this maniac.

"Struck in blood and time," she said.

The Ghost gave her a smile so wicked, she feared he might reach out and bite her. The mark on her arm throbbed with sudden ferocity and she felt reality twist. Her vision clouded for a moment and the Ghost's smile was gone.

Well hell, whatever she'd agreed to was done now. She might as well get on with it. The door that had frustrated her had blown off the roof. Hot water cascaded down the shattered staircase. Kiran would be lucky not to break a leg reaching the main floor. Jefferson's voice, shouting at the operatives she'd recruited, echoed from below. They must believe they were under attack.

She started down. "I'll go first. I need to explain why the roof exploded."

Chapter 8

Kiran shoved her way through the door at the bottom of the stairway into a dark hall. An overhead sprinkler promptly drenched her. The explosion had knocked out the electricity and triggered the fire suppression system. Given the lack of light, the backup generator had obviously failed to kick in. Perfect—a pitch black corridor full of nervous operatives, all experts at killing people, with guns likely aimed at her. She sloshed her way through to the main floor and froze as three red laser sights danced across her chest.

Luckily, Jefferson recognized her before anyone put a hole in her. "Patel, what the hell are you doing?" She emerged from the gloom and lowered her gun.

"I'm getting wet, Director. Please tell your super spies not to put a hole in my head before I can explain." The silhouette of a woman shifted against one of the windows. "Dr. Garner still has her sight trained on my shoulder. I don't think I've given her enough reason to kill me yet."

The last red dot slid to the floor, but it didn't vanish. Amongst the sprinkler spray and the steely streetlight shining through the windows, Kiran made out figures hanging back in the darkness.

Jefferson stepped in front of her, thankfully blocking the line of fire. "Is it Krol? Did he hit the roof?"

Kiran shook her head. Jefferson's question made it clear that she had always believed Anatol, even if she was too afraid to follow his plan. Kiran raised her forearm, displaying the mark. "It's the other one. We don't have much time."

The Irish jerk crossed the room to stand alongside Jefferson. His gun was still in his hand, but at least it was pointed at the floor. "I don't trust this

CHAPTER 8

woman, Jefferson. She's been lying since she arrived."

"I wish it was all a lie." Kiran tried to keep her voice even. That was always a good plan when people seemed ready to shoot you. "Director Jefferson, we need to go back to the Chief's office so I can explain."

"Let's do that." Jefferson wiped a sheen of sweat off her brow. Her voice sounded shaky for the first time in Kiran's memory. "This needs serious explaining."

The red dot of Dr. Garner's sight still played at Kiran's feet. "I thought we established Krol was dead, Director. Don't tell me we have an octogenarian mastermind to deal with?"

Jefferson didn't turn around. "The eighty-year-old might be the least of our problems, Doctor, and I asked you to stand down." The red dot on the floor vanished. "Patel, please tell me you didn't do anything extreme. We had a deal."

"We're going to need a new deal. Your team was about to lose any chance at saving those kids. Jefferson, he's coming down those stairs and there's nothing we can do to stop it. You've got to get these operatives back in that office now. If they start shooting, I don't know what he'll do. Anatol promised you would support me. I need the best two of them to help control him."

Jefferson's shoulders sank. "Everyone, back to the office. Put the guns away. Move. Now."

"Someone had better explain what the hell is happening." One of the Israeli twins was getting impatient.

The doorway at the end of the hallway squealed open followed by the sound of boots splashing through water.

Kiran felt herself go stiff. "It's late for explanations."

The Irish jerk aimed his gun at the approaching steps. "I'm not going to get cornered in that office, Director. I'm taking my own advice."

Dr. Garner took cover behind a desk and aimed down the hallway. "Who's behind you, Patel?"

Kiran stepped to the side and pulled Jefferson out of the line of fire. "Put the guns away. They are not going to be helpful. I promise you, Dr. Garner."

Water splashed, and she felt the Ghost's presence like an avalanche about to crash down upon her. Director Jefferson stared up with a look of terror on her face. Kiran fought not to turn and draw her own weapon.

A backup generator kicked in and half the lights flickered on. Kiran turned to see the Ghost marching down the hallway amidst the flickering lights, like the reincarnation of Death itself. The Ghost heaved his bag off his shoulder and sloshed toward them.

"Holy shit. What is that thing?" One of the Israeli brothers got a good look at the Ghost for the first time.

The Irishman fired three suppressed shots just before the Ghost's sack flew out of the darkness and floored him.

Kiran dove to the floor. This was not how she had planned it. She looked up to find the Ghost picking up his bag with one hand and the unconscious Irishman with the other.

The Ghost held up the limp body up as a shield as red dots danced across the hall. "This one has already failed his audition," he rasped. "Are you so sure, woman, that we have the best of the best to choose from?"

Kiran was still lying next to Jefferson in a pool of water. "The super best," she said. "Please don't kill them all before we choose two." She grabbed Jefferson's arm. "Director, you need to get them to fall back."

Jefferson didn't move. "Part of me never believed. No matter how much faith I had in Anatol." Then she came alive, got to her knees, and shouted across the room. "Put down your weapons, you idiots. Fall back to the Chief's room and wait."

"He's killed Seamus." One of the Israeli brothers was crouching behind an overturned desk with his gun pointed at the Ghost. Kiran gave thanks he was smart enough not to fire.

The Ghost sniffed the Irishman's hair. "His heart is still beating. Though he may be brain dead. Possibly an improvement."

Dr. Garner took two steps back. She had her weapon leveled at the Ghost's chest. "Director, you had better tell us what this thing is."

Jefferson stepped to Garner and forced down her arm. "You're going to find out, but first I'm going to keep you alive."

The Ghost dropped the Irishman into a puddle on the floor. "Alive for now.

CHAPTER 8

The woman and I will wait for you fools."

Kiran picked herself up. She didn't bother to wipe the water off her face. "This way and don't hurt anyone else. We're going to need two of these people."

They made it back to the Chief's office without anyone getting shot. Dr. Garner and one of the others carried Seamus and lowered him into a chair. The Irishman moaned and looked to be coming around. Le and the police chief had apparently already left the meeting.

Director Jefferson squeezed the edge of the Chief's desk like a plank of wood she was holding onto as the Titanic sank around her. "When I called you six here, I told you that you might be selected for an extraction team made up of three others. All of you understood the danger and still chose to come." She nodded toward the Ghost without looking at him directly. "This is the danger. Patel wasn't lying. She wasn't drugged during the church disaster. An enemy, perhaps augmented by foreign power or bionics if you care to call it that, is chewing up our best people. It's a threat we've never faced before. Our weapons, our usual methods are useless. This is who we've called in to counter that threat."

Kiran didn't miss that Jefferson had avoided any use of the word magic or summoning in her explanation.

One of the Israeli twins looked the Ghost up and down and shrugged. "My brother and I have had to work with every type of scoundrel the world has. If we must work with a lunatic dressed up in some bizarre costume, we are both ready."

At the word "costume", the necklace around Kiran's neck burned like ice cold death. She prayed it was protecting her from this monster she had no doubt wished to kill everyone in the room. She had never felt such menace.

The Ghost glared at them from a corner of the office, his bag over his shoulder. "Ready? Who are these people who you name worthy? Who you deem *ready*? Which of them is the Cup and the Sword?"

Jefferson looked like she was about to pass out, but her voice was even and steady. "These people are the best anywhere," she insisted. "Seamus was Irish special forces, but he looks like he'll need a while to recover before he joins any team. Dr. Garner is CIA. Parker, FBI, and former special forces. Smith is a Green Beret and a specialist in explosives. Akers is one of my own SWAT members. His men were killed in the last raid. He's the best we have standing. Yuri comes to us from Israeli special forces and Petrov is his brother. I wish you could take all of them, but Anatol insisted it could be only two."

The Ghost glared at each of the candidates in turn. "You bring soldiers good at killing. I need souls that fear no flame, hearts twisted beyond repair, bodies broken and born again."

Jefferson gestured around the room at the collected operatives. "You'll do no better than these. I swear it." Her hand became a resolute fist.

The Ghost lunged forward. "Parker, they call you. Qualifications?"

"Four years in the Bureau. Three before that on special forces as team leader and decorated in—"

"Enough." The Ghost leaned in until his face was inches from Parker's. "Were you once an arrogant king who wished to live forever? Have you forgiven yourself for your pride beyond measure? Did you lose your weapon in a cold lake deeper than a rich man's greed?"

Parker looked baffled. He turned to Jefferson for explanation, but the Ghost had already moved on.

"You, explosives man, were you shaped from mud on the banks of a river? Or trained by wild animals? Did you humble a tyrant? Are you a master of the flames of the jinn?"

Smith raised an eyebrow. "C4 mainly."

The Ghost shook his head. "SWAT man, you failed to save your friends. Why should we have faith in your friendship?"

Akers looked ready to draw his sidearm. "If this is intimidation you're trying to pull, I don't give a crap. Put me in front of that thing one more time, and you'll see what I can do."

The Ghost turned away. "Angry and overconfident."

He regarded the Israeli twins. "Brothers in arms. That is good. But I need brothers who've been together for thousands of years. Souls who could die in each other's arms. What would you do if one of you perished in front of the other? If he was torn to pieces and dragged through the dirt with you

CHAPTER 8

helpless to stop it?"

Yuri ignored the question. "This creature is insane, Anya."

The Ghost waved the twins away. "Sanity is overrated." He considered Dr. Garner last then shook his head. "We have one woman already."

"Enough." Kiran thread her fingers together and squeezed to control the feeling of being about to burst. "You've insulted them all. Now choose the two you think best before we run out of time. We made a deal in blood and plasma or whatever."

The Ghost folded his arms and threw himself into a chair. "Cowards and fools will not serve. None of these are acceptable."

Akers drew his Glock and leveled it at the Ghost's head. Anger and frustration played across his face. Jefferson dragged the man's arm down.

Kiran had had enough. "You promised you'd pick two from the people we had below us. That was our deal."

The Ghost's face was expressionless. "You fear betrayal? That I would break faith so swiftly on a pact sealed in time and blood? No, woman, there is too much you still owe me. All that was promised will be paid. But remember, you dragged me here to fight. Monsters aren't killed easily. Cunning, cruelty, and the black fire of hate are the tools we will need." He gave Kiran a stare that burned into her skull. "I have chosen who will join us from those who are here among us now. As I promised."

Faster than she could have imagined possible, the Ghost stood and thrust both his hands through the thin paneling that separated the room from the hallway. He shattered the partition with his shoulder and dragged in two men, covered in splinters and dust. The Ghost batted away the stunned men's guns before they could raise them.

Reese and Gonzales fought to keep their balance.

"They were listening outside the door?" Jefferson stammered her question.

"Sneaks and cheats are what I need," the Ghost said. He pushed the two officers away and they fought to gain their footing.

"No way." Kiran felt the world further collapsing around her. She was losing any chance she had to put things right. "These two are street detectives. You'll just get them both killed."

THE TOOLS OF THE GHOST

Reese straightened his shoulders and met her eyes. "Don't say one more damned word against street detectives. The street teaches a lot you'll never understand."

The Ghost walked around the two of them. He picked a bit of paneling out of Gonzales' hair. Brushed dirt off Reese's uniform.

Jefferson slammed a hand on the desk. "What are you joking at? These two are screw ups. They haven't done one useful thing on this case. Reese only cares about himself." She appeared to think about this. "And money. Gonzales just follows along with him and hides. Pick two of these agents and be done."

Reese's hands balled into fists as he glared at the FBI Director. "I am so sick and tired of people like you, Jefferson. You've got some big shot position and think you can look down on the rest of us, right? All my life people have underestimated me, told me what I couldn't do, what I could never become. My dad died on a cold bed and told me not to put up with the same shit he put up with his whole life." He shook his head. "I shouldn't be surprised you're like all the rest, Jefferson." He turned back to the Ghost. "You touch me again, and I'm putting you down."

Kiran had a terrible feeling Reese was going to get himself killed.

The Ghost slapped Reese in the chest.

Reese stumbled back. He recovered, in a moment and stepped forward with a knife in his hand. Kiran had no idea where he'd drawn it from. Gonzales had pulled a gun out of his boot and looked like he might not even need it to take down the Ghost. His hair stood up like a lion's mane. Hitting Reese was not a good idea around his partner.

The Ghost nodded in appreciation. "Good." He then proceeded to ignore both of them. "These screw up street cops followed us back to this room without one of you noticing." He pointed at Kiran. "Not even this woman, and she sees dead crows and the paleness of shadows. They had their guns pointed straight at my heart the entire time. Look at them. They are the only ones here not soaking wet. They disabled the water system wherever they were hiding. They are brothers in arrogance and ignorance made human. Sneaky, deceitful, full of spite. They are ever lost in a world they do not

CHAPTER 8

belong in, but what men on this earth are not lost in the end? I like their style." He met Kiran's eyes. "Our pact is sacred, and I hold you to it, woman. The Trinity is complete."

"Screw this," said Gonzales, which was at least a two-word sentence. His deep brown eyes shone with anger. "You'll get us killed for nothing."

The Ghost reached into the leather pouch at his side. He drew out his hand and displayed thick ancient coins filling his palm. "You'll earn enough for all you ever desired. Survive and you will never be called loser street cops again. Die and your families will never want for anything. Pledge yourselves and your names will be legend once more as kings and heroes. This I promise."

Both Reese and Gonzales were silent for a long time.

"Don't do this," Jefferson pleaded. "Anatol told me everything hinges on this decision. That we had to be sure. You're a rookie, Patel. And these two are disasters."

Reese glared at Jefferson. He drew himself straight and met the Ghost's eyes. "What if we say no?"

The Ghost pointed his chin at Seamus who had lapsed back into a semi-conscious state. "He said no, but I wouldn't have taken him anyway. If you deny me, you go back to your existence. Tell me no and I will be the one who is wrong. Refuse and be safe and quiet for all time. Protect no one. Heal no one. Forget who you were."

Reese looked to Gonzales. Gonzales picked up one of the silver coins and felt the weight of it. "Heavy."

"I'm tired of all the bullshit they give us," Reese said.

Gonzales tossed the coin high in the air. "Word."

Reese snatched the coin as it fell. "We might get ourselves killed, my brother."

Gonzales looked like half of him wanted to attack the Ghost and the other half wanted to run out of the room. He closed his eyes tight before speaking. "At least, we'll be paid."

Reese gave Jefferson a hard smile before he turned to the Ghost. "I've had enough of the crap. These people are no better than us." He examined the coin in his hand once more. "We're not coming cheap. But we're coming."

Kiran felt the air warp around her. Felt the weight of a mountain drop upon her shoulders.

Director Jefferson stood, looking unsure of her grip on reality. "Whatever madness you have planned here, Patel, let it go. We can coordinate our efforts. The Chief has gone to prepare the backup teams to surround the warehouse. We can end this together tonight."

The Ghost waved away Jefferson's speech before Kiran could respond. "Assault whatever you fools will. The girl has promises to keep." He slammed his fist on the desk and the wood cracked. "And I hold people to their promises."

Chapter 9

It was past one a.m. and everything had gone to hell. Crammed into the corner of a booth in Seattle's most run-down diner, Kiran felt trapped in a nightmare.

"More gravy. And pecan pie. Bring the whole thing," the Ghost shouted at the waitress then rubbed the back of his coat sleeve across his face, smearing it with grease. The table was piled high with the remains of his feast. He'd eaten everything from chocolate ice cream to the fish fry and showed no signs of stopping. Kiran had no idea someone already dead could have such an appetite.

The rest of the diner had long since emptied at the sight of the Ghost. The manager and the waitress had panicked and started to phone for the police until Reese flashed a badge. They were currently huddled behind the counter, likely praying no one would die tonight.

The Ghost had insisted they stop here before he would say another word. His coat with its six buttons, five shiny black and one a pale white, looked miraculously dry. While Kiran was still dripping water over the table.

Gonzales had squeezed his oversized muscles into her side of the booth, leaving Kiran enough space for a toddler. Reese balanced on the edge, next to his partner, one of his legs splayed in the aisle. Across from them all, the Ghost was stuffing the remnants of a roast turkey leg into his mouth and licking grease off his fingers. His enormous bag covered in buckles and zippers and pockets took up the rest of his side of the booth like another misshapen member of the team.

The waitress approached warily with the pie and gravy. She lowered them to the table before speaking. "The special you ordered comes with either a pork chop or chicken fried steak. I wasn't sure which—"

"Both." The Ghost emptied the gravy boat over his plate with one eye on the waitress's fast retreating figure. "Thou shall not covet. I was never clear whether that referred to a neighbor's wife or greed in general. Kind of takes the fun out of everything though." He lowered his face to the pie and inhaled. "Ahh the pleasures of the flesh. How I've missed them."

He tore off the aluminum shell surrounding the pie and took an enormous bite before lounging back. "I count this part of the promise as kept. The grease from this pie could oil an engine." He raised a full mug of burnt coffee to his lips and drained it in one long gulp.

Gonzales seemed at a loss. Reese looked like he was reconsidering the sway of money. The lives of eleven children hung in the balance and God only knew what Krol would do next. She had to get control of this team before it all fell apart. She shuddered to think what that might mean. What would this creature do if she lost control of him?

Kiran made herself stop clenching her teeth and got up the courage to say something. "You've had your pie. Now we should go." She started to get up, hoping the rest of them might follow her lead. "Those agents will be moving on Krol. We can get there in time to help get the kids out."

The Ghost waved a drumstick in the air and failed to get up. "Don't waste my time. Your precious children won't be there. The fools your director selected are dead already, or possessed by demons, or whatever Krol has planned for them. I don't get involved in lost causes."

"They weren't going to move until two. We still have time," she said.

The Ghost raised one eyebrow. "Do we, Wand Bearer?"

"What did you call me?" She was used to being called names, but this was a new one.

"Wand, Scepter, Bearer of the Mark, names fade and lose their meaning. You were ever ashamed of who you were, how your twisted mind worked. Your mind was ever on fire. Always fighting for other's acceptance. Fighting to be what you are not." The Ghost took another bite of pie. "How much time do we have? *You* tell me."

CHAPTER 9

Kiran had no idea what the Ghost meant by all his strange names. She let it go for now and turned her thoughts to Jefferson's team, felt the gears in her mind shift, going over the possibilities. Her mouth went dry. "Krol won't wait. He'll strike as they gather, take them one by one amidst the confusion." She sat back down.

The Ghost wiped crumbs off his face with the back of his hand. "Krol will feast on their corpses."

Kiran flashed back to the church and the image of an arm hanging out the window. It couldn't happen again. "We have to warn them."

The Ghost slammed the table with his fist and the gravy boat jumped. "Warn them? How many times will you waste your breath? They would steal your glory, claim your throne, cast you aside as a brown-skinned fool girl. You are nothing to them. Nothing."

Kiran took out her phone and dialed Jefferson. The call went straight to voicemail. She had no luck with reaching Le either.

"Why waste our time on the past?" The Ghost pointed a finger somewhere between Gonzales and Reese. "Would either of you plan an assault after you were warned you would be tortured, and your skin slowly removed?"

Gonzales and Reese shook their heads, eyes wide.

The Ghost bit down on the turkey leg, crunching bones and all. "Never be brave when you can be patient," he said while chewing. He nodded at Kiran. "And you should put on dry clothes. That has got to be unpleasant."

Kiran struggled to respond to this madness amidst the crunching and cracking. If it were too late to help Jefferson's team, that would leave only the four of them.

Reese spoke first, "What you got in the sack? Weapons?"

The Ghost licked his fingers and gave Reese a long stare. "Everything. All the tools I could ever need to destroy my enemies. But the only bag you need concern yourself with is this one." He patted the pouch at his belt. "Enough coin to ensure you never work again." The Ghost held up a finger. "Wait, one second." He unzipped one of the sack's countless pockets and removed a cell phone. "Do any of you know how to work this?"

"Where did you find that?" Reese asked. "They hand out cell phones in

Hell?"

"I took it off the fool who shot me. Thou shalt not steal no longer applies once they try to kill you. Does this play music?"

Reese nodded. "But it's useless without his password and..." The phone lit up in the Ghost's hand without the trouble of passcodes. "Wait, how the hell?"

The Ghost shrugged. "Show me how to acquire music and I will double your payout."

"We aren't here to play with toys," Kiran said. She tried to make it sound like an order, but as usual no one listened.

Reese picked the phone off the table. "I better get double for this."

"We need a plan. Now," Kiran insisted.

The Ghost pulled out a toothpick from one of the many pockets of his coat and started cleaning his teeth while Reese explained the workings of the phone and the earpieces the Ghost had managed to steal along with it.

Kiran felt like she was going to explode. Krol might be taking apart the entire assault team while they lounged over pie.

The Ghost pointed at the table. "What have you done with the silverware, woman? Is that supposed to mean something?"

Kiran stopped pulling at her hair. She'd arrange all the forks and knives in groups, organized the sugar packets, lined up the salt and pepper. All without realizing it.

"This entire demon act gets so old," the Ghost continued. "Cultists summon a monster like Krol who endeavors to open a gate and let in a major fiend through some sacrifice. They never think of anything new." He waved his hand at Gonzales and Reese. "We men will take care of it. Your female wiles will not be required."

Kiran narrowed her eyes. "And how exactly are you going to take care of it before they sacrifice those kids?"

The Ghost shrugged. "Work, work, work. You have to be more Zen about this, or is it Taoist? I forget. The man of Tao does nothing, and the wind drops carved steaks in his lap—that kind of thing. Feel the way the wind blows and swerve. Or was it bend?" The Ghost rubbed his chin. "I should

CHAPTER 9

have made that a haiku."

Gonzales whispered something to Reese, but Kiran failed to catch it.

"No, I think it was Chuang Tzu not Lao, third century, but you may be right, G," Reese replied.

The Ghost leaned back against his bag. "Anyways, Krol is out there. He's dropping clues, trying to draw in the opposition. He may unleash some minor demons he's brought along for us to deal with."

"Demons?" Gonzales' mouth hung open and he abandoned whatever discussion he was having with his partner.

Reese pointed a finger at the Ghost. "No one mentioned god-damned demons. What happens if we decide demons are not our thing?"

The Ghost stared at the finger until Reese pulled it back. "Your souls are forfeit if you abandon us. I am bound to hunt you down and destroy you. You have pledged yourselves to this task."

Reese straightened up in the booth. "You didn't say shit about killing us."

The Ghost shrugged. "Rules are rules. Did the Lion or the Tin Man abandon Dorothy? Be sure they would have been torn to pieces if they did."

"I'm no Scarecrow," Gonzales said.

The Ghost's face contorted into a sneer. "You're the Lion and your friend is the Tin Man. You should have guessed that."

Reese's face grew hard. "And what does that make you and Patel? Dorothy and Glinda?"

The Ghost laughed. "The girl is Toto, wounded and abandoned. Lost in the woods with no way home. I am the Wicked Witch of the West. Dorothy is dead."

Kiran shuddered. What did he mean by wounded and abandoned? He didn't know shit about her life. There was no way he could read her thoughts, was there? She had the distinct impression that if Reese managed to anger the Ghost enough, the monster would reach across and tear out his throat.

The Ghost leaned forward, resting his forearms on the table, and the three of them drew back, pressing themselves into the backrest.

"You two are the Sword and the Cup. The strength of honesty will be the sword that holds the Ghost down. Courage and tears for the downtrodden will fill the cup for those who brave the Ghost." The Ghost leaned back and the three of them collectively exhaled. "Those were the words written long ago that still bind you, though you are nothing more than shadows now. I would have recognized you if your faces were burned off and you were wearing wigs. I would recognize you in this universe or any other."

A fire lit behind Kiran eyes. She spoke before she thought better of it. "Listen. You should have chosen one of the crew Jefferson had picked out. Lives are at stake. These two can't help us. Gonzales' knee gives out. Reese can't throw trash into a garbage can. They never came up with one clue during the investigation. Their own boss took them off the case. They're not up to this."

Reese pointed a finger at her. "You have less experience than a fresh daisy. And you piss people off. We all know you're not meant for this. Sure, you can analyze data, but this is more than that. I'm the one who should be leading this team."

Oh, hell no. As if having the asshole Ghost thing to deal with wasn't enough. "You've got experience working with a creature who wants to kill you and fighting a priest who was already dead once? Because if you've earned that boy scout badge, Reese, you can have this shitshow. But if you're talking about your stolen car beat then you can—"

With a sweep of his arm, the Ghost sent all the plates flying off the table onto the floor. Food and gravy spattered the walls.

The manager of the restaurant stepped forward and looked about to protest, then stepped back again behind the counter as the Ghost turned his eye on him.

The Ghost returned his attention to the three of them. "All of you are useless. Your lack of faith in each other is justified. But do not worry. I am the miracle you need, and I have eaten. I can correct your weaknesses."

"You can't correct her lack of experience." Reese had to get the last word.

"Weaknesses?" Gonzales seemed more interested in what the Ghost had to offer. "How?"

"Your knee is ruined. Do you wish it healed? Wish the speed of the wind and lost youth?"

CHAPTER 9

Gonzales looked profoundly skeptical, but he nodded. "Claro, but—"
"Then it is done."
Gonzales cocked his head. "Get out…" He stopped talking as he lifted his knee and struck it against the table. "Move, Reese."
Reese slid aside as Gonzales pushed his way out of the booth. The big man lifted his knee up and down and stepped hard on it. He walked up and down the diner's aisle. He jumped over the mess the Ghost had created on the floor and landed without a sound. In a moment he was back at the booth, gripping the table with both hands. "It's like I'm fourteen again."
The Ghost ignored him and turned to Reese. "You wish that hand could hold a gun and never miss again? Could hold a paintbrush and call forth Van Gogh?"
Reese took a long look at Gonzales who was standing on one leg, testing it. Reese's eyes lit up as he placed both hands on the table, closed in tight fists. "Damn straight, I do." He sighed. "I don't tell anyone. It was never real sickle cell, it was just supposed to be sickle trait, but it did a job on my joints. Writing, drawing, aiming, anything is torture. If you can do something for it, it would make all the difference."
"Open your hands," the Ghost commanded.
Reese stretched open his fists and screamed as bone writhed and snapped under his skin. He held up his arms and his fingers extended with a final crack. Then his eyes went wide. He flexed and stretched his fingers again.
The Ghost offered Reese a fork. "Strike that picture."
Reese didn't hesitate. The steel fork flew the length of the diner and pierced a painting of a rooster, cracking the glass. The fork quivered, embedded in the bird's neck. Reese took in a sharp breath.
"An animal lover, clearly." The Ghost turned to Kiran. "And you? I can give each of you one wish. One only. What is it you desire?"
"Only one?" Gonzales looked confused.
"You two have chosen and will have nothing more from me in this lifetime. But you girl, think well. The Sword is right. You have no experience in any of this. But you need not worry, I have enough for all of us. You could ask for something far more interesting, strength to match two men, beauty to

beguile any victim, sight to reveal all you are too blind to understand."

This Ghost monster managed to insult her even when he offered her shit. She hadn't gotten through being pissed off at Reese and now this. But she didn't have to think about it. She knew what she wanted; she wanted all of this to never have happened and to be alone on her bed reading an old mystery novel she'd read a thousand times, she wanted her father back, wanted to never doubt herself again, to never fear enclosed spaces or worry all night about everything, to know what she was meant to do. But those weren't superpowers. Nothing good ever came from wishes in the stories. Gonzales' knee would probably turn into an iron weight that sank him in a river. Okay, that was pessimistic, but it was a gift from someone who admitted they wanted to kill you.

"What I want is for you to get to work and find Krol. You only seem interested in ogling the waitress and eating everything in sight."

The Ghost shrugged. "That can't count. I am already bound to do your bidding. It is a minor thing. But seize your wish while you can. Are you so boring, so empty of lust for what you cannot possess? I offer you a dream. Even Anatol chose something in the end."

An overwhelming sense of loss hit her. Anatol was supposed to have trained her until she was ready for anything. She'd had it all planned. Follow his lead for a couple years until she figured everything out and won the department's respect. Solve a few quiet cases and build up her skills until she could become a senior agent. And it had all blown up. Her partner was dead, and she was stuck with an insane monster. But she could change that. She could wish for the strength to fight Krol. For a weapon to take him down.

"What did Anatol wish for?" She had to know.

The Ghost looked past her, remembering a moment from long ago. "As a child, he first wished for his brother to live. That bound us together, but I could not count that." The Ghost shook his head, coming back to the present. "He did not trust my offer. I gave him a gun. A weapon that would not fail. You carry it at your side."

She placed the brass gun Anatol had left her on the table. Her own gun had been useless, but this one hadn't killed Krol either. "This heavy antique

CHAPTER 9

thing?"

"I see he gave it to you. But he was the one who tricked me. He insisted the gun was my choice, not his. He wished for something else in the end."

"What did that old scoundrel score off of you?" Reese asked.

"A beast. Nothing more. He was content with a shaggy dog to stay by his side. Anatol was a strange one."

The gun, suddenly, was the last thing Kiran wanted. A magicked item created by a foul creature who had committed who knew what crimes? She slid the gun to Reese.

"Take it," she said. "If your aim is as good as that, it'll be of more use to you. I'm not into sixteen-hundreds dueling junk."

For the first time the Ghost's superior expression vanished. "You would give up such a weapon to someone you can barely trust?"

"What do you mean, barely trust?" Reese had already taken the gun, pulled it close.

The Ghost seized the front of Reese's uniform before he could blink. "Arrogance and greed fuel you and always have. I chose you because I understand you to the bottom of your boots. The sword you wield is too cheap to disappoint me." He thrust Reese away and the man bristled, clutching Anatol's gun tight as if he might unload right there.

"And me?" Gonzales had stopped hopping and looked concerned.

The Ghost scoffed, "You've given up on most everything already, haven't you? All you have left is your silence and your fear. You have no room in your heart for the downtrodden. What do I have to fear from any cup you hold? Your control over me is a thin thread."

Kiran shivered. Who was this creature who had them at his mercy? Whoever he was, she was sick of his attitude. "What about you? Who were you in your past life? What crime was so terrible that it could never be forgiven, even by your god?"

The Ghost bent forward until his face was an inch from hers, his eyes burning black, like portals to Hell. "I seek no one's forgiveness! You wish to know who I am, who I was? I'm the nightmare that demons dream of. I am the creature who killed the Easter Bunny and ate his soul. Take off the necklace and I'll show you what my enemies see before their demise."

Kiran felt the burning cold pouring off him, threatening to extinguish her. Every atom in her body demanded she flee. But lives depended on her not running away. Anatol had chosen her for a reason. She was supposed to pull this team together even if they thought she was just a girl they had to bring along.

"Liar." The word came out too quiet, but it was a start. "Anatol told me you were once a man. A simple man, nothing more. The Easter Bunny would kick your ass. Enough threats. Whatever you are, eleven children's lives must mean something to you. This team has to work together."

The Ghost bared his teeth. "They can roast in Hell for all I care. And we are NOT a team. You are the master. I am the slave. Remove the necklace. See for yourself what the slave will do when free." He threw himself back in the booth. "Waitress, I am not done with you. Bring pie, bring coffee." He thought for a moment. "And those little bags that keep everything hot."

Sweat dripped down Kiran's cheeks. She wondered if she was hallucinating. The waitress brought pies and takeaway bags and a steel thermos full of hot coffee, all of which the Ghost stuffed away inside his bag.

"If you're supposed to obey me, then start taking orders. We're getting out of here, because if I were Krol, I wouldn't be satisfied with taking out that team. We're the ones who matter. I'd make sure we were all dead. We can't stand around and wait for him to move. I can't explain, but…"

Maybe it was a glimmer of light in the window overlooking the street, or the way the Ghost turned his head ever so slightly. Maybe it was sheer luck that made her move.

But Kiran cut short what she was about to say and stood up an instant before the window exploded.

Chapter 10

White fluff filled the air as bullets punctured the cushion. Gonzales dragged Kiran to the floor before she could react. Reese lay next to her, holding his arm. Blood poured down his wrist from a hole through the center of his palm.

The Ghost reached under the booth and ripped the table off its bolts. He smashed it into the window, blocking the shooter's view. "The man of Tao does nothing, and the wind drops everything in his lap," he said. "Definitely Taoism."

"Shit. He put a bullet through my hand." Reese rolled on the floor and moaned.

The Ghost shook his head. "God gave you two, Reese. Count yourself lucky."

The sound of a fully automatic roared outside and a long line of holes appeared in the table the Ghost held against the window. The sniper hadn't given up. They'd be shifting to a better angle soon. If Gonzales hadn't been so quick, Kiran would probably be dead. The combined smell of pecan pie, gravy, and Reese's blood filled her nostrils, and she almost threw up. Luckily, the manager and waitress were still unhurt behind the counter, but this was a crappy start.

"This couldn't be better." The Ghost took another bite of chicken leg.

"We're supposed to be hunting them," Reese protested. He opened and closed his hand and groaned. "This shit hurts."

The Ghost spared Reese a withering glance. He peeked through the window. "There's only two shooting at us from across the street, next to that lamppost.

THE TOOLS OF THE GHOST

See for yourself."

"No, I'm good. I'm not getting my head shot off. I only have one of those." Reese held his wounded hand to his chest.

Kiran crawled through the mess of food the Ghost had tossed on the floor. She picked up a pile of unused napkins and pressed them to Reese's hand. "Press this against the wound." She left Reese, crawled two booths down, and risked a look over the windowsill. Under the lamplight, a bald man in a T-shirt was leveling a rifle with a scope at the diner. Another stocky figure in a brown coat stood with what looked like a military grade assault weapon. She ducked back. "Two I can see. They've got the place covered. If they rush the door, we're dead."

Gonzales had his gun drawn. "Ay, Dios mío." Sweat poured down his face. "We're going to die."

"Let's shoot them first." The Ghost jammed the table into the window frame and left it there. Then he seized Reese's wounded hand and ignored the scream as he stuffed a napkin through the bullet hole. "Shoot him. Your aim is true."

Reese narrowed his eyes. "Damn fools. Time for some payback." He crawled toward the window and lifted Anatol's gun to the hole between the table and the outside world. He stole a glance and fired.

The man's scream was the next thing Kiran heard. She raised her head. One shooter was on the ground, the other running.

The Ghost pulled Reese's arm down before he got off another shot. "We need one alive." The Ghost pushed the table out the window, destroying the entire frame. "Gonzales, give chase. I'll pay the bill."

Gonzales stepped over the window frame, his gun in hand. "Dios me bendiga." He leaped through the window as if his knee had never bothered him.

She couldn't believe he'd just sent Gonzales running out into a middle of a firefight alone and that Gonzales had actually gone. The Ghost was going to get them all killed and probably didn't care. Kiran picked herself up and brushed a chunk of pie off her shirt. If she survived this, she was going to need a long shower.

CHAPTER 10

The Ghost reached into his pouch. Silver coins caught the light as he tossed them into the air. The waitress and cook took cover as the ancient coins banged against the counter, spun in frying pans, and clanked into empty coffee pots.

"No receipt required." The Ghost strode through the window as if he were going to a slow Sunday picnic, dragging his sack, glass and window frame trailing behind him.

Kiran grabbed Reese. "Come on."

Reese opened and closed his wounded hand. "Looks like it missed the bones. I'm straight." He picked himself off the floor. "Can't leave Gonzo out there alone. I'm going out the front. There might be a third shooter we haven't seen taking shots at my brother." Reese pulled out his phone. "I'll call for backup." He stayed low and headed for the door.

Kiran stepped through what was left of the window and sprinted to her car. Gonzales and the second shooter had already turned the corner. The Ghost's magic had put lightning into Gonzales' legs.

Kiran threw open the door of her car to find the Ghost already in the driver's seat. Before she could go around, Reese piled in the other side. She dove into the back as the Ghost shifted and the car lurched ahead. She slammed against the door as they whipped out of the parking lot and around the corner.

Reese stuck his head out the window. "He jumped on a Harley. Looks like Gonzo might catch his ass anyway."

Sure enough, Gonzales was about two hundred yards ahead, gaining on a square-built man on a motorcycle. The Ghost gunned the engine and managed to sideswipe two parked cars, drive onto the sidewalk, and narrowly miss a lamp pole. Kiran braced herself against the seat and tried to at least wrap an arm around a safety belt. Anatol's necklace might be protection against getting strangled, but it looked like the Ghost was allowed to smash her to death in a car crash.

They managed to overtake Gonzales just as the shooter jumped off the bike and dashed into a warehouse. The car slid sideways into the curb and screeched to a stop. Kiran succeeded in not throwing up.

"Unfortunate. I didn't hit anyone." The Ghost sounded disappointed. He threw open the driver's door and stepped out as Gonzales caught up.

Gonzales didn't even look winded. "Mierda. Almost got him."

The Ghost reached over his head and cracked his knuckles. "No need for haste, Gonzales. He won't have run far."

Kiran grabbed Reese. "Did you call SPD for backup? I can't get through."

Reese shook his head. "Dispatch won't answer. System must be down."

"Perfect, just perfect." Kiran's fingers had gone cold. She suspected that much more than dispatch might be down. Krol was moving faster than they were and taking out all their support.

She looked up at the warehouse. Four stories tall, it looked like an abandoned building out of a horror movie. The dark bricks were stained with soot as if the building had survived an inferno but retained the scars. Its windows were dark, half of them cracked. A black fire escape wound up the west side of the building. They probably should go around back or find another way in. This stank of another one of Krol's traps.

She squeezed the black mark over her forearm before she realized what she was doing. Anatol told her she would be able to sense magic, to feel when reality was bending. But the mark on her arm was as quiet as a shopping mall tattoo. Why was she still sure they were all going to get killed?

"I don't think Krol is here," she said.

The Ghost looked up at the sky and sighed. "Wand Bearer, your mind remains in shackles. You are lost to your true senses." He spread his arms wide and breathed deep. "Smell the shadows. Look to the sky. Krol cannot be here. The crows have not arrived, and they never miss a feast." He cracked his knuckles. "Without Krol, your guns should still kill people. This won't take long." The Ghost dragged his sack from the back seat and slung it over his shoulder. He leaned against the car door and pulled out the cell phone he'd stolen. He started scrolling with his thumb and kept talking. "I don't know why humans always long to open a portal and bring across some demigod to rule over them. But our part is easy. We go in, grab a cultist, and rip off his fingers until he tells us where the ritual will take place. Then we keep it simple and kill everyone. Do unto them before they do unto us. Embrace the chaos. Same routine every time."

CHAPTER 10

"It feels wrong," Kiran said. "I think we should—"

"You think too much." The Ghost adjusted the sack on his shoulder. "Feel free to doubt yourself as much as you like. Never doubt me."

Kiran threw up her hands. "Don't doubt the guy who wants to kill me, sure. Maybe, deep down you care about our safety, but someone should go around the back." Even if the evil jerk had all the experience, marching in there just seemed dumb. The night smelled of death.

Reese put a hand on her shoulder like a senior officer might to a dumb rookie, and she considered pepper spraying him. "Hold up. We stay behind the monster and live to collect the check."

"Greed is wisdom we can all appreciate." The Ghost marched up to the door the shooter had gone through and kicked it in. The door cracked in two and fell off its hinges. "Follow me and I will make you fishers of lousy men." He disappeared inside.

"Great." She was supposed to be leading and their secret weapon had already abandoned them. The Ghost clearly had different tactical training than she did.

Gonzales drew his gun and shrugged. "Vamos."

Reese nodded. "There's no telling that monster what to do." He looked up at second story windows. "I've been in this building. It's a junk-yard. Plenty of spots for a shooter to hide. That fire escape should get you in at a good angle."

Gonzales pointed to the black cast iron spiral on the far side of the building. "Cover us."

"Fool better not run out of money." Reese finished wrapping his wounded hand in a rag. "We're going to need a long vacation." He pulled out Anatol's gun.

The necklace went cold against Kiran's chest and her vision blurred for a moment. "Be careful. Something feels wrong about this."

Gonzales shrugged. "It all feels wrong. He shouldn't have picked me." Gonzales followed Reese toward the door. Sometimes Gonzales made Eeyore look cheery.

She headed for the fire escape, trying to stay close to the shadows and out of the sight of a potential sniper. Gonzales and Reese had already entered the building. She knew they were sending her around back to get her out of the way. With her luck there might not even be a back entrance and she'd be stuck outside and miss the whole thing.

The fire escape looked like it might collapse at any minute. Wrought iron creaked as she started to climb. With each step the necklace grew colder against her chest and her feeling of something terribly wrong grew with it. She imagined her dread the same way she had as a child, like a giant trembling shadow, following just behind, trying to hold her hand as she dashed up the stairs in fear of the basement. It tiptoed alongside like a completely wimpy monster, desperate for comfort.

Kiran paused on the second-floor landing and her dread paused with her. She imagined the shadow shaking its head frantically at the suspiciously ajar yellow door in front of her. She took a deep breath and did her best to ignore it. The black mark throbbed against her skin as she reached out for the handle, and hesitated. Some magic bullshit was clearly going on here. Whatever it was, she didn't have time for it. She grabbed the handle, and a voice rang out against the inside of her skull. She imagined her shadow monster holding her tight and telling her that it had told her so.

"*Bring me the traitor who executed the helpless. Glory shall be your reward.*" This wasn't Krol's half-human growl. This voice dripped with majesty. Kiran felt the sudden urge to bow, to surrender, to whoever the glorious speaker was. She had no doubt that he spoke the truth; whomever he named had committed the greatest of crimes and must face justice. She braced a hand against the wall and bit her tongue to shake her thoughts free.

The door shimmered before her in a golden yellow haze. If she opened it, she knew she would find herself in a land where the unrighteous would be punished and justice would be done. In a place where her deeds would be rewarded.

"Listen, whoever you are. I have enough voices in my head already. There's no space left for squatters." She clenched her jaw until the pain cleared her mind, and the door returned to cracked yellow paint once more. Damn. Someone or something had found a way inside her head. Either that or she

CHAPTER 10

was losing her grip on reality like her father had and that was not something she had time for. She gripped her gun in both hands and shouldered the door.

The door swung open without a sound, and she stepped onto ruined hardwood flooring. A corridor ran all along the four sides of the building overlooking the central floor. The building must have served as a grand hotel in some distant decade before the rooms were gutted. The enormous space, once a lobby, was now filled with cardboard boxes and junk furniture. It looked like a squatter settlement, a place where a hundred drug deals had already gone wrong. There were a million places for people to shoot at you.

But the chase was already over. Her paranoia evidently was misplaced. They'd succeeded in getting her out of the way and getting the job done.

She made out Reese, standing with his back against a column. Gonzales was maybe ten feet away. The Ghost stood in the middle of the squatters' lobby holding a short-haired man by his shoulders. She'd guess two hundred and eighty pounds of mostly muscle.

The Ghost shook him like a rag doll. "Don't think I don't enjoy this because I do. It's my favorite part, but it can't go on forever." He turned back to Reese and Gonzales. "You guys enjoy this part, don't you?"

Kiran was glad to see both detectives shake their heads 'no.' Gonzales and Reese looked as uncomfortable as she felt.

The Ghost shrugged. "Where is Krol?"

The man stayed silent as the Ghost continued to squeeze.

"Please, don't let the Ghost pull off his fingers," Kiran prayed silently with no idea who she was praying to or why she was praying for the jerk who had tried to kill them. She didn't even have an idea who the Ghost answered to in the end. She was fairly sure it wasn't any of her gods.

Sweat shone on the man's forehead as he trembled. "He'll kill me if I say one word. You don't understand."

The Ghost lifted the man off the ground until he was at eye level. "I understand the language of threats and killing people all the way down to commas and semicolons. What is your name?"

The man hesitated until the Ghost shook him again. "Ryder. It's Ryder."

"Ryder, the Lord gives you life, and the Lord taketh it away." The Ghost twisted and there was a sickening crack.

The man screamed as his left shoulder popped out of its socket and hung limp at his side.

"Reese, bring this loser a chair before I throw him on the floor."

The Ghost dropped the man into the chair Reese supplied. "I believe there was a question you wished to answer?"

It was like watching a horror movie she couldn't stop. Kiran felt like she should be rescuing the man, even though he'd been trying to put holes in them minutes before. Why didn't he just answer the damn question?

The man's eyes were desperate. "Krol sent us. He told us to kill as many of you as we could."

She scanned the area for anyone who might get behind them. It was too dark to see much. A giant ruined chandelier hung by a worn cable and shed scattered light down below. She hated this place. There were too many spots where someone could hide.

"How did the priest return to this world?" the Ghost asked.

Ryder lifted his head. His face struck Kiran as oddly placid for someone who just had his shoulder forcibly dislocated.

"Krol is no priest. Krol is vengeance." Ryder chuckled despite having one shoulder hanging at an odd angle. "You think you know everything. Think we're some stupid cult, performing empty rituals. That we don't understand what we're getting into."

The Ghost worked his tongue over his teeth and dislodged a stuck piece of pork chop. "Where is he? Tell me and I may let you keep your fingers."

The Ghost finished his latest threat and Kiran drew in a quick breath at a sudden pain in her arm. The lines of the black mark began to twist along her forearm as if they were alive. She looked down to see steam gust up through the cracks in the floor. What the hell was going on? She ignored the pain and pressed herself against the railing, searching below for a disaster she felt certain was coming.

Ryder leaned forward, grinning in a way that sent a shiver through her. The cultist was supposed to be losing his shit, not gaining confidence. Without thinking, she trained her side arm on the restrained man in the chair.

CHAPTER 10

With a sickening pop, Ryder's shoulder snapped back into place. He reached out his arm and flexed his fingers, still smiling. "Much better. You see, I'm going to need this arm." He seized the Ghost by his coat. "Let's get to know each other better until Krol arrives."

The Ghost tilted his head ever so slightly. "You truly desire to know what I am?"

Ryder's eyes began to glow with a sickly yellow light. "I would much rather break your bones."

The air shimmered as the floor beneath them rotated like the stage of a Broadway play. Damn. The entire thing had been a set up. They were waiting for the Ghost all this time.

Kiran fired and Ryder jerked. Reese emptied three more rounds into him before Ryder and the Ghost disappeared behind a white veil of steam. Kiran felt every neuron in her body dump their adrenalin load at once. It was another twisted situation where anything could go wrong. She almost punched the wall.

The back door opened, and a gust of fresh air sent the smoke swirling. She lost sight of Reese and Gonzales. She realized they were both screwed.

"Behind you!" She emptied her magazine and managed to hit one of the cultists rushing into the building, but there were so damn many of them. A huge gust of steam welled up from the floor as gunfire erupted. She aimed into the mist. Sweat rolled down her back as she waited. Any shot she fired now was likely to kill the people she was trying to protect.

The smoke cleared to reveal a ten by ten-foot steel cage in the center of the room. The Ghost and Ryder were trapped, and things were not going well for her side. Ryder's muscles had bulged to impossible proportions. He had the Ghost by the back of his coat and was clearly enjoying slamming his skull into the bars. At least ten cultists were watching the show. Gonzales and Reese were both on the floor, their hands zip tied behind them, knives held to their necks. It had all gone horribly sideways.

Ryder shook the Ghost and slammed him into the cage one more time. "Krol wanted us to find out how to kill him? It doesn't seem hard." He pressed the Ghost's face against the bars and whipped around in a circle, grinding him against the steel. He finished by lifting him overhead and smashing him against the floor. It was a scene out of a WrestleMania nightmare.

Her breath caught as two of the cultists shoved long guns through the bars. She crouched and ran down the corridor to get an angle on them but was too late. She peeked over the banister as they unloaded a stream of bullets into the Ghost. His body flipped over with the force of the impacts until their guns clicked empty. Finally, Ryder kicked him in the gut as a finishing touch, launching him into the bars once more. Kiran took aim at Ryder's head. He'd killed the Ghost and she was going to make him pay for that. She was only going to get one chance before they knew she was up here. She hesitated as the broken figure raised a hand to grab a bar of the cage. Something inside her told her to wait.

"Get up," Kiran whispered, willing the Ghost to rise.

"The freak is still moving? I'll fix that." Ryder pulled a long gun through the bars and proceeded to beat the Ghost with it until the assault weapon fell to pieces. The Ghost scratched a hand across the stone floor.

Ryder leaned back against the bars and flexed his out-of-proportion muscles. "He's over-advertised, Collins. The spell Krol gave us is all we needed. He's half-dead already. Let's drop the cage and baptize him."

One of the cultists, who looked far too much like Abraham Lincoln with a shaggy beard, stepped close to the bars. "The fire first. I want to see him suffer for what he's done."

The Ghost's hand fell upon his bag.

One of the cultists stepped forward with what appeared to be a flamethrower with a pair of old-fashioned bellows attached to the back. "Give me a second," he said.

The Ghost drew a five-foot-long iron rod out of his sack and brought himself to one knee. He slammed the rod onto the cracked marble.

Kiran fired three times as the cultist aimed the flamethrower. The first bullet hit the stones at the cultist's feet. The flamethrower roared. Her second shot hit him in the leg and the man screamed. Her third shot hit Ryder at the base of his skull. He grabbed his head and fell to the floor.

Kiran ducked as a barrage of gunfire sprayed the walls of the second floor.

CHAPTER 10

How had everything gone so wrong so quickly? At least her last shot had put Ryder down. She crawled to a new position and reloaded. Before she peeked over the railing, she heard the Ghost's gravelly voice.

"You are lucky I didn't lose a button." The Ghost's black coat was on fire, his scalp was on fire, his lips were on fire, but he didn't seem to mind. In his hand he held the iron rod.

Ryder got up off the floor and shook his head as if the bullet had merely dazed him. "I'm just getting warmed up."

"But I'm already on fire." The Ghost whipped the iron rod in a vicious arc, catching Ryder on the jaw, sending teeth flying across the room.

Ryder staggered but didn't fall. He threw two punches so fast that they blurred, but the Ghost simply accepted them, spun with the force of the blows, and cracked the rod into Ryder's ribs, his arms, his legs, each time with the sound of bone breaking. The monster that Ryder had become rebounded off the iron bars again and again to find that iron rod aimed at him, surgically crashing into bones, until he finally slumped to the floor. The Ghost picked Ryder up, gave him a final shake, then wedged his head between the steel bars of the cage, where it stuck like a mounted trophy.

The Ghost blew on his flaming sleeve, but the fire kept burning. He started counting buttons on his coat. "All there. My luck holds." Then he slid the iron rod through the bars of the cage and started bending the steel.

Kiran froze as the cultists dragged Reese and Gonzales in front of the cage, long knives pressed to their necks. It was all going to end like it had with Anatol.

Abe Lincoln pointed at the Ghost. "Drop your weapon, Assassin. Or we cut their throats in your honor. Your friends will die before you."

The Ghost stopped tearing the cage to pieces and Kiran resumed breathing. She thought he wasn't going to stop or care for a moment, but she'd been wrong. The monster did have a conscience somewhere deep in his soul.

The Ghost removed his hat and took a moment to scratch his silver scalp. "Wait, don't use knives. Too boring. You could hang them by their ankles and feed them to lions. Do you have lions? I loved that the last time I saw it." He yawned as flames danced across his back. "You see, I don't have friends."

THE TOOLS OF THE GHOST

He lifted the rod once more and slammed it through the bars with a clang. "But I promise you this: in two minutes, I will have this cage open, and I will squeeze every one of you fools completely through the tiny spaces between these bars until you tell me where Krol is."

Reese cried out despite the knife to his throat. "You bastard. You got us into this. I hope they find a way to make you rot in hell."

The Ghost seemed to consider Reese's raving. "You're right. I owe you something, even though you were both useless. I promise to kill the two losers who cut your throats first, and I'll push them all the way through the narrowest gap in the bars, legs, and all, even if it's messy. And I'll put all the money I owe you in your pockets afterwards, Reese. But remember this and let it be the last thought you have in that greedy arrogant mind of yours. I DON'T CARE." The first of the cage's steel bars broke off and clattered to the floor.

The two cultists who were supposed to kill Reese and Gonzales looked at the fallen bar, rolling across the floor, and then at each other. They didn't move to cut any throats.

Kiran took aim. She bit her lip and fought to keep her hands steady. It was a complete shitshow. Her team was going to be slaughtered before they accomplished anything.

The cult leader stepped forward, blocking her line of fire. He looked strangely calm despite Ryder being very dead. "Your luck has run out, Oath Breaker. All of this was preamble to ensure you suffered. Every monster has its kryptonite. Krol has readied your grave."

The Ghost shook his arm, but that only served to fan the flames eating their way across his back. "Tell me about it while I break out. Then I'm going to tear your lungs out through your ribs."

The cult leader tried to maintain a brave face but stepping back screwed up the effect. "Your threats are empty, Ghost. This will be your baptism and Hell shall receive you." He raised his right hand and one of the cultists threw a switch on the wall. A partition in the floor slid open and the cage began to tip. "A pool of holy water for your baptismal drowning, your secret weakness. Welcome to the final resting place of your soul."

CHAPTER 10

The flames reached the Ghost's other sleeve, and he gave up on extinguishing them. He adjusted his bag on his burning shoulder as the cage tipped forward and plunged into the gaping hole in the floor. The Ghost disappeared in a puff of steam as the cage sank deep below the water.

Shit. It was all on her now.

Evil President Lincoln pointed again and the tear in the floor closed over. "It is done. Krol will be pleased. All shall be ready for the King's arrival." He coughed into his hand. "Someone kill the two cops and let's get out of this shit hole. I can't take the—"

The cultists' further words were drowned out by gunshots as Kiran fired three times. Her last shot hit the mark and the ruined fixture holding up the chandelier shattered. The electric monstrosity flared bright then flickered to death as it crashed to the floor. One of the cultists standing directly below it screamed in the sudden darkness. No one was killing the two cops if she could help it.

Kiran groped her way down the stair railing, her heart slamming against her chest. She couldn't see a thing and hoped the cultists couldn't either. Everything had gone far beyond hell. The Ghost was gone, her team neutralized, and she was surrounded by people who wanted to kill her. And there was no back up coming. She reached the lower level and took cover behind the stairwell to reload.

She heard someone bump into something. "Find whoever is shooting at us." It sounded like the voice of the fake Abraham Lincoln. There was some moaning from the unfortunate person crushed by the chandelier.

Kiran took out her cellphone, covered the light with her thumb, and hit the flashlight button. With a hard twist of her wrist, she sent the phone spinning across the floor toward the voices. It was just enough light. She took aim at shoulder level.

Reese and Gonzales were lying on the floor, being ignored. The cultists were clustered near the area where the cage had been. She really hated these people.

"Which one of you idiots dropped a phone?" Abraham Lincoln was evidently not quick on the uptake. One of the cultists actually turned on their phone's light to scan the darkness, giving her an even better view.

Kiran fired twice.

Someone screamed and their phone went flying, sending arcs of faint silver spiraling across the walls. Luckily, the phone landed with its light shining toward the ceiling. It was faint, but she had a good angle if anyone came toward the stairwell. With the two SPD detectives on the floor, she didn't have to worry about hitting anyone she cared about.

She swept the gun in a chest-level arc and unloaded.

A scream preceded a thud as a body hit the floor. Kiran ducked behind the stairwell to reload.

She was about to fire again, when the sounds of cultists cursing and scrambling in the dark were interrupted by a loud thumping, getting ever closer. Kiran imagined a giant approaching, its footsteps louder by the moment. The image of Krol shaking the life out of Anatol came back to her. He was coming to kill them all.

As the thumping grew louder, one of the cultists managed to find the door and throw it open. Gray light from the streetlamps outside spilled into the room and Kiran imagined Krol's arrival, his body filling the doorframe like an overgrown Hunchback of Notre Dame. He would tear the gun out of her hands and laugh. Would tell her that she should have run away when she had the chance.

Her eyes were locked on the doorway when the floor cracked open, and a hand reached up from the tear in the ground, like the claw of a demon from the abyss. The cultist who'd opened the door screamed, was dragged down, and disappeared.

The Ghost emerged from the hole, shook himself like a dog, and slammed a dripping wet hat onto his head. He reached into his bag and pulled out his cell phone before scrolling through the screen. Then he struck his iron rod against the floor and Kiran realized what the thumping had been.

The Ghost spit out a mouthful of water. "Thou shalt not kill. That one always cracks me up."

One of the cultists threw a spear straight at the Ghost's chest.

He batted it away. "Just a moment. Gotta get the volume right on this song."

CHAPTER 10

The Ghost swiped at the phone a few times. "There, got it."

He exploded into action.

Kiran could only catch glimpses amidst the stretch of streetlight and the cellphone beams, but she could hear well enough. Cultists screamed. Bones cracked. A body struck the stairwell and slid to the floor. The Ghost ran up a wall and leaped through the air, his coat spread wide like the wings of a great silver bat. The iron rod lashed out and spun in the cell phone light and cultists went flying. The final image she saw was the Ghost holding one of the cultists up by his shirt and shaking him before dropping his limp body into the hole in the floor.

The Ghost slid the iron rod back into his bag and stared in Kiran's direction despite the darkness. "Come out from there, woman." He looked around at the dead bodies. "I got carried away. I meant to leave one alive for questioning. Untie Reese and Gonzales and let's get out of here. I want more pie."

She waited for her hand to stop trembling before she holstered her gun. She'd almost lost them all. Of course, the jerk wanted more pie.

Chapter 11

Kiran found herself in a coffee shop with Supertramp playing in the background. Her father was sitting across the table. She knew it was a dream because he told her so.

"This is just a dream." Her father took a big sip of coffee from a paper cup and his face went into panic mode, eyes dilating. "Whoa, mamma, that was hot. I won't be able to taste anything for the rest of the day." In front of her father were eleven aged and worn tarot cards, drawn by hand on plain cardboard. The suits of the tarot deck, coins and swords, cups and wands, had been colored in with what looked like glitter crayon. Over the pictures were names written in black magic marker—Petra, Andrea, Juan, Jamie, Thaddeus, and Felipe, Bar, Mateo, Thomas, Simon, and Paul. Her father slid the cards around in front of him and the glitter caught the light and made the worn cards shimmer before her.

Her father furrowed his brow. "Most of the deck is missing. I fear someone has stolen it. There are three names to each suit; swords, cups, wands, but only two for coins. They mean to take one more child, don't they?" He rearranged the cards again. "There's something about these names, isn't there? Why take these kids in particular?"

Kiran grabbed one of the cards, the ace of wands, it had little Juan's name scrawled across it. She ran her fingers over a few of the others. The drawings upon them were not the usual Marseilles deck; this was an edition she had never seen before. She picked up the two of coins upon which a man in chains with coins drawn on his back was climbing what she swore was the Space Needle. The priestess of wands displayed a young girl digging her way

CHAPTER 11

deep under what appeared to be Pike Place market with a giant wand-shaped shovel. The king of swords bore a black king brandishing a blue sword with a wall of gum behind him. And the knight of cups showed a lion lounging in a teacup with the arches of Pioneer Square as the background. The arches were on fire, which made it weirder, but it was clearly a Seattle edition.

"I hate tarot cards, Baba. They're all about fate and destiny, just like Mom with her faith in astrology. As if nothing in life was about choices."

Her father took another sip of his coffee and tapped the cards. "What choice did those kids have?"

She put the card in her hand back down, wanting to be rid of it. "Nothing connects those children. I've looked at those names for hours. There's no pattern I can find." She said it, but she didn't quite believe it. She'd spent more nights puzzling over those names than she cared to remember. The kidnappings had never seemed random to her. They had sought out eleven children in particular, even crossing state lines to take the ones they'd chosen. What on earth connected them?

Her father slid the cards around again and kept drinking,

Kiran looked around the shop. An old man in traditional Chinese robes was sitting nearby talking to someone dressed like Santa Claus. They were eating brownies that looked very tempting. The Hindu god Ganesha sat in the corner holding a teacup with his trunk while he spooned in a tremendous amount of sugar. The only other table was taken up by Reese and Gonzales, who were eating donuts. Reese was turning over a golden crown in his hands and Gonzales had twigs in his hair and was wearing what appeared to be a lion's hide over his shoulders. They both looked half dead, riddled with bullet holes and claw marks. Gonzales was missing a leg. None of this seemed to bother them. They waved at her. She knew how these dreams with her father went and tried not to start speaking too quickly, tried to just sit and not move at all. However strange it was, she wanted it to last.

"Who's the guy in the robes?" she asked. A cup of hot chocolate had appeared in front of her with one of those delicious brownies. She tried the brownie first. It didn't disappoint.

"That's Confucius. Man plays a mean game of chess. Look, I know it seems all relaxed in here, like we have all the time in the world, but I've got to tell you something while I can."

"There's plenty of time for that." She looked around for anything she could distract him with, sure that as soon as he told her whatever dream nonsense he needed to, she would wake up and it would all be over. "Hey, what is this place, the future or something? Reese and Gonzales look dead."

"You know those guys?" her father asked. "They're in here all the time. Never stop squabbling. I don't know why they sit together. You can't fix stupid."

Reese looked over at their table and gave her father the finger. He shook his head at them and turned away.

"But maybe you're right. This could be the future." Her father looked around the shop. "I'm not sure where this dream is to tell you the truth. It's on the other side of the penny, I'm sure." His brow furrowed and a look full of pain flashed across his face. "I've been in the dark, far below, lost in this neighborhood a long time."

She tried changing the subject to buy time. "Hey, do you remember when you would pick me up from school on your motorcycle?" She always used to worry when her father picked her up from school. When her mother came, the ride was predictable, filled with questions about classes and test scores and friends. Nothing to worry about. But her father picked her up on his bike, and he was a horrible driver.

"I would forget my helmet half the time and you would insist we walk home. Two miles pushing a bike the whole way." He smiled. "Cars would stop and ask if we needed a hand."

"And you would say, 'The bike is fine, but I'll take any help I can get with this stubborn girl.' And I would die of embarrassment." If she kept talking, she was going to start crying, so she took a sip of hot chocolate and managed to burn half her tongue.

"Watch it. I told you they make the drinks too hot here. Look, that stubborn part, it's the best part of you. I always knew it." Worry crossed her father's face. "I remembered what I was going to tell you. It was something about enemies and the other side." He leaned in close over the table. "There was a

CHAPTER 11

man in here recently I'd not seen before. Dressed all in white, middle-aged but impressively fit, called himself the white king. He asked me to give you a message, something biblical. He said, "Remind her of Matthew 10:36. 'A man's foes shall be those of his own household.' Or something like that. He said he would try to help you, to keep some other fellow, Krol, I think his name was, away from you. What do you think of that?"

Kiran considered it. She had no idea who this white king was. Something told her she should take any help she could get, even if it was from a Christian god she knew nothing about. But warning her that her enemies were close was a complete waste of time. She knew the Ghost was an ass who would kill her at the first chance. That was the one good thing about him, he didn't keep his malice hidden. She knew who to watch out for. This white king, on the other hand, she wasn't so sure of. In chess, she preferred playing black.

Kiran took another sip of cocoa. "He said, a man's foes, didn't he?" She put the cup down and savored the taste. "I'm no man. And that entire message sounds very fortune cookie."

Her father laughed. "It would be better if he'd made it a haiku." He blew out a long stream of breath. "I think you already know what's important in life, Kiran. Hold that close and you'll be alright." He drank the last of his coffee and turned the cup upside down on the table. "All done."

She couldn't hold the tears back any longer. "I can't do this alone, Baba. I don't think I'm the one to do it at all." There was so much she wanted to tell him.

Her father lifted one of the cards in front of him. The two of wands displayed great scepters held up at a crossroads. "Don't give up on the pawns. We should be able to figure out who the twelfth child will be. You were always the one to solve the hardest puzzles." He took her hand and squeezed. "I'm sorry. You're waking up now. Time's up."

"Just a second." She drank her hot chocolate down to the bottom and flipped the cup upside down. "All done."

* * *

Gonzales stepped out of the coffee shop, and leaned on the heavy branch like a cane. It wasn't easy to walk with only one leg in actual life, but in the dream, it didn't seem to be bothering him. He adjusted the lion skin over his shoulder. It felt right being there.

"That was Kiran inside the coffeeshop, wasn't it?" he asked.

Reese pocketed the golden crown in his robe. "She was there for a moment, then she disappeared." He scratched his beard which had twisted itself into braids and grown at least a foot long. "This is a strange dream, Gonzo. I feel like I've been waiting my entire life to get here." He rubbed a hand over a particularly large hole in his side. "Are we dead, my brother?"

Gonzales had never felt more alive. His heart beat like the heart of a great beast. He felt ready to take on an army and had no idea why. "Not dead yet, hermano. Strange that we've been waiting our entire lives to go to a coffee shop, isn't it?" All his life he'd been quiet, scared to speak too much, to reveal what was inside. Here he felt no fear. He felt wild and ready to scream. He shaded his eyes and looked into the distance where only eagles could see.

"I see a man, robed in white, coming toward us from far off. Shall we fight him when he arrives?"

Reese squinted, trying to see what Gonzales had found. "Your eyes were always better than mine. Ahhh, I see him now. He has a silver crown on his head. That's the dude they were talking about in the coffee shop, the white king. I don't like the look of him, Gonzo."

Gonzales looked down at all the holes currently in his body, not to mention the missing leg. "Fight or run, looks like we die soon, hermano." Oddly, he wasn't worried about dying for once.

Reese sighed. "I bet we're never gonna get paid." He took out the crown and slipped it on his head. "But let's wait and see what this white king has to say. I mean, it's a dream, right? How much can he hurt us?"

Gonzales readjusted the branch and wondered how he had lost his leg in this dream. "A lot. I'm pretty sure."

The two of them waited patiently. Gonzales felt certain they had been waiting for centuries already. A little more waiting would make no difference.

CHAPTER 11

* * *

Kiran woke on an inflatable mattress, staring at her kitchen ceiling with the smell of damp dog filling her nostrils. She closed her eyes and tried her best to hold onto the dream, to remember what her father had said, to taste the cocoa a little longer, but it was no use.

She opened her eyes to a kitchen clock that read eight A.M. Spartacus was lounging across her legs and threatening her blood circulation. Sometime during the night, she had put on her flannel nightgown and sweatpants. The sound of snoring in the next room robbed her of any hope that their near-death failure with a supernatural killer was part of her dream.

A peek over the countertop confirmed her fears. Reese and the Ghost were playing chess on her bed while Gonzales slept on the floor with a pillow over his head. Just perfect. An evil monster was playing chess with an SPD detective on her bed. The bastards had ruined the game she'd been in the middle of for a month. Worse, they were touching her chess set. She would have to soak the chess pieces in bleach and burn the bed sheets.

Everything from last night came back to her. They'd had no luck contacting Jefferson or any of their police contacts after the church disaster. Going back to her place was the last thing she remembered. She'd never felt so tired.

"Do any of you have a concept of privacy? Or personal space?" she yelled at the ceiling. "That's my bed. The place where I stare at the wall and pretend to sleep."

"Whatcha got for breakfast?" Reese called out. "I'd get donuts, but this Ghost dude might think I was ditching you and kill me. We haven't heard from SPD. Coms are dead."

Kiran opened a cabinet without getting off the floor and launched a box of cereal over the counter. "No one better ask for coffee."

She sat on the kitchen floor and leaned against Spartacus's back. Krol had cut them off. How the hell were they supposed to find the kids without help from the department and no leads? And the creature who was supposed to be their secret weapon had almost gotten them killed. Her enemy was definitely in her household, or at least her apartment. She clutched Anatol's necklace and remembered how easily the Ghost had destroyed all those people. For all she knew, the spirit of Hitler or Jack the Ripper was lounging on her bed. She said a silent prayer to Ganesha to protect her and the lost children. Who could have been evil enough for Hell to fear him?

"Cocoa puffs. Excellent," the Ghost rasped.

The crunching of dry cereal alternated with Gonzales' snoring. There was no point in ignoring reality any longer. She got up and marched into the bathroom. Spartacus came along and flopped down in front of the bathroom door.

The mirror revealed an exhausted face that looked like it had slept fitfully on an air mattress. Her blue jacket and orange scarf were on a hanger suspended over the shower railing. They looked washed and dried. The rip in the jacket had been sewn over. She refused to consider which of the three in the other room carried a sewing kit in their pockets and had taken the time to fix her clothes after they almost died. Maybe there were elves that did laundry in her apartment that were part of this whole nightmare.

She ran a toothbrush over her teeth to give herself time to think. Finding the kids hadn't been the cake walk the Ghost had promised. The cultists had expected him. Krol was way ahead of them. She had to find a way to outthink him, had to take control of her team.

She emerged with minty breath and partially tamed hair to a scene out of the Twilight Zone. The Ghost had thrown his duffle bag across her bed and was lounging against it as he stuffed Cocoa Puffs into his mouth. Reese had his hand on his chin, examining the board. His bandaged hand had stopped bleeding. He looked more at peace than she'd ever seen him. Gonzales had woken up and was watching the game while he also ate Cocoa Puffs. The chess board caught her attention as the Ghost made his move and captured Reese's rook.

"Knight f3," Gonzales said.

"Strong move, G." Reese's hand hovered over his black knight. "But there's no way to win." He made a fist as his face grew grim. "I'm out."

"You've got mate in four, Reese. Look harder," Kiran announced. She found

CHAPTER 11

a Butterfingers bar and figured it would do for breakfast. She pulled one of the kitchen chairs against the wall and put her feet on a bean bag. Spartacus flopped himself between her and the bed and fell asleep.

"He cannot win." The Ghost raised himself up, glaring at the board.

"Says the one who almost got us all killed," Kiran said. "You don't understand the game as well as you think."

The Ghost gave her a stare that would burn through the polar ice caps. "I understand you, woman. I hear the sucking hole of doubt that screams every time your heart beats. I smell your fear. I see the wound in your soul you hope to heal by bringing those children home."

"And you taste the delicious chocolate crunch of Cocoa Puffs." The Ghost's words pissed her off more than she wanted to admit. He didn't know a damn thing about her. He was guessing and it was all psycho bullshit. "It's not about me, is it? It's about your ego and thinking you always know everything. But you don't. You were shocked Krol even came back. You have no idea how to find him or what he has planned."

Reese held up a finger. "Wait. I think the FBI is right for once. Gonzo's knight move was on track. Mate in four, maybe." He jumped the black knight to f3.

"There is only doom for you on this board, Reese. The woman lies as she does about everything. She will lead you to despair."

Kiran closed her eyes and envisioned the pieces swimming in a sea of rain. Somewhere amongst them were eleven pawns she needed to bring home, and another whole side whose mission it was to keep them away. But where in hell were her pawns and why had they taken them?

Reese slid his queen into the fray, but he looked unsure. She *had* lied about his chances. In fact, his position stunk, but you needed confidence to attack, to make the other side panic and make mistakes.

"Alright, so you know everything about taking down the killers. Tell us, who Krol was, really?" she asked, still looking at the ceiling. *And who the hell are you, sitting on my bed?* The last thing she wanted to do was look into those dead eyes again.

The Ghost jumped a knight over his enemy's forces in an ill-considered attack. Reese's chances went up. "Krol was a priest with a taste for hurting people. A brilliant mathematician with a bent mind. He made a deal with a greater demon for protection and the Polish cops who went after him ended up extremely dead. Back then, the necklace was in their hands. They summoned me and I sent Krol to a long-deserved sentence in Hell. Anatol was there. He should have explained." The Ghost rubbed the white button on his long coat. He looked strangely thoughtful.

Kiran reached over while Reese scratched his head and moved a pawn for him. Just talking to this monster made her sweat. "And he's come back for what? Revenge? To destroy you once and for all?"

The Ghost slid his pawn forward. "I cannot be destroyed. Hell has learned that lesson many times. They would not have released Krol for such a foolish mission. They do not free any soul lightly."

She took the Ghost's pawn with Reese's bishop. "Check. Then why?"

"That was a stupid move," Reese said. "He's just going to—"

The Ghost captured her bishop with his knight. "Why do you care so much? Do you even know?" He waved a hand around the tight space. "You have pictures of the kids scattered about, notes about possibilities, theories that fill your papers. Some of them, I admit, are clever, almost mad. Why do you care, woman?"

The board swam before her, a swamp of squares with helpless figures sinking into the mud, demanding her protection, amidst a barrier full of enemies she had to penetrate. She slid a pawn forward, opening a path for Reese's queen. "Because the kids are what matters." She closed her eyes and promised herself she wasn't going to start yelling. The necklace grew uncomfortably cold against her skin. "You've been through this before. You said they were all so predictable. What will they do next?"

The Ghost stared at the chessboard. He slid his queen forward, capturing her queen with no apparent cost. "My question first. You refused my offer of a wish? Why? No one refuses in the end."

She examined the board and couldn't understand why she had made such a stupid move. She had tried to protect a lone pawn she was sure could reach the other side and win the game, but she had missed seeing half the board.

CHAPTER 11

It was the same error her father had started making when he had launched entire attacks to take out a knight, only to lose his king in the end. The kind of mistake he made before he lost his grip on reality and fled.

"It's cheating," she said. "There's got to be some price you're not mentioning for a wish. But I asked you first."

The Ghost waved a hand at her. "You are the bearer of the Wand, the revealer of mysteries. Your purpose on this earth is to unravel the knots. Am I right? You live for it, obsess about it, would die to solve the problems around you. Most like you are more than a little mad. They see things that may or may not be there. When they push themselves too hard, their minds shatter. Be careful what puzzles you try to unravel, woman. No mystery you solve will fill the hole inside you. No problem you solve will buy forgiveness."

Something inside her snapped. "Whoever you were, you're an asshole. I've got no reason to ask for forgiveness. You don't know anything about me." She felt like he could see the hole inside her and was enjoying twisting his hand within it.

The Ghost shrugged. "Should I tell you lies instead, Kiran Patel?"

Her name sounded strange in his hoarse rasp. Wand Bearer? He could call her whatever he wanted if he answered her questions and helped find the kids?

"How did they know you were coming?" she asked.

"It doesn't matter. I find him, kill him again, and collect whatever's left over. That's why I was summoned, isn't it?"

Her stomach turned over at his words. 'Collect whatever's left over.' The monster truly didn't care about the children as long as his contract was fulfilled. "What if Krol's not so easy to kill this time?"

The Ghost yawned, then patted his bag of tools. "I have whatever I need to send him back. Demons, devils, madmen, murderers—they all go down in the end." He moved a bishop on the board. "Checkmate. Your vision is poor, woman."

She had miscalculated. Her pawn was one square away from reaching the other side. One square short of safety and victory. She tipped her king over. "And if he's found a way to destroy you?"

"Then I'll finally be free from slavery, and you'll be on your own." The Ghost looked into the distance. "But if there's a way to do so, I don't know it. Flame, cold iron, cannon balls, and the edges of a thousand weapons have all failed. Lions, bears, demons, dragons, none of their teeth have left a mark upon me. I am what I have always been; cursed to be a tool until the end of time."

"We're not here for a mass murderer's pity show." Kiran braved the Ghost's glare and the necklace burned against her chest. She had no doubt in the world he would have killed her at that moment if he could have. "We screwed up back there because we listened to you and underestimated them. We don't even have a witness to question. We need to anticipate their next move."

The Ghost met her stare. "Alright, you lead. What would you do if you were Krol, and had the help of Hell? If you could possess souls and crush everyone in your path and your only goal was suffering?"

"I would attack. I would find my strongest targets and eliminate them." The realization hit her. "We've got to find out what happened to the others last night. Can you go to police headquarters and see what happened without killing anyone?"

"Is that a command, Master?"

She ground her teeth at his tone. If she was going to take control of this team, she had to sound like she knew what she was doing. "It is."

"Then I will leave you and take a stroll." The Ghost got up and opened her fourth-floor window. He slung his bag over his shoulder. "Your wish is my command, General." He put a leg through the open window, slid over the edge, and was gone.

Reese hurried to the sill and looked down. "He's climbing down the wall."

Gonzales threw himself onto the bean bag and sighed. "We should run." She wasn't sure if he meant it. He clearly wasn't in a running position.

Reese was still leaning out the window. "Ghost Monster's turned the corner. If we're going to run, this is our best chance."

Gonzales folded his arms behind his head. "He'll find us."

Reese started pacing the room, examining Kiran's disarray. "While you were snoring, he told us he'd remove our intestines if we took off. I told him

CHAPTER 11

we weren't going anywhere until we got paid in full."

Kiran opened her desk drawer and found her last pack of clove gum. She ripped it open like the addict she was. "You're in it for the money, Reese? All you care about is your good looks and what you get out of it?"

"So, you admit I'm good looking?" Reese smiled at her. "But it's not just the money. There's the glory too."

"All I admit is you're conceited and shallow." Kiran put the first piece of gum in her mouth and felt the palpable relief. She had to find a way to pull this ramshackle team together.

Reese's smile vanished. "What's wrong with money and finally getting some credit for what we do? Who doesn't need money?" He pointed his chin at his partner. "Gonzo sends cash back to his sister in Mexico. I've got a mother in a facility that costs more per month than most people make in a year. My father never got the money or recognition he was worth his whole life. I promised him I would do better. Make sure I got credit where credit was due. Money can make all the difference in the world."

"Not for those kids, it won't." Kiran chewed harder. She didn't care what the two of them were in it for, or at least she shouldn't. They hadn't been much use so far, but Anatol had insisted it was the force of their combined wills that kept the Ghost in line. She thought about it. Well, Gonzales had saved her from getting shot in the diner and if Reese hadn't taken down the cultist with the crossbow, she might have died before Anatol.

"Would have been a great chance to run," Gonzales insisted.

Reese slammed his hand down on her counter, spilling the Cocoa Puffs. "No more running. This is what the curandera warned you was coming, all those years ago, back in Oaxaca."

Gonzales closed his eyes and balled his hands into fists. "Mierda."

"Did you know Gonzo was once the fastest kid in Oaxaca?" Reese smiled, looking proud of his partner.

Kiran looked at the wall of muscle that was Gonzales. Strongest she might have believed. Fastest seemed a stretch.

Gonzales closed his eyes and leaned back. "In Oaxaca, there were lots of runners. People who trained up in the mountains and got fast. None of them could catch me. I was sure I'd make the Olympics until I hurt my knee. But my crazy cousin told me not to worry. He took me to an old curandera, but she wouldn't touch me. Said my future was written and all she could do was tell it to me. I didn't want to hear it. I didn't want to give up the few pesos I had for lies.

"The old lady leaned in close. I could smell tequila on her breath. Told me to keep my pesos. My future was plain to see. I was the wild man of the woods, and the dragon was coming for me. Dragon's flames would cook my flesh, dragon's claws would tear me open, and I would never run fast enough to get away. I would die in my brother's arms once again. She blew smoke into my face, and I ran. I ran out of there even though my knee hurt like hell, but I couldn't run fast enough. She yelled after me that this would be the last time my soul would be reborn. The dragon would find me, and I would fail to do what I was meant to. Somehow, I knew she spoke the truth. It's all been wrong since then. Scared me so bad I almost died right there."

Gonzales' confession was more words than she'd ever heard the man speak combined.

Kiran rolled her eyes. "A dragon? You can't live your life based on what a fake fortune teller said, Enrique. I mean, you refused to pay her. Of course, she was going to curse you with some random dragon stuff and blow smoke in your face."

Gonzales stared at the ceiling. "You saved us back there, Kiran. You were right, we shouldn't have rushed in. You shooting at them was the only thing that stopped them from slitting our throats. That's what Reese said when you were sleeping. I just say gracias."

Reese bit his upper lip. "Okay, you're not all bad. We get what you're trying to do here. It's a messed-up situation. You saved our asses. We'll watch your back." Reese cracked his knuckles. "I'm sorry I said you were batshit crazy."

She didn't remember the batshit part. "I'm sorry I said you were both just street detectives and not up for any of this."

Reese raised his eyebrows. "Damn. That hurt a little."

"A little," Gonzales agreed.

Kiran bit her lip. "If you hadn't sent me up the fire escape, we all would

CHAPTER 11

have ended up zip tied to the floor."

Reese straightened his shoulders. "Maybe if we're all together in this, we'll be able to rein him in a little and won't get killed in the first few hours. And I've been thinking. This Ghost, I think he's Genghis Khan. When that knife was against my neck, and I was sure I was going to die, I looked into his eyes. It was like looking into a black hole."

"Hitler was short." Gonzales tapped his finger on the chess board making his point. "But I say Hitler."

Kiran sat on the floor. Well, at least they didn't think she was all bad anymore, and now she had two goofballs to watch her back. It was better than nothing. "I don't think that was his human body. He could have been anyone, any race, any time."

"King Leopold of Belgium," Reese countered, pointing at his partner. "He had millions of people's hands cut off in the Congo. He's worse than Genghis Khan and Hitler."

Gonzales rubbed his chin, considering. "A bad one."

Kiran was surprised that they knew who King Leopold was and that Reese played chess so well. She was surprised she could carry on a conversation with both of them for so long.

"Maybe a murderer." Gonzales spread both hands wide. "Someone who ate people. Maybe Dahmer."

Reese shook his head, rejecting the guess. "Stalin. He said millions of deaths were just a statistic." Reese pondered his statement for a moment, then shook his head. "I take that back if we get take backs. I'd go with Vlad the Impaler. The Ghost doesn't have that Stalin vibe."

"Pol Pot?" Gonzales shook his finger at Reese. "Puede ser."

Kiran realized she didn't know these two at all. "I think he's someone out of the Bible. Maybe Jesus or some Roman guy who killed everyone."

"Not Jesus." Gonzales looked panicked as the one Christian in the room. "Por Dios."

"Okay, didn't mean to offend, Enrique. Maybe Lucifer or some devil or I don't know. He quotes scripture all the time." Kiran sighed. "But we have to find out. Anatol said it mattered. If we know who he was, maybe we can predict what he's going to do, control him, prevent him from turning on us." Something deep inside her insisted it was vital. They had to understand the Ghost.

Kiran lost her train of thought as the mark on her arm began to throb. She felt it calling to her, demanding that she listen. Spartacus raised his head as if listening to some far-off sound.

"What is it?" Reese asked.

Kiran ignored him. Anatol told her the mark would change her if she opened herself to it. She clasped her hands together, not certain what to do. The damned thing might try and take her over, but she felt certain the mark knew something she needed to find out. She closed her eyes and let the magic in.

A black swirl of ink and smoke formed in her mind's eye. She followed it as it threaded through the keyhole in her door, wound its way down three flights of stairs, and hesitated. A hard knock sounded on the street.

"Someone's coming." Part of her was aware of Reese drawing her gun and Gonzales getting to his feet. Another part of her passed through the outside door and saw the two people trying to enter her building. The two Israeli brothers Jefferson had introduced her to stood next to each other. One of them reached for the buzzer.

"How do you know?" Reese asked.

The magic released her, and Kiran snapped back to full awareness. She stared at the mark on her arm. "It's this thing on my arm. I don't know what it's doing to me." She still felt disoriented.

A moment later, the buzzer to her room rang. The brothers didn't say a word into the intercom.

"I think it's the Israeli brothers. But not really them." The bible verses her father quoted came back to her. She wasn't sure if what she'd seen had been a hallucination or reality. How the hell could she know?

"What do you mean?" Reese gripped his gun harder.

"We should get out of here." Kiran opened the door. The hallway was empty. She considered the elevator as a last resort, but a crash from below changed her mind. Footsteps hit the stairs. She slammed the door shut and threw the

CHAPTER 11

bolt.

"It's probably your mother," Reese said, but he leveled his gun all the same. "But just in case, get behind the counter. You can get a good shot from there. We've got you."

Gonzales lifted her bed and slammed it against the door. He took up a position to the right of the door and drew his gun.

"Don't you dare shoot her if it's my mother." She hated that Reese was trying to shield her like a knight in black leather armor, but she was glad they were both here. She'd made a terrible mistake sending the Ghost away. Whoever was coming up the stairs, she felt certain they did not wish them well.

She ran for her gun as Spartacus heaved himself off the floor, a low growl rumbling in his throat.

The door burst open with the sound of splintering plywood and scraping metal. A blast of heat struck her face as the wood tore off its hinges. The room filled with the smell of sulfur and rot.

It definitely wasn't her mother.

Chapter 12

A piece of the door struck Kiran in the chest and hurt so bad her vision went black. She stumbled over a coffee table covered in books and hit the floor. She regained her vision just in time to see the disaster unfold.

In the doorway stood Yuri, of the Israeli paramilitary, glaring at them. His eyes were glowing, his face twisted in a mask of rage. She caught a glimpse of his brother, Anya, pressing in behind before Yuri glared at Reese and began to raise a long automatic weapon.

Kiran felt time slow as her body tried to keep up with her mind. She had to move before Reese got shot and the weapon swung across the room and claim them all. Her hand closed on her volume of *The Collected Stories of Sherlock Holmes,* and she threw it across the room at Yuri. A shot rang out and pages of book blew across the room. A black flash filled her vision and thunder crashed moments before the bullets struck.

Luckily for her, the sound of thunder was the growl of an exceptionally large dog.

Spartacus, who Kiran couldn't get to move fast with any command, struck Yuri like a bolt of black lightning. The giant dog latched onto the Israeli commando's shoulder and dragged him to the floor, still snarling. Anya stepped in behind his brother, weapon in hand, and staggered back as two golf ball size holes appeared in his chest.

The sound of Reese's shots deafened Kiran. The SPD detective stepped over her and kept firing as pages continued to float around the apartment.

The fact that this only seemed to slow Anya down was a big clue that they were all screwed. Anya bounced off the door frame, glanced at the holes

CHAPTER 12

in his chest, and raised his gun. Gonzales dove across the room screaming something Kiran could no longer hear now that Reese's gun had deafened her. He tackled Anya as Reese put another bullet into him.

The studio apartment was not big enough for five people and a dog in the best of circumstances. All she registered were flashes of color, pressure waves of gunshots, book pages drifting down, and pieces of broken furniture spinning through the air.

Kiran had no idea where her gun was, but she found a broken chair leg and swung it with all her strength at Yuri's head. The chair leg shattered provoking Yuri to pause for a brief moment in his efforts to dislodge her dog from his shoulder. He elbowed Kiran in the ribs, sent her slamming into the floor, and resumed trying to kill Spartacus.

She spit out some blood and rolled back up. Gonzales flew over her head and crashed against the wall. She got to one knee and tried to make it to the kitchen and find her damn gun. Before she took a step, Spartacus's rear end slammed her into the bedside table as Yuri swung the dog around, trying to dislodge him.

Another gunshot registered as the faintest of sounds, then Reese's brass gun spun over the kitchen counter and disappeared. Hot blood sprayed her face. She had no idea whose blood it was. Spartacus crashed to the ground in front of her with Yuri on top of him. Blood seeped into her eyes as she pushed herself against the wall and tried to stand.

She fumbled on the counter for anything she could grab, anything she could use as a weapon.

Anya slammed something onto Reese's head then seized him by the neck. She could see through Anya's chest where Reese's shots had torn holes into him. They'd had some effect. Anya seemed to be moving slower, but Reese wasn't moving at all.

Her hand closed on the brass Ganesha.

Gonzales grabbed Anya around the waist. Anya slipped to his knees, but his hands were still wrapped around Reese's neck, squeezing the life out of him.

Kiran hit Anya with the Ganesha on the back of the head and felt a shock run up her arm and course down her spine. Anya's head snapped forward and his neck stiffened. He slumped down and thankfully didn't move again. The place where the Ganesha had struck his head was smoldering. Kiran dropped to her knees as the smell of burning hair filled the room.

The last of the pages of Sherlock Holmes spiraled to the floor.

Gonzales was already laying Reese on the floor, preparing to do CPR. He yelled something about getting help, she thought. Her hearing was returning. Or maybe he needed help with the CPR? Her hand burned terribly. Gonzales yelled again, and this time she was certain it was something about an ambulance. She felt a desperate need to sit down as the room wobbled before her.

The floor reverberated with pounding, and everything stopped. She turned.

The Ghost was crouched on the windowsill, pounding his iron rod against the floor. The tails of his ruined coat streamed behind him in the wind. "Don't press on his chest unless you enjoy breaking ribs. It won't do any good, he's still breathing."

Reese promptly coughed in his partner's face.

Gonzales went limp and slumped against the wall. He waved a hand at the Ghost. "Por Dios, you were sitting there all this time?"

The Ghost pointed his iron rod at the unmoving form of Yuri. His throat had been torn out. "I thought our fearless leader had things under control. Though it looks like her brilliant idea to separate the team almost finished all of you. Luckily, the dog took care of half the problem."

Spartacus lay unmoving in a heap amongst a pile of furniture. He'd killed one of the demon-possessed brothers on his own and paid a heavy price. His ribs were bare, he was covered in blood, and he did not appear to be breathing. Kiran dropped and threw her arms around the black dog. She buried her face in his neck and was surprised to find herself shaking. He was Anatol's last gift to her, steady and faithful. She was the one who was supposed to be taking care of him, not the other way around.

The Ghost slid down from the windowsill and prodded Yuri. "The dog finished this one." He slid the rod under Anya and flipped him over. "This one you hit with a holy symbol. A very heavy holy symbol. 'Thou shalt worship

CHAPTER 12

no other god before me for I am your Lord God.' Was that ever a lie. You're lucky your own god didn't let you down."

"What the hell did they put on me?" Reese tried to remove whatever Anya had thrust over his forehead.

The Ghost jerked forward and tore the object away, ignoring Reese's scream and the blood trickling down his forehead. He stared at the crown of thorns before tossing it to the floor. "What are you playing at, Krol?" He looked shaken.

Reese wiped the blood out of his eyes and regarded the Ghost. "Hitler. He was Hitler. I knew it."

Kiran got to her feet and didn't hesitate. "I want that wish now."

The Ghost nodded. "We all have desire in the end. You wish for power to crush your enemies. For lightning to fly from your fingers. For the Earth to shake with your step."

"Shut up and save my dog. He's still breathing. Fix him now." She felt her lip trembling, but she kept her eyes on the Ghost.

The Ghost froze. "What kind of joke is this? Aren't you saving the wish for some grand moment where you unleash it upon Krol and send him back to the Pit? Some wish to save yourself from me when I find a way to destroy the three of you? Some gesture to—"

"Enough. Heal him before it's too late," Kiran demanded. "He didn't deserve any of this."

The Ghost went silent. He bent down and ran his gray hand through Spartacus's fur. "Two wishes. Two for one dog. Not even a magical dog. Just a great old sheep dog mutt." He shook his head and regarded Yuri's dead form. "But only a great heart could take down such a demon alone. Anatol must have foreseen it." He took hold of Spartacus's bloody ruff and lifted him off the ground. He blew into his face.

Spartacus growled and his upper lip lifted back. The Ghost lowered him and retreated as Spartacus rolled to his feet. He wobbled once then looked around for Kiran. He made his way to her, gave her a look that made clear she owed him a chicken dinner, and wandered over to his water bowl. Blood still stained his coat, but the wounds had closed over.

"We won't have a hope of using that dog against Krol," the Ghost said. "If this is some grand strategy to use the dog as a weapon, it's nonsense."

Kiran couldn't believe this crap. He actually thought she wanted to use poor Spartacus as a weapon? "Spartacus is going to my mother's place, and he's going to sleep as much as he wants, eat whatever he wants, and she's not going to say a goddamned thing about it, or she can kiss her dreams of medical school and marriage goodbye." She realized now why Anatol had made her watch Spartacus and made up that shit about his joints aching. He'd wanted someone to watch over her.

The Ghost took a deep breath. "What a waste of a wish."

Kiran ignored him. "We have to get Reese and Gonzales to a hospital," she announced to the room. She helped Gonzales get Reese onto the bed. Then she wiped his forehead with a kitchen towel. Reese still looked dazed.

The Ghost looked them over. "None of you are dead yet and the dog is fine. We have work to do while you three still live. The woman has failed at leading. I will be the one making the decisions from now on."

She almost stuck a finger in his chest but touching him seemed like the worst idea ever. "Spartacus tore apart one of those demons and I killed the other. You did nothing. You're not making any more decisions that are going to get us all killed."

The Ghost's eyes flickered with black fire. "Fine, you can make the decisions that get you killed."

"Screw off," Kiran said. Something outside the window caught her attention. "Wait, what is that sound?"

She wasn't sure, but she thought she heard someone screaming for help. She bent over the windowsill and looked down. She startled at seeing, a man hanging by the collar of his coat four stories off the ground. A screwdriver, driven into the brickwork looked to be the only thing preventing his fall.

The Ghost seemed to remember something. "I forgot about him." He leaned out the window as far out as he could and dragged in the unfortunate man that he'd left hanging. Without a word he tossed him on the floor, amidst the dead bodies.

"You sent me to find out what remained of your police department. The

CHAPTER 12

answer is—nothing worth saving. Police cars are smashed against the building. Ambulances are taking away the dead. They'd forgotten this cultist in a cell by himself."

The cultist bared his teeth like a cornered beast. "You'll die for this. They'll possess your souls. They'll turn you into their playthings."

The Ghost leaned over him. "I have been dragged across the Coliseum in chains, burned and stabbed by Vlad the Impaler, thrown into vats of hot oil, and pierced with a thousand arrows of English kings, yet somehow I am still here in this body I cannot escape." He picked up the cultist by his collar and lifted him into the air. "I am tired for the first time in many years, and I do not know why. You will answer this girl's questions now." The Ghost turned to Kiran and nodded.

"Where are the children? Are they alive?" Her voice cracked as she spoke. Almost losing Spartacus had shaken her not to mention almost getting killed herself.

The cultist regarded her with undisguised disdain. "They're alive for three more days, but you will never find them. They're far below where the spirits walk. They await their time to be summoned for the King."

The Ghost shook the man. "One more mysterious response and I throw you out the window. Where?"

The man narrowed his eyes. "Deep under the church there is another city where the tunnels converge. In the bowels of the Earth where the dead sleep. That is where they are."

Oh, great. Deep underground in the crypts. What could be better? Kiran hands started to sweat at the thought of dark tunnels where you could be lost and buried forever. Three more days. She could hear her heart pounding, trying to beat its way out of her chest, and hide.

"You were so close but never heard them cry." The cultist laughed at this point.

Kiran wanted to choke the man. Those kids were waiting for someone to help them. Deep under the earth they were praying for someone to come for them.

"Why did Krol take those children? What does he want?" She tried to keep herself from growling at him.

The cultist didn't hesitate. "He wants the King to be redeemed and reign again. The King will complete the sacrifice and restore the balance that was destroyed."

Kiran shuddered at the word sacrifice. "What King?"

The Ghost sighed. "I told you, it never changes. He'll be some great devil of Hell or Satan himself to rule over the earth or some such nonsense. This fool won't know. He'll think he's going to get some great reward and then pow, the demon shows up and promptly eats the cultist's head right off his shoulders and laughs. I've stopped this plan more times than I can count."

Kiran started pacing. "Under the church there is another city? They must mean the old city under Seattle. The entrances were closed after the plague in the early nineteen hundreds. There are tunnels down there all over the place."

The cultist spat on the floor and Kiran smacked him. Her place was messed up, true, but he wasn't allowed to mess it up further. The cultist narrowed his eyes at her. "The undercity is ours now, woman. Nothing will stop the King when he returns."

"Is there anything else you wish to learn from this gentleman?" the Ghost asked.

Kiran examined her nightgown. She was a mess of tears and blood. Every bit of her furniture was destroyed, and two very dead men lay on the floor. The Ghost was right, she'd screwed up. They'd almost all been killed. She leaned down and picked up a half-chewed GRE book and flipped through the pages. Spartacus had eaten the answers in the back and left only questions with drool on them. How appropriate. All she had were questions and the answers she was getting did not satisfy.

Some part of her brain warned her that they didn't have the whole story. The Ghost could be wrong. This king the cultists were waiting for could be far worse than Krol. He could be the one who had found a way into her head. She laughed and was afraid of the sound she made.

"I have to call my mother to take Spartacus. She's going to be so pissed. I can't think of any more questions."

CHAPTER 12

The Ghost exhaled. "Then we're done." He spun and with one heave tossed the man through the open fourth-floor window. The scream was short lived.

Kiran stared at the Ghost in disbelief.

The Ghost straightened his coat. "You said you were done."

Reese turned to Gonzales. "Vlad the Impaler was 1400s."

Gonzales picked his gun off the floor and holstered it. "Mierda. That ends the Pol Pot theory."

The Ghost slid his iron rod back into his bag. "I killed Hitler when he fled his bunker in 1945. Stuffed him into a toilet and flushed until I got bored. They just made up the suicide story."

"I've got dibs on Attila the Hun." Reese laid back on the bed and rested his head against Kiran's bloody pillow. "I have never felt so close to dying before."

"Genghis Khan is still possible." Gonzales put a hand on Reese's shoulder. "You are not allowed to die, hermano, until we fight the dragon together."

Kiran stepped to the window. Her hands were still wet with Spartacus's blood. She looked down. A crowd of people were on their cell phones probably trying to call 911 and getting no response. There was a body splayed on the street below and Kiran was surprised to find that she didn't care. That man deserved worse than a sudden fall.

"What do we do now?" Gonzales asked.

"We go under the city and kill them all." The Ghost picked up the circlet of thorns again and examined it. "What is there to understand? Destroying the things that are trying to kill you is always the right plan."

She took a deep breath and tried to stop her hand from shaking. "First, I'm going to shower and wash this blood off. Then I need to drop off Spartacus at my mom's place." Her mouth went dry at the next thing she'd have to do. The word tunnels combined with underground was not something she wanted to think about. She bent down and picked up one of the pages of *The Collected Stories of Sherlock Holmes*. It was the last present her father had given her. She folded the page neatly and slid it into a pocket. "If Krol's down there, there's no choice. We need to stop getting the shit beat out of us, find those kids, and pound Krol so hard that the last thing he ever wants to do is come back to this world again. We don't run, we don't hide. Castling early is a fool's move."

THE TOOLS OF THE GHOST

The Ghost gave a low short laugh which sounded like the last thing you might hear before you died. "Now that is just my style."

Chapter 13

Kiran sent the others ahead, before she went home, but thankfully, her mother wasn't there. If she'd seen the Ghost, she'd either have had a heart attack or invited him to dinner. It wouldn't have gone well either way.

She wrote a note explaining as little as possible while Spartacus climbed onto the sofa and crushed the cushions. She looked around at all the diplomas on the walls, Hindu idols looking down on her, and the spotless floors. The place already smelled of wet dog. Her mother was going to go ballistic.

Kiran closed the door behind her and took a slow breath to ward off the oncoming panic. So little time to find the children somewhere underneath the city. The thought of dropping into those tunnels, undoubtedly full of giant brucellosis-infested rats, made her mouth go dry. Being trapped in the darkness with the Ghost was like twisting a knife in a fresh wound.

Overhead giant clouds blanketed the sky amidst flashes of strange daytime lightning. She checked her watch as she headed toward Pioneer Square. Three o'clock and the streets were already empty. As she hurried, she tried to phone the bureau, the SPD, anyone in authority, but nothing went through. Either Krol had taken out communications or he'd worked some kind of magic to isolate them. On her final call to Jefferson, she made it to voicemail.

"Director, two of your spy guys tried to kill us. Get the hell away from them. We're following up on a lead. They have the kids in the tunnels below the city. Damn. I hope you're alive, Jefferson. I can't do this alone. I mean I have Reese and Gonzales and the evil killer monster guy, but you know what I mean."

She imagined the rest of her 'team' had found the entrance to the tunnels by now. Tour groups used to start at Pioneer Square before the kidnappings drove them off. With any luck the Ghost had already led them down, found the kids, and brought them back. She could skip the whole wandering around in a dark pit thing and send the Ghost back to whatever evil dimension he hung out in. It was probably some alternate dive bar where drunks everyone hated were sent forever and the Ghost was the bouncer. Or maybe the bartender, doomed to listen to them all. She wasn't sure what would be worse.

Two blocks from Pioneer Square, she found Reese, sitting in front of a storefront, holding his head in his hands. The store's glass window had been smashed to pieces.

"What happened?" she asked. Had Krol found them already?

Reese pointed over his shoulder. "He wouldn't listen once you were gone. Looks in at every window. He lifted an entire cake out of a bakery and stuffed it in his bag. He saw a guitar here and just broke the glass and grabbed it. He's in there."

"Where's Gonzales?"

"He made Gonzo go with him. Said he would tear the entire place apart if we didn't do what he said. We told him those kids are running out of time, but he said he's got all the time in the world." Reese shook his head. "I'm not going back in there. He said he'd kill me if I try to drag him out again. You better go. He likes you."

"He hates me," Kiran protested.

Reese lifted his eyebrows. "Hate's the way it comes out, that's all. At least he doesn't threaten to kill you anymore. He told me he'd tear off my arms if I didn't leave him alone."

The wail of an electric guitar blared out of the store. He hadn't threatened to tear her to pieces in the last couple of hours, that was true. But she wasn't into abusive relationships with potential mass murderers. She just had to get her queen and bishops back into position. They'd wandered off the damn board.

"He won't be hard to find." Kiran stepped through the broken glass and followed the music past knocked over shelves of score books and a drum the Ghost had undoubtedly kicked to pieces. Piano chords joined the guitar's

CHAPTER 13

wail in an eerie harmony before she found the two of them in the back of the store.

Gonzales sat at a piano, his brow covered in sweat, his eyes half closed. The Ghost was leaning back with a dark blue V-shaped electric guitar screaming at maximum volume. Gonzales' hands flew over the keys, matching the Ghost note for note. Whatever they were playing stopped her in her tracks, threatening to transport her to a place she had no desire to enter, a place where the Ghost lived for eternity.

Tears ran down Kiran's face as the Ghost sang in a language she'd never heard. In her mind's eye she saw a village far away, an ocean with a ship far out to sea, its sails in tatters. Then Gonzales stopped playing all at once and the guitar went silent.

The Ghost raised a fist to the ceiling. "He never needed anything. Not one thing. I was the one who needed everything, yet you were silent." He lifted his hand as if he were about to launch into another guitar solo.

They didn't have time for this. The children didn't have time for an evil killer's emotional breakdown.

"You two have no rhythm," Kiran said.

The Ghost's hand froze mid strum. He kicked over the amp and it went silent. "Gonzales is incredible though."

"I mean, you have some intense emotional expression." She didn't want to totally piss him off again. "Maybe you could have a future in hard metal or techno."

"You mean that?" the Ghost was already stuffing the guitar into his sack.

"Look, you've got some obvious anger issues, hey I've got some too. Let's face it, music that doesn't say something is boring. I mean, you'd have to practice. After you're done killing Krol."

The Ghost shrugged. "I've got centuries."

"I don't have centuries." Gonzales wiped his forehead with his sleeve. "Maybe we can do it again when this is over."

Kiran pointed to the shop's entrance and tried to will them outside. "Okay, deal. We finish this we can have a garage band."

"You play?" the Ghost asked.

"My mother made me take a lot of lessons. Come on, let's go."

The Ghost still didn't move. "Down there, I lead. You have no experience in the darkness, no understanding of the world below. I promised to follow your orders when you know what needed to be done, but you understand too little."

"Go ahead and walk in front." Kiran silently thanked every Hindu god she'd ever prayed to. The idea of being first through the tunnels and crypts was about as appetizing as eating bat guano. Let the combat expert grope his way ahead. "But I'm the one leading. No more 'embracing the chaos' crap and trying to get us all killed. At least not if you ever want me to teach you some licks on that guitar."

The Ghost finished closing his bag and hefted it onto his shoulder. "We shall see."

They walked back through the display case and found Reese.

The Ghost reached into his pouch and tossed a handful of silver coins through the broken glass. "Thou shall not steal." He examined the destroyed window and threw in a few more. "I wanted an accordion, but those are harder to find."

"Sold out, I'm sure," Kiran said. "Pioneer Square is right there. Let's go."

The entrance to the tunnels was marked with a sign and about a hundred warnings not to proceed without a certified tour guide or you were likely to die, and it would not be the tour company's fault according to their lawyers.

"Whoever follows me will not walk in darkness." The Ghost jumped from street level and dropped into a pit that extended deep below street level. "It's darker than Hell down here," he yelled back up to the three of them.

Reese shrugged before turning and descending the ladder. "It'll be a shit show finding our way across town through these tunnels. We should have hit the church and found the basement."

"The SWAT guys who tried the direct assault method are all dead, Reese," Kiran reminded him. "Some of them got possessed by demons and that looked like it really sucked. But the very next time we summon a monster with a ragged coat who wants to kill all of us, you be in charge, ok?"

She followed Reese and Gonzales brought up the rear. Their flashlights lit

CHAPTER 13

up a wreck of narrow tunnels winding off in every direction. The cold air smelled of seaweed, wet earth, and the grave.

"Reminds me of Oaxaca." Gonzales said.

"Or some of the rougher parts of Detroit," Reese added.

Kiran was already starting to hyperventilate. The mark on her arm throbbed, and she had no idea what it was trying to tell her. She could swear the walls were closing in around them, swear the ceiling was dropping. She shone her light over the wet brick festooned with multi-colored chewing gum. "This was once part of Seattle until some great fire in the 1800s," she explained. "They built up after that, but they still used this underground portion, shopped here and everything. Most people forgot it ever existed." She certainly wished it didn't exist anymore.

"Everyone forgot except our nerd FBI researcher," Reese added.

Kiran pulled out a map. She'd highlighted a likely route that should get them below their target. All they had to do was follow the simple path and they wouldn't be buried freaking alive. By entering here, she planned to avoid any traps Krol had set. If she got her bearings, she could...

The Ghost rapped upon one of the brick walls with his knuckles. He ran a finger down the grimy surface then plunged it in his mouth. "We have a problem."

"What sort of problem? Are the walls unsound or something?" she asked while she imagined the walls collapsing around them.

The Ghost raised an eyebrow. "The world itself is not as sound as you might hope. It'll be extremely hard going back now."

"Hard like, 'Wow, it's so much fun that I don't want to leave this place hard.' Or hard like, 'We're all permanently trapped hard?'" She was quite sure she already knew the answer.

A cloud passed over the sun at that moment and darkened the one patch of light shining from above. Kiran stepped back to the ladder and examined the sky. A thick fog had rolled in; not that unusual for Seattle, she told herself. She couldn't make out much of anything.

The Ghost tapped the cobblestones that lined the floor with his iron rod, listening to the echoes. "Something has woken these tunnels. Either Krol has been here for an awfully long time, years perhaps, or they are more haunted than I suspected. You said a plague killed a great number of people? The walls taste haunted. The stones shift beneath my feet. The passages twist as we speak. Going through won't be easy if we hope to ever come out."

"Bad path then." Gonzales started back to the ladder.

Reese grabbed him by the sleeve before he could start climbing. "We said enough running, brother. I feel something calling to me down here."

"Don't want anything calling me," Gonzales said.

"I don't think we'll find the children another way." Kiran said.

"If they're still alive." The Ghost dropped to one knee and pulled up one of the cobblestones from the floor. He scooped out gravel and mud and held it in his palm. "Krol is playing a well thought out game. He has laid his traps down here. There is old blood and pain mixed into this place. The ocean has flooded it and left its mark. Shipwrecks and sailors, plagues and deals gone bad stalk these ways. We need your chess game to improve."

She tried to hand him the map, but he ignored it. "Can you find the path? I mean, I have the map all marked out and everything, but maybe you could just walk a little ahead, not too far, and we could come behind."

"No map will help here." A gust of cold air welled up from somewhere far ahead and whipped the Ghost's coat about him. He pulled his hat down tight about his head before he stood. "I know places like this, half stone, half spirit. We will not get far without a guide."

Kiran felt her current deep unease increase logarithmically. The wet cold of this place cut through her clothes and found her bones as if she were naked. She looked to Reese who seemed the only calm at the moment. "What do you think, Super Detective?"

Reese didn't seem surprised she asked his opinion. "I've always thought the world was full of spirits. My mother was from Barbados. She said our ancestors watched over us in the dark. Those are hot Barbados ghosts. Even their ancestors were from warm places. This doesn't seem like anywhere I would find them. Still, I don't mind meeting whoever died here. Maybe they would know the others."

Gonzales shook his head. "Lousy place for una reunión familiar."

CHAPTER 13

Kiran sighed. "Family reunions are always messy."

The Ghost raised his rod. "Fools. I am always cast with a host of fools. There is only one way to find a guide." He brought the rod down upon the cobblestones three times and the tunnel rang like a cracked iron bell.

Kiran stepped away from the walls as pearl gray tendrils of smoke and shadows began to seep from between the bricks.

The Ghost waved his hat through the tendrils, and they swirled away from him. "Awake, you lazy bastards. We do not come unaware to be sucked dry as your snack. Test us and see what happens. We seek a guide. Come now, before I smash this place to pieces, and let the ocean in once more." He slammed his rod into the cobblestones one last time.

Smoke and shadows coalesced before them then divided into three separate shapes. As Kiran watched, the shapes took form, diaphanous and tenuous, but the forms of people, nonetheless. Kiran made out a tall dark-skinned woman, dressed in long velvet sleeves, her hair tied back in a tight bun. A pale man, near as wide as the tunnel, with an open shirt and a beard that reached halfway down his chest, and an old man dressed in a vested suit with glasses and a silver-tipped walking stick.

"Which one of you dead will guide us?" the Ghost asked. "We will pay your price."

The spirit of the bearded man bent his head back and laughed. The sound boomed through the tunnels and a brick fell from the wall. "Pay us, Ghost? What will you pay with? You are empty inside. You cannot even bleed." He stepped past the other two summoned spirits and leaned over the Ghost, taking up most of the tunnel. "What can you do to those who are already dead? We need take no orders from you. We need not guide you anywhere."

The Ghost adjusted the sack over his shoulder. "I can stuff your soul in here and close it for all time. I can put you in my hat and take you out for party tricks. Try my patience. See what happens."

The spirit brought up both his giant fists. "You do not belong here, Ghost. Your crimes are no secret to the dead. Why do you trouble us?"

The Ghost waved a hand in Kiran's direction. "Look on the unfortunate souls who travel with me and you will know."

The woman put a hand on the bearded man's shoulder and dragged him back. She stepped forward and peered at them through misty brass spectacles. "The Wand, the Sword, the Cup, and the Coin here once more after so very long." She leaned forward, narrowing her eyes. "The Wand is here as a woman. I would never have believed it if I had not seen it with my own dead eyes. She examined Kiran with an intensity that burned. "It is strange, both halves of you are combined in this form. You ever came as the Priestess or the Star, now I am uncertain what you are."

The spirit stepped in front of Gonzales and ran a spectral hand down his cheek. Gonzales pulled away. "You did not pull away from me before, Enkidu." She looked hurt. "Long ago, I brought you out of the wilderness and tamed you. I will not do so again, for the dragon comes for you, and the dragon will not be denied." She turned back to the Ghost. "I will be your guide the final time you enter this place, Coin Bearer. That time you and the Wand will come here to die. Until then, I will see you no more." She gave a last fond look at Gonzales. "Take care of him for me until I return. A shame he has to die so often." The spirit raised a hand and began to fade into mist. She dropped down between the cracks in the cobblestones and was gone.

"Ay, Dios mío," Gonzales said. "Sucks to be confused with dead women's lovers. She was joking about the dragon, right?"

The bearded man stepped forward and put a finger to Reese's chest. "Your Sword is gone, dropped in a lake, shattered and given to Hell, King of Kings. Your friend's hands are empty. His Cup was broken. He will not heal you or anyone else ever again until it is remade. Do not let them herd you when you should be leading at the head of armies. When you should be ruling us all."

Reese didn't flinch. "I'm not here to rule anyone, friend. We're here to find some lost kids, that's all. I don't know who you think I am, but no one's here to hurt you."

Gonzales stepped next to Reese like a protective shadow. "Except maybe me."

The bearded man shook his head. "I will not guide any of you. Krol has been here. I have heard his words. He has called forth a true king who will right the Ghost's great mistake and free us. I will not be part of your folly." He

CHAPTER 13

turned, walked straight into one of the walls, and disappeared before Kiran could ask him what he meant. What king had Krol called into this world? What other disaster had he brought here for them to deal with?

The last spirit looked them over one by one before he spoke. "What will you pay, Ghost? I will not take your gold." He glided closer and pointed with his cane. "I will guide you in the darkness for your white button. It looks fine to one who has not touched bread in a long while."

The Ghost turned on maximum glare. "It is mine and will stay mine. Do not ask again." He reached into his pouch. "This will be more to your liking." He tossed a coin high into the air.

The spirit caught the coin and bit down on it with teeth that passed through the metal but left it whole. "The Coin Bearer pays with Silver of the Dead, the purest in all the world. This will serve. Your passage is paid." He waved his cane at the rest of them. "I will take nothing from the Wand. She has lost too much already and can see too far into my soul. Her Wand rests in Hell and awaits her there. The others have misplaced their weapons and will not find them again until they are remade once more with blood that has never flowed in any vein. I take pity on them." The spirit opened his coat, revealing huge gashes in his side and ribs laid bare. He fastened his coat again and straightened his shoulders. "My price is to be healed one day when the Cup is remade and to be stricken down and never rise again when the Sword is held in your hands."

Reese and Gonzales looked at each other and shrugged.

"They have agreed," the Ghost said. "Be it in this life or some other."

The spirit raised his cane. "I am Hans Svenson. I will guide you into the undercity, but each must find their own way out. No spirit here knows that path or we would have left long ago. Follow me now and lose your last chance to turn back."

The Ghost waved a hand at him. "Enough talk. We have places to go and assholes to kill."

The spirit pointed with his cane and the tunnels ahead shifted and slid together, drawing into one. "Walk and listen." He started ahead into the darkness.

THE TOOLS OF THE GHOST

They followed the spirit a long way while water dripped, and the tunnels grew colder. No one spoke, and Kiran lost her sense of time as the tunnels turned again and again. She felt certain that the oxygen must be decreasing despite the gusts of wet air that blew though the tunnels. She guessed they had traveled under half the city by the time they stopped, but they were still in the middle of a long tunnel with no way out. Then she heard it—a whisper, a faint cry, a sob far off at the limits of imagination.

"What was that?" she asked.

The Ghost rushed ahead without so much as a flashlight. "That is a sound no parent can ever forget, the sound of a child crying. It does not stop and does not waver. I heard that cry years ago when Krol was alive. I used it to hunt him when all else failed."

Kiran felt the shiver start in her scalp and make its way down her spine to her toes. She closed her eyes in the darkness and felt a burning in her chest as the cry rose and faded. Krol would pay for this. She would find a way to make him pay. Hans Svenson had already gone ahead.

"We're here, Kiran." Gonzales looked as terrified as she felt, but he said it. Reese just nodded, but she knew what they meant, and it was a lot. She shined her light on the uneven cobblestones and hurried to keep up.

The tunnel sloped relentlessly down until they came to a circular room where four paths branched off. Candles sconces flickered along the walls. A worn painting of some saint decorated the wet brick. Far overhead, a circle of gray light filtered down through an ill-fitting manhole cover.

"You charge too much for your wares, young man. I am not about to pay so much for candles, no matter what world they may illuminate," a deep voice down one of the corridors continued to haggle for a price he was content with.

Kiran peered down the tunnel and saw a host of people dressed in clothes from an era long gone. They trudged through alleyways, some holding groceries, others carrying buckets of water or bales of cloth into storefronts. Chickens pecked their way between the stores and children sprinted through the lane. People were climbing ladders to go up and down from the store fronts to the street level above. The candle seller looked up at someone and

CHAPTER 13

smiled, and Kiran caught a glimpse of a young lady looking down at him admiringly from above.

"What is this place?" she asked their guide.

The spirit of Hans Svenson gazed down the tunnel fondly. "People were not always dying here. That way leads to the markets of old. The spirits there go on living their past lives, climbing ladders to a world that is gone, ever returning to the world below. But that is not your path today."

"What about this messed-up way?" Reese asked. "This better not be our path, either."

Kiran looked over Reese's shoulder to find a tunnel bathed in flame. People shouted and poured buckets of water upon a fire that they had no hope to extinguish. A charred man stumbled out of a storefront and collapsed on the street. A crowd of people stepped over him as they ran.

"No, Hero of old, I will not lead you into that fire. It consumed many of us, but it will not touch you while I lead this party."

"Can we help?" Gonzales took a step toward the fire and clenched his fists. "That man is still alive."

Their guide shook his head. "He has been dead for centuries and cannot be saved without the Cup, Healer. And countless armies have searched for it in vain. Come away. You can do nothing for them but join in their demise."

He led them down an empty tunnel for a few paces before Kiran grabbed Reese's shirt. "Wait," she insisted, seeing that the Ghost had hung back, gazing down the third tunnel, frozen as if by some spell. "Are you coming?" Kiran asked.

The Ghost rubbed a hand over his face and turned away. He joined them, his face expressionless.

"What was down that way?" she asked.

"A family eating dinner, nothing more." The Ghost's voice was barely a whisper. He coughed. "I must be hungry again. I should have snatched their dessert."

"Better that you did not," their guide said. "Even the Ghost himself might be trapped here. This might be where your story ends. How sad if it should be over a piece of cake."

133

The Ghost laughed at that. "I can think of no finer end. Knives and flame and the weight of mountains could not end me. But cake and pie might find a way. That would be beyond fitting."

They found themselves in a long narrow tunnel that finally sloped upward. Water rushed somewhere far in the distance.

"Is it much further?" Kiran didn't like this path at all. If the tunnel flooded, if they were attacked from either end, it would be a bad place to find themselves in.

Their guide shook his head. "Quite far, Wand Bearer. This path cannot be made any shorter. It leads underneath Broadway and winds toward the catacombs beneath the church. There I will leave you to your fate."

Kiran didn't like the sound of the word "fate." Before she could obsess about it, her cell phone rang.

Reese lifted his eyebrows. "Our phones have been dead for ages, and you get reception? I've got to get whichever your carrier is."

"Word," Gonzales agreed.

Kiran pulled the phone out of her pocket. She should have known. Her mother could reach her in any dimension.

"Yes, Amma."

"This dog, Kiran, I mean have you ever bathed it? I kept it in the bath for twenty minutes and I will never get the stain out of that tub. But its smell is not so bad now. I poured rosewater on it and oiled its fur. It loves my cooking."

"Amma, I can't talk now."

"Yes, yes, always too busy for your mother. I just wanted to give you some much needed advice. To tell you to go slow for once. Take care of yourself. Eat properly. The grad school tests are not till February. You still have three months left to study if you—"

"Amma, *this* is my job. It's what I'm best at. What I've got to do. Look, I've got a bunch of kids to find and a city to save so can you just give it a rest?"

"That's what I'm trying to say, Kiran. You should rest a little. You should—"

The voice cut out. Kiran wished she could reach out for it and pull it back. Her mother might annoy the hell out of her, might never appreciate her for

CHAPTER 13

who she was, but she was her mother. She tried calling back, tried dialing 911. Nothing. She speed-dialed her brother, the pizza place, the drug store without any luck. The phone was dead to the world but somehow her mother could still call to harass her. She turned it off.

"Honor thy father and thy mother," the Ghost said to no one in particular.

"Whatever," Kiran said. "My father disappeared years ago. And my mother would love it if I built a golden altar to her. Then you'd start talking about false idols or something, right?"

The Ghost shrugged. "I always liked idols. The little ones you could put in your pockets. The big ones were good for kids to ride on. We should never have gotten rid of the idols."

Hans Svenson didn't even turn. He spoke to the tunnel and his words echoed in her skull. "Your father was here once, Wand Bearer. I remember him walking these paths, lost and afraid."

Blood rushed to Kiran's ears. Her heart stopped beating. She grabbed for the spirit's arm and her hand passed through him. "Say that again."

The spirit of Hans Svenson turned toward her with wraith-like arthritis. "Time is fluid here, like the path of waves it recedes and comes again, I could not tell you when, but I saw him wandering, searching for a path."

"Could you find him again?" She imagined her father, falling from the sky, landing somehow in this underworld, disoriented, with the weight of a million tons of stone pressing down around him, surrounded by spirits. Her father was confused on a good day when he'd slept, when she'd managed to trick him into eating breakfast with her. How could he survive down here, alone? "How do we find him?"

"Find him?" Hans Svenson opened an empty palm. "To find him, you have to know where he wished to go." He waved a hand at the walls, and they fell away into mist. In their place reappeared dozens of tunnels spinning off in every direction. A sulfurous wind blew up from a route that sloped down to only Hell knew where. She leaned into another tunnel and listened to the screams of seagulls. The tunnel led to an ocean, but she felt certain it was no ocean she'd heard of. Her father could have taken any of them.

"He would be searching for a safe place, a place to rest, to hide. He could be hurt. Which path would he have taken?" Her mind raced with the possibilities. They had to do something.

The Ghost spoke in a harsh whisper. "No choice here leads to safety. Everywhere in the maze is but another place to run from."

"Then we find where he's hiding." Kiran spun to face the Ghost. "We drag him out and take him with us. He's sharper than any of us, he'll help with all of this." They would damn well find a way.

The Ghost pulled off his hat and waved with it in the direction of one of the tunnels. "This way you will find markets where people are bought and sold like animals. You can buy a rug to carry you on the wind or a pen that writes only lies." He aimed his hat again. "Down this path you will find a red ocean where gray ships sail and are dragged under when the winds fail." He replaced the hat on his head. "The other choices are worse. Doubt if you will. You need not believe me. Use your true vision, open yourself to the power of the mark. See with the eyes you were born to see with."

Kiran pulled her sleeve down further, hiding the mark, as if she could keep it hidden, keep it from hearing the words they spoke. "What do you mean?" she asked.

The Ghost shook his head in disappointment. "Anatol told you so little. He had too much faith that you would understand on your own. The mark gives you vision and creates a path. You forged a path into my prison and called me here. You can use the magic to see into other realms, even into the minds of others. It can grant you great power but take care. The power will tempt you. Look too far and you will be lost. Extend yourself into the mind of a demon or creature you could never comprehend, and you will lose your sanity before you can return. But look now, if only to convince yourself of your folly."

Kiran raised her hand and let her sleeve fall. The mark shone like black mercury in the darkness. Forged by angels and demons, it was a living thing she could not trust, Anatol had warned her. She felt it calling to her, tempting her with a promise to see farther than she had ever dreamed possible. She reached out and let the magic in.

A rush of dizziness swept over her as her vision swam. She blinked and the

CHAPTER 13

world shifted. The Ghost and the others still stood before her but something about them had changed. Around the Ghost a gray halo shimmered in the gloom. Reese stood tall and regal, brandishing a long sword he seemed completely unaware of while Gonzales was leaning on a sapling, ripped from the ground, and holding a golden cup. Hans Svenson appeared just as before, but solid. Beyond them stretched a dozen tunnels twisting into the distance. The mark called to her, and she let her mind fly.

Like a first-time sailor, she rode the wave of magic, sending her sight far ahead. The tunnel twisted and turned, ever onward, through darkness and mist. She sailed on for what seemed like miles, until finally the tunnels ended, and a cavern lay before her. Long curving wooden tables filled the cavern, scattered amongst stalagmites thrusting up from the floor. At each table sat people in tattered clothes, huddled over steaming bowls, spooning some kind of stew into their mouths. Kiran trembled as one of the people turned toward her, revealing a curved horn sprouting from the center of her forehead. Between the sinuous tables weaved hulking figures with steel pots on their hips from which they ladled servings half into bowls and half across the cavern floor.

A dull panic washed over her as if she was in a fog and it might be some other person far away, seeing all this. Her heart told her to run from this place with horned people, but she couldn't flee yet. Whatever these people were, they might know where her father was, might have seen him. The mark tempted her, promising she could read their minds if she only stretched further, drew deeper on the power. Before her was a young girl with a spoon to her lips. Kiran reached out with magic of the mark.

The girl with the horn in the center of her forehead dropped her spoon before Kiran could try to read her mind. The horned girl stared off into space and at the same time straight into Kiran's eyes. She reached out a hand. "You there, come here. You should not be doing that."

Kiran felt a tug as if the girl had a hold of her. Something lurched in her chest as the girl pulled. Kiran felt her mind, her entire soul, being dragged down the tunnel. She was filled with a certainty that the girl would tear her in half, and she would never return whole again.

She strained to break free, and her opponent fought back. The horned girl planted both her hands on the table and surged to her feet, pulling harder. Kiran felt herself slipping away, losing touch with her body. Her life would end here in some underground tunnel. She would become a spirit and never see her old world again.

In desperation she thrust her mind forward and visualized striking the girl with all her focus, pounding her with a fist between her eyes. The horned girl reached up to her face as if she'd been slapped and Kiran felt the hold on her loosen. She drew herself back and fled. Down the tunnel, not caring which path she chose, racing to get as far away as possible.

She lost count of how many turns she'd taken and realized she was lost. Her last turn ended in a long passageway filled with the smell of the sea and a cool wind. The stone floor gave way to gravel then sand as the tunnel sloped down and opened wide, revealing a black beach where water stretched to the horizon. Kiran gathered herself and let the panic wash away, tried to gather herself to follow the thread of magic back to her body.

A dark shape on the ocean caught her attention. She stretched her awareness high and flew over the gray water. The cold wind tried to beat her back, but it could do nothing against spirit and thought. She went on past the great waves until the black shape grew into a mountain in the middle of the sea. Far below, a lone skiff rode the waves, and she knew in her heart who sailed upon it.

She plunged like a hawk down through the mist until she felt herself touch down on the hard wooden deck with feet of spirit. The man at the helm turned, his shirt was ragged, his beard was unkept, and his face was worn and haggard. But his eyes saw her, spirit or not, and they grew bright as the dawn. Her father stepped toward her and stretched out his hand. His mouth opened as he mouthed her name.

She reached out with a hand of spirit and felt her grip pass through his fingers. She tried again, tried to hold him, but her arms found no purchase. Her heart ached terribly. But she'd found him. They could get him home.

"Baba, where are we? How do we get you out of this place?" She felt herself trembling.

CHAPTER 13

Her father's look of surprise changed to concern. "Kiran, I can just make out the outlines of you. How did you come here? What have you done?"

"Baba, listen. Just tell me how we can find you. I've come with friends. We can get you out. Get you home."

"My stubborn troublemaker. Even here, you cannot be kept away." He shook his head. "You came all this way to find me? Sent your spirit and left your body behind?"

Kiran ran her hands through hair that was not there. "It's a long story, Baba. We came to find lost children who've been taken. Someone told me you were lost here too. I'm taking you back with me. I'm sorry I couldn't find you last time. I'm sorry I didn't realize you were in trouble. This time I'm taking you home."

Her father tried to run a hand over her shoulder. "You aren't the one who should be sorry for anything, Kiran." He looked around at the ship and out at the ocean beyond. "Everything here is so clouded. I've been searching for the wand for so long I forget at times who I am or why I even came." He shook his head as if trying to bring his thoughts into order. "They took children? Pawns in some game, I'm sure. I've heard of these lost children, I think. He closed his eyes tight for a moment then turned to her. "Kiran you must go now. If there are children waiting for you, relying on you, you must find them. You've stretched yourself too thin. Any longer and you will never return."

She shook her head no. "I'm going to find them, Baba. But I'm taking you with me. I can't do this alone."

Her father pointed high into the air. "Look, the magic fades. You have little time left to decide. To come here with your body and your friends will take ages. To bring me home, you will have to abandon whatever path you first set on. The children will stay lost."

She looked behind her. The black thread of the mark's magic stretched away into the sky. It was growing ever fainter, a wisp of spirit dissolving away.

"I'm not leaving you here, Baba, all alone." She willed those words to be true.

"I'm never quite alone, Kiran, while I know you're out there. But those

139

kids are more important than I will ever be. They are the ones you cannot abandon, whatever you may want. I taught you not to abandon the pawns."

She felt the pull of the mark upon her, a final warning, a last chance to return. She grabbed for her father and felt her fingertips brush his. Her voice cracked. "I love you, Baba. Stay safe and I'll come back for you."

Her father frowned. "You can't always stay safe, Kiran. When everything is lost, you attack. Do what you have to. Get those kids back."

Kiran let the mark pull her back as she drifted up and away and felt her heart break completely.

Her father raised a hand in farewell then turned and took the helm again, steering toward the black mountain.

The thread led her on and she flew carelessly, careening down tunnel after tunnel, her eyes wet with spirit tears until she slammed back into her own body and released the power of the mark.

She covered her face with both hands, wiping away sweat and tears, searching her brow to make certain there was no horn plastered to her forehead. When she looked up, she found the Ghost watching.

"You knew just how dangerous that was and you still let me do it." Her voice had no strength whatsoever.

The Ghost shrugged. "You didn't summon a babysitter. You saw what you needed to see. You won't make the same mistake again." He gestured down one of the tunnels. "These paths are not ours. I am here to kill and to kill only. Not to protect you. Not to heal old wounds or find lost souls. None of these paths lead to Krol."

"And I don't care what your agenda is." Kiran wanted to shake the Ghost by the shoulders, but barely felt strong enough to stand. "I found him there. My father is lost, all alone, and we can bring him back. We are not abandoning him in some stinking sewer realm where arthritic spirits spend their forevers." She pointed at the Ghost's chest. "Do you understand me, or did the brain in that skull turn to dust long ago?"

She expected the Ghost to unleash his usual glare of a thousand dead suns, but his eyes stayed locked on the floor. "You are the Wand, the Priestess, the Star. Ever lost, you were always meant to lead." He took in a deep breath

CHAPTER 13

and shuddered. "I have made many countless mistakes in both my life and death. My choices have seldom led me out of darkness. I am no arbiter of anyone's fate. Those who wander from the way of understanding will rest in the assembly of the dead."

"All right then." She wasn't sure what he meant by "assembly of the dead," but she wasn't going to dwell on it now. She considered the routes before her, and her mind spun, trying to remember the path back.

"What did your father say when you found him?" Gonzales stepped in front of her in his maroon shirt, fingering his wooden bead necklace. "Did he say now was the time to come for him?"

Kiran felt the ground slipping beneath her. "What does it matter, Enrique? How would a man who's been lost all this time know what the right thing to do is? I mentioned the children and he said…" Her legs lost the strength to hold her. She felt herself falling.

Reese caught her and held her tight as she shook.

She buried her face in Reese's shoulder and gave thanks she didn't have to rely on her legs to keep her off the ground. "He said to never abandon the pawns. He told me to go."

"Hey, hey there." Reese squeezed her then stood her up and brushed the hair out of her eyes, but he didn't let go. "We're here for you."

She looked up and saw that Reese's eyes were wet too.

"My father died of leukemia when he was in his forties," Reese said. "It was a bad way to go. I was a kid, and he was a young man with lots of life ahead and it all vanished. I wish I could go back for him too. I'd go anywhere to find him. Gonzo's father got shot in Oaxaca when he was in eighth grade. Imagine that and the cops did nothing. He always thought maybe they were involved in the whole thing. That's why he wastes his time with me, trying to do a little better. We both understand."

Gonzales clutched his wooden beads and abandoned his world of monosyllables. "You fear losing him again. I get that. I'm afraid of so many things. When I speak, the fears come back to me. In silence I can push them down, so I stay silent when I can. But this place, this place makes me remember them all."

"Word," Reese ran his eyes over the walls and shivered.

"You two are throwing me off with the role reversal," Kiran said.

"I'm afraid of this place," Gonzales continued. "I'm not ashamed to admit it. Reese joined the police thinking he could earn respect, be rewarded for who he is. That was all wrong. I joined thinking I could face my fear, do better, but I was just as wrong. The fear never left. Somewhere on these paths death waits for me, I am sure, like it waited for mi padre. But if we survive what is ahead, we will return with you and help find your father. After we bring those kids home we will return. Te lo prometo."

She held up a hand. "You don't have to say 'Word,' Reese."

Reese closed his mouth.

Kiran realized she was clenching both her hands in front of her like she might punch Reese or Gonzales. Thankfully, they didn't seem to mind.

"Shit, shit, shit," she said. Something inside of her split open and bled out completely; she suspected it was her aorta, but she managed to keep standing despite the fact that she must have absolutely zero blood flow now. Reese grabbed her again and she shook free. She needed to stand on her own.

Her brother, the doctor, sure as hell wouldn't be able to explain it, but there it was, she was a goddamn medical miracle, standing with no aorta. Her father was gone, and he was going to have to stay gone for a little while longer. She couldn't abandon the pawns out there, in the dark, waiting for her.

"Make these go away, Hans." She waved a hand at the myriad of paths, and they disappeared, leaving only the one they were already traveling upon. A feeling of emptiness swept over her like the last bit was being drained away. Her voice cracked as she spoke. "I'm holding you to that promise, Gonzales."

"Word," Gonzales said, and the world was right again.

Reese raised a hand, gesturing at the Ghost. "Hey, this is one of those open you heart moments, you know? I talk about my dad, who always got treated like he was something lesser than everyone else, who left this world too early. Gonzo talks about why he doesn't talk much. Now maybe you mention why you're such an ass or something?"

The growl that emanated from the Ghost's throat was low and menacing enough to momentarily replace Kiran's despair with sheer terror. Even Hans

CHAPTER 13

Svenson turned away.

Reese stepped back. "Or you don't talk at all."

The Ghost leaned over him. "And you all stay alive a little longer."

Hans Svenson waved them on. "Come now, no need to fight amongst yourselves when there are so many other ways here to die." He led them on, and with every step Kiran felt the final drops of her blood drip out of her ruined aorta, or maybe it was a jugular vein, she had no idea; they all connected to the heart somewhere, she figured. She imagined her father somewhere in a market where people were bought and sold, where pens that wrote only lies were bartered, playing chess for his life and a scrap of spirit bread. "Survive, Baba. I'll be back for you as soon as I can."

Her eyes were trained on her feet, so she barely noticed when they reached the end of the tunnel and arrived in a small alcove.

"This is where I leave you," the spirit said. Their guide pointed down a stairwell that ended in an ornate wooden door with an enormous iron padlock.

"That lock should not prove any trouble, I'm sure." He held up his silver coin. "Payment has been made. May you find your way to the other side."

The Ghost waved a hand at the spirit, dismissing him.

The spirit seemed upset at being sent away so unceremoniously. He pointed his cane. "You, Ghost. May your past deeds haunt you until your miserable end."

"Screw you, Hans," the Ghost replied.

The spirit slipped away beneath the cobblestones, and they were alone. The look he gave the Ghost when he left was devoid of anything but wrath.

"Come on. Let's get this over with." The Ghost started down the stairs.

"Wait." Kiran held up a hand.

"For what?" the Ghost asked. "I can crack that lock with one blow."

"Don't touch it." Kiran stared at the door, wondering. "Please."

The Ghost looked up at her from the bottom of the stairs. "Why?"

Kiran didn't have a good reason, but she seldom did when she got these feelings. She thought back to her mother's voice, telling her to take care of herself, to go slow for once. She didn't like Hans Svenson, that was the only thing she was sure of.

"If I was Krol, or whoever we're up against, I'd bring us to a door where we couldn't escape, where there was no other path out. I'd set up a guide to bring us here and make it all seem straightforward. Krol fears you. You already killed him once. But down here, rules are different. He could lose you in some other dimension forever, couldn't he?"

"I don't trust that guy," Reese said. "He took his money and split before we opened the door. He never wanted to help those people in the fire."

Gonzales nodded. "Mentiroso."

"Where would you have us go?" the Ghost asked. "This place is an infinite maze without a guide. Every wrong turn is your last."

"I want us to take our time." Kiran felt her mind slip into high gear, a sudden jolt of adrenaline speeding her thoughts. "You have tracked Krol before. Can you still hear those children? Can you hear them through that door?"

The Ghost put his ear to the door. He shook his head. "I hear an endless wind on the other side." He rapped his knuckles on the door. "Do not stretch yourself beyond this door with the mark. Krol may have foreseen that."

"Agreed. I don't like the sound of endless wind." She shuddered, imagining her mind being trapped on the other side of the door, her body left behind. It would be the perfect trap. "I think we should go back to the place where the path first forked. There were voices we ignored back there." She took another look at the door with the giant padlock. Something about it seemed wrong. "I don't trust Hans' choices."

The Ghost shifted his bag to his other shoulder. "Lost here or any other place in this universe, is all the same to me."

They made their way back down the tunnel and Kiran doubted herself the entire way. They reached the branching point, and she asked the Ghost to listen again. He placed his ear to the ground while they waited.

He straightened and pointed to the street where people were still milling about hawking their wares from a Seattle two centuries ago. "Down that path, I hear children shouting, but their voices hold no sorrow." He nodded toward the other path where orange fire bathed the tunnel and smoke billowed. "There, I hear the cry we heard before, a lost child desperate for his mother.

CHAPTER 13

It may be from another time, I cannot say. I am the bludgeon, nothing more. You must be your own guide."

Kiran had had enough. "Don't give me that bullshit. Bludgeon, hammer, screwdriver, whatever. You sound like a professional wrestler. The three of us have never traveled in another dimension with spirits and dead people. We need your mind, not your bravado. What do you think?"

The Ghost raised his chin and stared at her a long while. "I think Hans was an asshole and a liar."

"Then we're in agreement. We take the road less traveled." She took a deep breath and gazed into the flames and smoke. "Out of the Lying Han, into the fire."

The Ghost growled under his breath. "Your mind is more twisted than I feared."

Kiran raised a palm. "Don't say 'word,' Gonzales. Please."

Chapter 14

The walls of the tunnel radiated heat like a brick oven. They passed empty shop windows where chairs and tables had been knocked over in a rush to escape, to run from a fire that never ceased plaguing them. At the end of the tunnel, they stepped into a courtyard where people dressed in clothes from another century fled in every direction, racing up ladders to escape the flames. Kiran's eyes stung with smoke. Even the cobblestones under her feet felt hot. She inhaled and went into a fit of coughing. If this was an illusion, it was very convincing.

All she could hear were desperate shouts as people fled. "Can you follow the sound through this?" she asked.

The Ghost pointed across the courtyard. "Somewhere there, amongst the madness. There's too much noise to make sense of anything now. This place is about to die. Everyone here has perished before in flames and will soon perish again. This is a place where death never ends, where no savior ever comes."

Kiran didn't say it, but the truth was inescapable. The flames were jumping from building to building, surrounding the courtyard. They would soon be among the dead if they didn't find a way through this nightmare.

Gonzales grabbed her arm. "Wait. It's like a movie."

"This is no movie." Kiran pulled her arm free. "The fires are getting closer."

Gonzales shook his head. "No, I mean I've seen it before. When I looked down the tunnel earlier. These same people were dying. I've seen it in my dreams a million times. This is the dragon. The dragon is coming for me." His face was covered in sweat.

CHAPTER 14

"Keep it together, my brother." Reese put a hand on his partner's shoulder. "There's no dragon here. We've just got to find our way through."

The glass of a nearby storefront exploded and flames licked the street. A woman screamed in another store, trapped inside by the fire.

"No. These are the ancestors, hermano. They may not be ours, but they die in front of us, victims of the dragon. No puede ser." Gonzales shrugged off Reese's hand and took off at a dead sprint.

Her team was going insane.

The Ghost sighed. "He's dumber than I thought. He cannot touch them. No one can change the fate of the dead."

Gonzales crashed into a door that was already aflame. The door burst to pieces, and he disappeared inside. Reese took off behind him. Kiran hesitated. If these were the dead, what could they possibly change?

Gonzales tumbled out of the doorway holding a woman in his arms. He hit the ground with the woman atop him, trying to put out the fire eating its way up his pant leg.

Reese threw his jacket over him and beat out the flames. He helped Gonzales to his feet and put out the last of the sparks.

Kiran held out a hand and the woman took it. Her grip was surprisingly real.

The woman was trembling. "Where do we go? Where?" Kiran had no idea what to tell her.

"You cannot save the dead." The Ghost looked angrier than usual.

"We can try." Gonzales ripped off the tatters of burned pantleg. "Kiran, we could get them into that other tunnel where there's no fire. They don't need to die here again."

"My brother is right," Reese said. "We can't leave the ancestors like this."

The Ghost glared at the two SPD officers. "You idiots have taken us too deep into this story already. The touch of doomed souls is real to you now. Their fires will be your end." He turned his glare on Kiran. "Talk sense into these fools, woman."

The spirit was still clutching Kiran's hand. The look of desperation in her eyes made Kiran's decision for her. Why did the stupid heart defy logic most

THE TOOLS OF THE GHOST

of the time?

She gauged the distance from the approaching fire to the way they've come. "If we could do something quick. Lead them to the other tunnel before the fire takes everything—"

That was all Gonzales needed to hear. "Vamos, hermano." They dashed across the courtyard and Reese started shouting.

The Ghost shook his head. "Idiots. Why do I always work with idiots?"

"Why do I always work with jerks?" Kiran asked. "I mean, usually." She nodded toward Reese and Gonzales. "Those two at least have beating hearts. Whatever they're doing, it's working."

The crowd looked to be listening to Reese and heading their way. She watched as Gonzales lifted an injured woman onto his shoulders. Her face was charred black. Kiran couldn't bear to look at the rest of her.

"Come on. Don't be useless." Kiran sprinted toward two children headed in the wrong direction, down an alleyway she felt certain would end in fire. She grabbed their arms before they could get away. "You two are coming with me." Their wide eyes held maximum terror already. They didn't resist.

With the children in tow, Kiran sprinted in the direction of the tunnel they'd come through. Gonzales was already there with the burned woman over his shoulder. A crowd of others streamed after them as Reese herded them through none too soon.

Kiran was not so lucky. The fire raced after her across the courtyard like a living thing, dancing over stone that couldn't possibly burn, jumping from roof to roof like a monster denied its prey, coming to seek its vengeance. She ran with flames just behind her. Heat pressed against her, whispering a promise of her death.

Ahead, Gonzales handed the burned woman to Reese and waved them on. "Faster, Kiran!" Gonzales screamed.

She made the mistake of looking behind her and stumbled at the sight. As she watched, the fire pulled together and took the shape of a creature of living flame and destruction. The newly formed dragon reared above the courtyard, spreading dark wings tipped with fire from building to building, setting everything ablaze. Streaks of red light ran along the monster's scales

CHAPTER 14

as if a furnace within was straining to break free. The dragon stretched its neck high above the courtyard and glared down at her with coal eyes set in a black horned skull. It snorted and flames shot from its nostrils.

Just her luck. Gonzales' stupid dragon had to find them here. Like she really needed this now.

Kiran dragged the kids behind her, afraid she might pull off their arms, as she sprinted for the tunnel that was much too far.

The dragon's tail lashed out, smashing into a wooden cart, transforming it into a burning missile, rocketing toward Kiran with the certainty of death. She dove to the ground with her arms around the children and rolled, her eyes never leaving the approaching fireball.

The cart struck the Ghost first. She was never certain if he had been standing in its path and failed to move or whether he had stepped in front of it, but it hit him and burst into kindling as the Ghost was thrown across the courtyard.

Kiran had no time to look for what was left of the Ghost. She dragged the children off the ground and dashed past Gonzales, into the mouth of the tunnel. Another glance behind and Kiran realized they were unlikely to ever make it out.

"They are mine to burn. Mine to consume! You cannot deny me what is mine." The dragon lowered its head, its yellow eyes glaring straight into the tunnel like headlights in the darkness.

Gonzales kicked in a door and dragged the whole thing off its hinges. He left the door at the mouth of the alleyway and stepped out of the tunnel like a complete fool, waving his arms overhead, making the fatal mistake of catching the dragon's attention. "Vales verga! You've nothing better to do than burn this place over and over? Why not pick on someone your own size?"

Kiran almost pulled out a chunk of her hair. How big did Gonzales think he was?

The dragon tilted its horned head, as if sizing up the fool who'd dared speak to it.

"I know you, Enkidu, Son of Anu. Why have you come here again, defenseless? You cannot face me without the Cup. I will char your soul so you can never return."

"Enrique!" Kiran screamed. "Get back here." The tunnel was almost clear of the spirits. She needed Gonzales to follow them before he got himself barbecued.

"The curandera was wrong! You don't look so fast to me, lizard! Come on." Gonzales took off across the courtyard, weaving between tipped over carts, jumping over benches, as the dragon spun to catch him.

Kiran watched as Gonzales dodged the dragon's claws and made a full circle around the courtyard, using all the speed the Ghost had given him. Kiran held her breath as the dragon's chest swelled, preparing to incinerate Gonzales in a blast of fire.

But as Gonzales reached the tunnel, he picked up the door and braced it across the entrance. The flames struck the wood like a thunderbolt. Reese leaped to help Gonzales support the door. His arms trembled as he held the barrier up to the flames.

Kiran tensed to run but froze instead. Through the gap between the door and the wall she glimpsed the courtyard beyond.

The Ghost stood alone in front of the dragon. In one hand he held his iron rod, in the other a charred piece of wood that looked like the shaft of a spear. He was facing the monster like a matador confronting a bull, and he looked terribly small and frail in comparison to the juggernaut confronting him.

The dragon stretched its wings wide across the courtyard. "What business have you here, Ghost? You have no heart, no soul, no stake in this game. Enkidu is mine. They are all mine."

Kiran held her breath as the Ghost stood silent; his coat whipped by the wind of the dragon's flames. He kept his rod held out to his left and the spear shaft pointing at the monster, a matador ready for the charge.

The dragon lowered its massive horned head and released a cloud of steam through its nostrils. "Leave this place, Ghost and you will be free. Those who have enslaved you for centuries will die in flames, as they deserve. Why attempt to deny me what is mine?"

The Ghost shrugged his shoulders. "Because you're an asshole, dragon."

CHAPTER 14

The dragon charged. At the same instant Reese pushed Kiran back away from the door.

"Run, Kiran. Get the kids out."

Shit. Shit. Shit. The Ghost was dead. He had to be dead. Kiran ran.

She tumbled out into the central passageway and found a host of confused and burned spirits milling about. She dragged her forearm across her eyes and blinked away the tears. Gonzales and Reese had bought them the time they needed. The Ghost's sacrifice had bought them all time.

"For God's sake, that way," Kiran ordered. "Don't let them get burned to ashes for nothing." She started directing everyone into the other tunnel.

The dead stumbled down the new passageway and into the arms of long-lost spirits who embraced them. The two children Kiran had pulled through dashed ahead and disappeared in the crowd amidst screams of recognition.

"They are no good to me barbecued." A rasp she would recognize anywhere made Kiran spin.

The Ghost stalked out of the fiery tunnel, his hat ablaze, dragging Reese and Gonzales behind him. He tossed both detectives onto the floor in a heap. Kiran gave thanks to Ganesha that the Ghost was not easy to kill.

Gonzales' face was covered in soot and his right leg was terribly burned, but he didn't seem to care. "The dragon will not eat today." He lay on the ground and laughed until he cried and his face became a mess of wet ash. "I am still alive. The curandera lied."

Reese coughed and sputtered. He rubbed his eyes. "I must look like shit, for the very first time. It's not easy being so good looking."

Gonzales was still laughing. "Word."

Reese heaved himself up and pulled Gonzales off the floor. "Flattering me will get you everywhere, my brother." Covered in ash, Reese still looked amazing. He turned to Kiran and half-smiled. "We were impressive in there, hey? You run like a beautiful gazelle, K."

Kiran couldn't believe Reese was flashing that smile after almost dying. "That's the first time someone has compared me to an antelope, Reese."

Reese raised an eyebrow. "So how about dinner, if one of us survives after all this?"

Kiran stepped forward and brushed a mess of ash out of Reese's hair. She fixed Gonzales' wooden beads which had gotten all tangled. "First we survive, Reese, then maybe we'll grab a bite. And it had better not be at that crappy diner."

Reese's smile grew. "Now we have something to survive for."

Kiran turned to the Ghost and stopped herself from grabbing his coat and shaking him. "What happened back there? How did it not kill you?"

The Ghost met her eyes for a moment before turning away. "It charged like a bull and missed. Unfortunately, I don't die as easily as everyone would like me to."

Before Kiran could question him further, the last of the spirits disappeared down the alleyway and Kiran heard the sound again. Coming from somewhere in the inferno was a child's cry. The sound the Ghost had been following.

The Ghost beat out his flaming hat against the wall. He had heard it as well. "Come on," he said. "If you thought you were done with your dragon, you were wrong. It still has a good chance to eat you. That was round one."

"Mierda." Gonzales stopped laughing.

They trudged through the tunnel again to find the courtyard empty; the flames receded. The scene had started over again from the beginning like a movie reel, but the spirits were gone. They would never burn again.

"I'd say we have about five minutes before this place goes to hell and that asshole dragon comes back for revenge," Kiran said. "He likes it served hot."

The Ghost started across the square. "Then let's get moving before these two fools try saving the furniture." He led them to a tailor's shop where blue dresses hung in the window alongside wide hats covered in lace. He kicked in the door. "It's coming from somewhere in there."

Kiran followed behind Reese as they stepped into a room filled with mannequins, bundles of cloth, and dresses in every stage of production.

"Just our luck," said Reese. "Let me guess. The sound is coming from behind one of those."

The far wall stretched to an impossible distance and was covered in at least a hundred doors of every shape and size.

CHAPTER 14

The Ghost nodded. "I have no idea which one."

They stood staring at the doors as the sound of the fire grew behind them, eating the buildings, roaring back for vengeance.

"I believe you will need a guide." They turned at the sound of a gentle voice.

A young woman who looked to be in her early twenties was examining them. She didn't seem threatening, but everything was deceptive here.

"Where did you come from?" Kiran asked.

The woman raised a chin in Gonzales' direction. "He carried me on his shoulders out of this disaster. I was dead and burned once again as I was bound to be for all eternity. But somehow, when I stepped into that other tunnel, I became whole again. It is written that all living spirits need a guide in this world. I owe you that and more." She pointed at a small door with a polished wooden knob. "Through there you will find your path. I cannot come for the way out must be found on your own. But that is your door. You must go no further in this realm of fire."

"How will you make it back?" Gonzales looked worried.

The woman smiled at him. "You've shown me the way. The flames will never catch me again." She walked up to Gonzales. "You suffered burns for me. Their mark will ever be upon you as a mark of my debt. If you are ever in this realm again, dear Enkidu, come find me." She kissed him on the cheek, then turned and walked back the way she had come.

"Everyone here keeps confusing me with someone else," Gonzales said.

Reese grinned. "Whoever this Enkidu was, he was a real ladies' man."

The Ghost shoved his hat deeper onto his head. "Where do I find these people?" He put his hand on the wooden doorknob as flames roared up outside the store. "Let's get out of the frying pan."

Chapter 15

They closed the door behind them and found themselves in an enormous underground chamber with barrels of wine stacked against the walls. Sixty feet above, pipes and wires traced the ceiling. In its center, a manhole cover sat ajar, revealing the night sky and a world Kiran would sorely love to return to. They'd been down here longer than she thought.

"We've arrived despite all of your nonsense." The Ghost gave a long exhale. "These are the catacombs and tunnels under the church. Krol will be here. This will all be over soon." He reached into his sack and drew out the long iron rod. It was the first time Kiran had gotten a close look at it. It was dented and scratched all along its length. She wondered how many people had perished under its blows.

At that moment, the clouds outside uncovered the moon and a perfect shaft of light slipped through the manhole, illuminating the Ghost's gray face. He shone silver, for a moment, like a strange alien, a fallen angel, a person she'd known long ago she couldn't quite remember, whose name was on the tip of her tongue. The music he'd played, and his mournful voice came back to her, lamenting some tragedy he could never make right again. In the next moment, the light faded, and the Ghost looked up, baring his teeth at the unseen sky, and she remembered who he really was. "Take off the necklace for an instant and he will rip out your beating heart," Anatol had promised. This creature was no one she'd ever known. He was a monster, a killer, someone she would flee from on any other day.

Kiran drew her gun. Reese and Gonzales already had their weapons in hand. The Ghost led the way down a winding stone staircase to a heavy wooden

CHAPTER 15

door armed with a rusted padlock. He struck the lock once with his iron rod and it shattered along with the door handle. So much for doing this quietly. He pushed the door open, and they were bathed in an unexpected light.

The room beyond the door was nothing Kiran could have imagined, and she had imagined some weird stuff. It was as if a gigantic hidden chapel had been built beneath the city and they had tried to win the Guinness Book of Records for the heading *Baroque Shit*. Shining brass candles blazed in sconces in every direction, far more candles than any church needed. Every column was carved with tiny figures who looked extremely busy doing religious things. The walls arched up to a ceiling depicting some scene from the Bible Kiran didn't recognize where a man she assumed was Jesus was bathed in light, floating above a crowd of people. It was far beyond gaudy and overdone. The room was deprived of pews or chairs, but an altar stood at the far end. Two passageways curved off to either side. A wide stone staircase a few feet to their right descended straight down before bending and continuing into the darkness like a route direct to the Abyss.

Reese spun around slowly examining all the ornamentation. "Well, shit. They've got a whole stinking Roman Catholic world down here."

"Madre santa." Gonzales' jaw hung open.

Kiran still felt like her aorta was missing. She'd traded the chance of finding her father for this. It was damn well not going to be for nothing. "Can you hear the children?" Kiran asked.

The Ghost turned his head from side to side, listening. "Terrible acoustics in here." He held up a hand. "Wait."

A tap, tap, tap of heels on stone echoed throughout the chamber. They stepped back into the shadows just as an extremely short nun dressed in her habit emerged from one of the passageways near the altar. Kiran recognized her. She was one of the few people who'd helped her during her investigation. The nun had wrung her hands and admitted that things weren't as they'd always been, though she'd blamed all the changes on renting out space to shady community groups for money. Kiran remembered she'd been half blind, her glasses so thick they pressed indentations into her nose. She'd wondered if the woman was the slightest bit addled by age. Sister Edith, that was her name.

The nun hummed to herself as she bent and lit a few more candles before picking up a tall brass candlestick. She started across the room toward the staircase at the far end, headed straight for them. She passed within six feet, still humming to herself, before she stopped and realized they were there.

Her eyes went wide, and she stumbled, but caught herself before falling. Kiran figured that would have been the last thing they needed, a nun with a hip fracture to carry out of here. Sister Edith held up the brass candlestick and peered at them through immense lenses. "Oh, I'm sorry. I hadn't noticed you there. How can I help you all?" Her lips spread in a genuine smile, revealing rather stained dentures.

"Sister Edith," Kiran began. "You might remember when—"

The Ghost interrupted her by stepping forward and kicking Sister Edith in the sternum hard enough to lift her entire small frame off the ground. Edith hit the wall and tumbled down the staircase like a sack full of smashed nun. Kiran heard every thud and crack as her tiny body bounced off stone and crashed on the platform below.

Kiran ran to the edge of the stairs, but Gonzales got there first.

Gonzales peered down. "Mierda."

"Damn." Reese shook his head. "You just cold-heartedly kicked a nun down the stairs. Allah is going to curse us."

The nun was twisted at all the wrong angles, her neck and pelvis and legs bent in positions incompatible with life. The brass candlestick lay near her head, already stained by a pool of blood.

The Ghost shrugged. "She had a candlestick." He peered down the stairs at her. "And I hate nuns."

Reese threw up his hands. "It wasn't a gun. It wasn't even a knife. Would you kill someone for carrying a gallon of milk?"

The Ghost bit his lower lip. "I may have overreacted."

He was interrupted by the disturbing sound of bone cracking. The Ghost ducked as something flew past his head. They turned as one to see the brass candlestick quivering in the wall. They spun back to look down the staircase.

Sister Edith's neck had snapped back into alignment. She was heaving

CHAPTER 15

herself up on her elbows as her pelvis slowly rotated back into place.

The Ghost shrugged. "Then again, maybe I didn't." He leapt down the stairs, landing with one boot on the nun's sternum, and raised his weapon.

The nun opened a bloody mouth and spoke in a voice that was far too deep. "We have had enough of you, Betrayer. You will find that—"

None of them ever learned what the Ghost was supposed to find out because he chose that moment to smash his iron rod upon the nun's forehead. He brought the weapon down several more times before he was satisfied. Kiran looked away before the nausea hit.

Reese shrugged. "He hates nuns."

The Ghost wiped the weapon on the nun's robes and rejoined them. "I won't wait so long when we see the next nun. Have you chosen a direction?"

Kiran looked down the stairs at what was left of the woman and fought down the sudden surge of nausea. That woman had been alive and normal a week ago. She took in a sharp breath. Unless the nun had already been possessed when Kiran had interviewed her, and she'd been sitting across from a demon. She really needed some gum about now before she ground her teeth away.

"Let's try the direction Demon Nun came from," she said. "I don't like the look of the stairs going down." Going further below would be adding to the nightmare.

They skirted the perimeter of the chapel and entered one of the tunnels behind the altar. The air here smelled of far too much incense mixed with the scent of a cold morgue. The cobblestones were slick, and long puddles traced their way up and down the halls. Water had found its way to this level and flooded it recently.

The Ghost narrowed his eyes. "The crying gets louder this way. I hear footsteps as well. The children are not far, and they are not alone."

She could hear it now too, faint enough that it almost seemed like her imagination: the sound of a child whimpering.

They'd found them.

Chapter 16

The door at the end of the corridor was made of blood-red steel inlaid with filigrees of gold. It looked like it could withstand the direct charge of a tank.

The Ghost put a hand to the door and closed his eyes. "On the other side of this door, we are going to find a shit storm. I sense the presence of a greater demon. Whatever summoning ritual they were planning on is probably complete."

"You sense it just like that?" Gonzales asked. "I mean, like spider-sense or something."

The Ghost sighed. "Or something."

Kiran could feel it as well. The mark on her forearm pulsed with energy and she felt the ache in her bones. "Could it be Krol?" She had a sense that this was it, the end of their search, that the children would be on the other side of that door and that they would either fail or bring them home.

The Ghost shrugged. "I hear the voices of children. Krol may be amongst them. If so, I will send him back where he belongs, and our pact will end. You will not see me again."

Reese flattened himself against the wall. "This is where it goes down. The true test of our worth."

The Ghost sighed. "You've watched too many movies."

Kiran's mouth had gone dry. The kids were on the other side of that door. Possibly hurt. "Break it down," she ordered. She hoped the Ghost could get through before it was too late.

"Just a second." The Ghost reached into one of his coat pockets and pulled out his cell phone and headset.

CHAPTER 16

"What are you doing?" Kiran asked. "Wait. I don't care. Just get through the door."

"Yes, master," the Ghost put his hand on the doorknob, and it turned with a click. The Ghost gave a rare smile. "Demons always forget to lock the door."

The door opened to reveal a forty by forty-foot chamber lit with torches with a throne at its center. Crucifixes covered the back wall, and none of them looked like they were there for decoration. Kiran was struck at once by the scent of rotten flowers and ashes. Cultists dressed in stupid robes were arrayed in a semicircle around the throne. They turned as one to face the door and started shouting and reaching for weapons. Much more concerning was the black-horned demon sitting on the throne with a spiked mace in its lap and an overly eager expression on its face. Krol was nowhere in sight.

A cage in the room's center held the children she'd so longed to see. They sat huddled in a mass that simultaneously caused Kiran's heart to stop beating and made her want to personally smash the face of everyone else in the room.

The Ghost swung his sack in front of the door and two spears slammed into it. "Free weapons." He swung the door half closed and pulled out the spears. He tossed one to Gonzales, the other to Kiran. "Only Reese's gun will work in there with a greater demon present." Another spear slammed into his bag while he was talking. "I'll kill the demon. You three try not to die." He raised a finger as if he had a sudden thought. "Wait. Reese, you do the prove-yourself-thing, like in the movies. It'll make it fun if you get killed and make a final speech."

Reese held up his middle finger. "I'm charging you extra for always being an ass."

The Ghost regarded the finger. "There's no clause for workplace harassment. I have to put up with you for free."

Kiran squeezed the shaft of the spear as her mind raced. "Just make sure the kids aren't hurt, no matter what happens." The Ghost wouldn't give a damn about the children. She had to get them out of that room and survive long enough to get them home.

The Ghost threw the door open and hurled his bag straight into one of the cultists who never got up again. He swung his iron rod in a wide arc,

THE TOOLS OF THE GHOST

smashing the skull of another. The rest scattered like tiny boats racing to get out of the way of an angry iceberg. The demon didn't even move.

The Ghost marched straight for the black-horned monster on the throne. Kiran followed in his wake for as long as she could. She kept her eye on the children as spears flew overhead and gunshots exploded. Out of the side of her eye she glimpsed Gonzales leaping like a hundred-meter track star, smacking down cultists before they knew what he was.

She turned away from the protection of the Ghost's shadow toward the cage and dodged a cultist jabbing at her with a spear. The man went down as one of Reese's shots hit him in the leg. Kiran found herself alone in front of the cage with the one cultist who'd stayed to guard it. A six-foot-tall woman stood before her, a long knife in each hand. Kiran had never felt more pissed off at anyone.

The cultist took a step forward, swirling the knives in a hypnotic pattern of steel. "Just in time to join the sacrifice," the woman said.

Kiran pepper sprayed the hell out of her. She was pleased to find that capsaicin worked fine in magical places. The woman dropped her knives and scrambled back, covering her eyes. Kiran flipped the spear around and slammed the butt into the cultist's forehead which ended her flailing around. Then she tried the cage and found it, of course, locked. The children crouched inside, covering their ears as Reese's gun fired again.

She needed the Ghost to rip off the stupid door of this cage. She turned in time to see the demon get out of his chair and lift his spiked club.

"So good of you to come, Dearest Ghost. I am Albazaran, third hand of the original Host. You've missed the others, so the pleasure of killing you will be all mine." He waved a claw at the walls of the chamber. "You see, all of this is planned: the crucifixions, the death of your friends. Wait, my mistake. You don't have friends anymore, do you?" The demon smiled, displaying a mouth full of yellowed teeth. "I have waited eons for this, battled countless other demons for the honor to finish you. You have no idea how much you are hated."

The Ghost pointed to his headset. "Music's really loud. Let me know when the soliloquy is over. A hand gesture or a little wave of the horns would do."

CHAPTER 16

Albazaran's smile vanished. His wings spread wide, casting a black shadow across the room. He lifted his spiked mace and came down on the Ghost like the vengeance of Hell.

Kiran flinched as the Ghost folded like a paper doll and went down under the assault. All she could make out was a crumpled figure getting the shit pummeled out of him while the demon raised his mace again and again. She grabbed the padlock on the cage and shook it, feeling completely useless.

One of the children reached through the bars and seized her wrist. She recognized Jamie Winters, age eight, third grade, two older brothers, a cat, and parents so devastated that they had trouble forming sentences.

Jamie pointed at the demon smashing the Ghost with his red mace. "It's on his belt, lady."

And indeed, it was. A gold key shining on a black leather cord tied about the demon's waist. There was about as much chance of Kiran getting that key as there was of her defeating the demon herself. She was so tired of these damned cultist and demons. She raised the spear and slammed it down upon the lock with every ounce of her frustration. The damned thing cracked down the middle and opened. So much for having to find a magic key and defeating a demon to open the cage. Kiran tore open the door and Jamie jumped into her arms.

"Damn. Who said you need a key?" Reese knelt and started helping the others. He took a look at how the Ghost was faring. "Allah help us. Let's get out of here before their demon thing finishes killing our devil thing. It's not going well."

Albazaran currently had the Ghost by the foot and was spinning him in a circle, intermittently smashing him against the wall. The demon had inadvertently killed the last cultists by flattening them with the Ghost's body. He ended with a final throw that sent the Ghost straight into the ceiling before he came crashing down again.

Albazaran leaned on his mace. "You are not what you once were, Ghost. Time has taken its toll. You were so fierce and enraged in days gone by. What has happened to the infamous warrior?" He snatched up the Ghost's limp body once more and yelled into his face. "The White King is here, Ghost. The

Lord of the Silver Lake, the one who haunted you before, has returned in glory. He has the blessing of the angels. Krol is nothing but his servant, sent to pound you to dust. But that honor will be mine." He dropkicked the Ghost into a wall.

Gonzales grabbed two of the children in his arms and sprinted for the door. He was back in a flash for two more.

Kiran grabbed the last two children and realized there were only six inside the cage. Inside her chest, her heart crumbled. She felt the mark on her arm start to burn once more, felt the world shift.

"None of you need die," the voice that had spoken to her in the warehouse found its way into her head again, except this time she saw who it belonged to. The room faded and before her stood a white king. Not at all like a chess piece, more like a man with a silver crown and a trim beard, with rather pale skin.

"I told you, no one new is allowed inside my head." Kiran tried to pinch herself, but she couldn't see her body at the moment and that made it hard.

The king looked sadly disappointed. *"Would you throw away the lives of your companions so easily? Would you doom your father for so little? I can return him to you, guide him out of the maze, restore his mind. All I ask is the life of the murderer, the wretch, the source of the evil that afflicts this world. Let him die here, and you shall live. Sacrifice one for the good of all."*

"Like I would give up the one thing you fear, my only weapon, for your promise to stop being an evil bastard who steals children. Who the hell are you? Where's Krol?"

"Krol brought me here. Soon, I will right the mistakes of the past, and all of this will be mine once more." The king turned away from her and walked toward a forested horizon. *"Your fate is for you to decide."*

Kiran returned to her body to find Reese shaking her by the shoulders. "I said get out, Kiran. Take the last two kids. Don't die here."

In front of them, the Ghost was in the process of being pulverized. The demon lifted his mace for yet another blow. Something inside her knew the Ghost could not take much more.

But the kids were not going to stay here a second longer. She ran for the

CHAPTER 16

door and herded the children toward Gonzales. She was sure Reese was right behind her until she heard his voice.

"Why don't you pick on someone who hasn't been dead for a million years?" Reese stood next to the cage. He was twirling the brass gun around his finger.

Albazaran turned away from the Ghost's crumpled form and balanced his mace over a shoulder. Kiran felt her stomach drop. The stupidly brave SPD detective was about to become a former detective and the bastard never looked more handsome doing it. She wanted to kill him.

The demon tilted his head and examined Reese. Kiran wasn't certain, but she thought she saw the briefest moment of fear flash across the monster's face. "He brought you both, I see. Weaponless and afraid, what threat are you to me, Sumerian? Your sword was lost long ago. Its shattered shards adorn the walls of a fortress in Hell. You will never wield it again."

"Good. I don't know shit about swords." He leveled the gun and fired twice.

Albazaran collapsed. Reese had shot him in both of his knees. Kiran released the breath she'd been holding. Maybe they still had time to run.

But it could never be straightforward, could it? Before she could grab Reese and get him out of there, the asshole demon snarled and raised an empty hand. The gun flew out of his grip and into the claws of the monster. Then the demon threw the mace. The weapon spun across the chamber. Kiran braced herself to run.

At the last moment, Reese threw himself to the floor and the mace struck the cage, sending iron shrapnel flying. He snatched up the cultist's long knives and scrambled back to his feet as Albazaran rose, his wounds already healed.

Reese clutched a knife in each hand. "Kiran, I told you to get out of here," he yelled and spun the blades. "I'm good with knives, Albaza Ugly. Come play with me."

The Ghost still lay on the floor, unmoving.

"Get up, Ghost!" Kiran screamed. "You're not allowed to give up. That's an order. You're not allowed to die." She had very little idea what to do with a spear, but she aimed it at the demon and threw.

The spear arced high and true before Alabazaran snatched it out of the air and made it explode into flames. The demon cocked his horned head in her direction. "Still more of you to kill. Which one are you?"

Before Kiran could answer, a rasping voice responded.

"I'm the bullet. She's the gun." The Ghost rolled to his knees. "She's the bearer of the mark, the holder of the seal." He grabbed one of the crucifixes fastened to the wall and pulled himself up. "The Wand, the Star, the Summoner, and the Exorcist. She's the god damned Ball and Chain." He finished getting to his feet and cracked his neck side to side. "And she's terribly annoying." He adjusted his hat and tapped his iron rod on the floor. "Round two, Red."

The mace flew across the room and into the demon's hands. He swung it with enough force to decapitate an elephant.

The Ghost ducked and Albazaran's weapon struck the wall, crushing stone and launching a cloud of dust into the air. The Ghost stepped through the dust and thrust the end of his rod under the demon's chin. The demon's horned head snapped back. Then the Ghost let loose.

The iron rod fell mercilessly, rhythmically, like a demon jackhammer, as the Ghost lurched and danced like a drunken kung fu disaster. The swings of the mace grew erratic as the Ghost crushed knees, smashed wrists, and cracked off both horns for good measure. The demon's weapon clattered to the floor as the rod struck like gray lightning.

The Ghost straightened his hat and stared at the crucifixes. He stroked the wood, then tore one from the wall. "I am never allowed to die." He picked his bag up off the floor. "Please, next time, ask them to come up with something new." With a final dull thwack, the Ghost split the demon's skull like a melon and the giant red body began to dissolve into mist. The Ghost stepped through the evaporating demon spray and stood before her.

Reese dropped the knives and picked up his gun. "Thanks for waiting until my death speech to show up."

The Ghost shrugged. "I got distracted." He pointed to his headset. "The internet."

She'd gotten distracted too, by a white chess king in her head. She still needed to figure out who in Hell that was. "I need you to carry these two," she said. "They're too tired to run."

CHAPTER 16

The Ghost examined the two kids hiding behind Kiran. Juan and Andrea couldn't have been older than five. "Hmmm," he said in a voice that reminded her of the wind sighing in a horror movie and which had the effect of making the kids clutch her tighter.

"I am the weapon, the axe, the—"

"Enough. Don't scare them with the speech. Come on." She lifted Juan first. "You ride here in the crook of his arm, and you Andrea ride right next to him. Juan, hold the strap of this cool bag. Yes, he'll let you play with the zippers. Andrea, you hug Juan tight. He won't let you fall." They both fit on the Ghost's long arm if he held it exactly right. "Don't worry about how silly he looks. The costume is to scare the bad guys. You should see him on Halloween."

The Ghost aimed a stare at her that would melt an ice floe. "Let's go before I have to pull out pumpkins and candy."

Kiran tried to match the Ghost's glare with her own and got him to at least raise an eyebrow. "Why did you let him almost kill you? What were you thinking?"

The Ghost shrugged. "I have fought for eons. I wonder, at times, if I have any fight left." He met Kiran's eyes. "And demons say the most foolish things when they are certain you are near death. Krol is up to something."

"Of course, he is," Kiran said. "There's some other jerk behind it. Didn't you say he'd try to summon some ass who wants to rule the world? It's someone who believes he's a king already. You know him?"

The Ghost looked strangely thoughtful. "I might. I will have to ask the crows."

Gonzales was breathing hard when they emerged from the room. He'd herded the children into a corner and was standing in front of them. Around him were six cultists in various states of unconsciousness.

Reese nodded in appreciation. "You do not mess with my brother when he's babysitting."

"He's not dead?" Gonzales looked the Ghost up and down.

"I was always dead," the Ghost replied.

Kiran went to one knee and hugged the children. They looked beyond

THE TOOLS OF THE GHOST

frightened. She gave the Ghost a hard stare. "Don't scare them. Remember, we're the good guys." She figured that part would be hard for him.

"This is his Halloween costume," Juan explained from the comfort of the Ghost's arm. "His mom made it for him."

A bell began to toll, and if a bell could be furious, that would be how it sounded. Kiran cringed then forced herself to smile. "Don't worry about that, guys. That's probably to tell time."

"Krol is coming" The Ghost ruined her white lie. "The crows were not here. Whatever else they summoned will be with them." The bell tolled again. "This was all a distraction. The crows never miss a feast."

Kiran gave up on trying to sound reassuring and focused on running. "Well then, let's get out of here."

The KLANG of the bell only got louder as they neared the chapel. Some of the children covered their ears in a futile attempt to shut out the banging as they rushed across the candle-lit chamber. Gonzales led the way and leaped to the door leading to the halls outside. He threw it open then slammed it closed just as fast.

"Angry people with torches. Running this way. Something big is with them. This door is not going to hold them."

The Ghost set the two children down with surprising care then drew his iron rod out of his sack. "Move." Gonzales stepped aside. The Ghost's first blow was to the ceiling in front of the door.

"What are you doing?" Reese asked. "We'll be trapped."

"We're already trapped," the Ghost said. Two more blows of the iron rod and the walls around the door caved in, a ton of stone blocking the tunnel. The Ghost returned the rod to the sack and picked up the children again. "Now we must choose a path." He turned to Kiran and raised an eyebrow.

She looked back the way they'd come and at the other tunnel leading away from the altar. "Where would they have kept the other children?" Kiran asked.

"If they are alive?" The Ghost shrugged.

This resulted in four of the children starting to sob while the other two in the Ghost's arms trembled. She decided again that the Ghost was a complete

CHAPTER 16

asshole.

"Gonzales, how fast can you check those three tunnels?"

"Fast." The big man dashed off down as the rest waited, listening to the sound of the bell and footsteps approaching.

"I'd like to beat the hell out of whoever is ringing that bell," Reese said.

Kiran glared at him. "Reese, the kids."

Reese shrugged. "I'm sure they feel the same."

Gonzales appeared and shook his head before dashing into the second tunnel. He was even faster rejecting it and the third.

Reese unholstered his gun. "They're coming down all three. We'll have to fight."

"Not this time." They would be overwhelmed. She wasn't losing these kids now that she'd found them. "We go down." She pointed to the stairway the Ghost had kicked the nun down.

"That looks like it leads straight into—" Reese began.

She poked him in the chest. "Don't say it."

The body of the nun had disappeared, but the blood stain remained. They wound their way down three flights as the noise above grew louder, with cultists shouting amidst the tolling of the bell. The stairway narrowed as they descended until they could only proceed single file. As they reached the bottom, the bell went silent, which somehow made everything worse.

"They've taken the stairs. We have them," someone shouted from above.

The Ghost set the kids down and peered up the stairs. "I sense another demon coming. This will be as good a place as any to face it."

"We're not facing anything," she said. The kids would not survive if they fought here. Kiran peered into the darkness of the tunnel ahead. Cold air blew up at her with the smell of saltwater and sewer. There must be a way out toward the water. She pointed to the ceiling. "Destroy the stairwell. We'll find another way."

The Ghost examined the narrow passageway at the base of the stairs. "Move back. This will get messy." He leaped up a flight of stairs and started smashing the walls to bits with his iron rod. An especially eager cultist dashed down before he'd finished. The Ghost punched him once and the man fell flat on

his back, kicked out, and lay very still.
   Then the stairwell collapsed.

Chapter 17

"The kids can't walk another step. We need to rest," Kiran announced. She wasn't sure she could take many more steps either. She would have added a few choice words to describe how spent she was and how walking through sewers was maximally shitty, but she was making a supreme effort not to swear around the kids.

She leaned against a wall, ignoring the black-green slime coating everything, and caught her breath. The path they'd taken sloped relentlessly upward which was hell on the legs, yet they seemed no nearer to the surface than when they started. The children looked ready to drop and she figured they were finally okay to take a break. The Ghost had demolished the tunnel behind them in three different locations. They should be safe for now.

Reese shone a flashlight around the chamber they'd arrived in. The beam extended into inky darkness with no sign of a ceiling. "Some kind of shaft," he said. "Seems as good a place as any. If we could climb these walls about a hundred feet, had a jackhammer, and ropes and a platform to lift these kids, we could stage a breakout to the surface."

The scent of ocean and cool air drifted up from the only tunnel leading out of the chamber. It sloped down as far as their flashlights would shine. She imagined it led to the sewer system and eventually into the Puget Sound. They should be able to find a way out through a drainage connector.

The Ghost dropped his sack and lowered the two children. He slid to the ground and braced himself against the wall with his legs stretched out. The children huddled together, sitting on and around the Ghost's sack of tools as if it were a giant bean bag. She made sure they turned off two of the flashlights to save the batteries. The children started to whimper as soon as the last one went out, so she turned it back on.

"I'm hungry," was followed by a very quiet, "Me too," from another child.

Kiran felt inside her pockets, completely empty of gum or anything to eat, and felt her heart breaking keenly. God only knew when the last time the kids ate, or what they were given. Six of the children; Petra, Andrea, Juan, Jamie, Thaddeus, and Felipe were here. Bar, Mateo, Thomas, Simon, and Paul were somewhere still alive, they had to be. She wiped at her eyes in the darkness, trying not to think of what might have happened to the five who weren't with them. She had to get these kids out of here and soon.

The Ghost unzipped his sack and pulled out a paper bag Kiran recognized from the diner. The paper was stained and torn, but the pie he slid out from it was miraculously in one piece. He stared at the pie for a long while without moving, then broke off an irregular slice with his hand and offered it to one of the children. "Dutch Apple," he declared.

Juan took a tentative bite and announced, "Oooh," in the most pathetic voice Kiran had ever heard. She forced herself not to cry as the little boy took another bite and she failed miserably. She hoped no one noticed in the dark.

The Ghost reached inside his bag again and pulled out the entire chocolate cake he'd lifted from a bakery along with yet another apple pie. He was kept busy handing out broken slices to children who were suddenly stuffing baked goods into their faces. The Ghost was immediately the most popular of any of the team. She remembered Anatol's words and gave thanks that the Tools of the Ghost included cake and pie, even if they were recently stolen.

Gonzales handed Kiran a piece of the pie that was somehow still warm. She wondered if the fires of Hell burned inside the Ghost's bag, or if he'd stolen a toaster oven when she wasn't looking. She looked around to make sure the kids had enough to eat, then she stared at the piece of pie a long while before biting it. It tasted of nutmeg and sugar and memories of childhood. The sugar rush pushed back her exhaustion and the world came a bit more into focus. She licked her fingers. Gonzales handed her a bit of chocolate cake.

"I want a story," Andrea said. "It's still night. I'm tired of night."

CHAPTER 17

No one answered the boy's request for a story for a long while, during which water dripped and the darkness grew deeper.

"Gonzo tells the best stories," Reese whispered. "Give them one, brother." Gonzales shook his head in the darkness, but Reese just elbowed him. "Go ahead, these kids won't mind. Just not one of the tough Oaxaca ones, eh?"

Gonzales cleared his throat. "We didn't spend all our time in the city when I was a kid. Sometimes, on the weekends, we'd go out to the rancho that my tío owned."

"This is a good one," Reese broke in with a big smile.

"When I was maybe ten, my tío came by in his old red truck to take us out. He had a tiny brown dog named Lulu with big ears that would sit in the truck bed with us, and we'd head out of the city. We'd pass big fields and trees with avocados and lemons and herds of cows. His farm was way out there, and it was huge. Well, it seemed big to us. One day, just before we got to the farm, mi tío spotted a turkey way out by itself and he says, 'Hey kids, you all want turkey for dinner? Then you better go out and catch that wild turkey.' Me and my cousins jumped out of that truck, and we started chasing that turkey all over the place up and down the field. You never imagined how fast a turkey can run. Lulu was chasing after it too, but it just kept ahead of us no matter how fast we ran."

At this point, Reese put his hand on Gonzales' shoulder. "Is this like the story where you made sausage at the farm with the pig you had become friends with?"

Gonzales considered for a moment before he continued. "We were dashing this way and that and falling all over ourselves until finally that turkey flew up into a tree and we never could catch it. My tío caught up with us though, and he had a great big picnic basket with lemonade made with real lemons and sandwiches for us all. And that night we had a great turkey mole that my tía made, and it was awesome."

"But did that turkey ever come down?" one of the kids asked.

"Oh, that one got away. My tía had some frozen turkey in the freezer."

One of the girls started to cry. Kiran hugged her, felt each sob, and fought to keep herself from falling apart. There was nothing wrong with Gonzales' story, but it hadn't been enough. They needed something to soothe them and drive away the nightmares of what had happened to them. She wracked her brain for some tale that would do the trick but came up with nothing.

A hoarse voice rasped in the dark. It took Kiran a moment before she realized the Ghost was speaking.

"This story is true. I was there. Many years ago, there was a man, a great musician, who loved the sound of crickets."

The Ghost paused and the room went completely silent except for the drip of water in the distance and the soft breath of children. Kiran imagined a gentle musician, lying in a field of crickets in the starlight. Imagined the Ghost telling a story of this man and lulling the children to sleep with a tale full of meaning that would reveal and redeem the monster inside. She propped herself on her elbows to better listen.

The Ghost rose to his feet and continued, "This musician loved the sound of crickets, their shiny carapaces snapping between his thick fingers. He thrilled at the crack and pop. He smirked as their legs twitched when separated from their tiny unfortunate heads."

Kiran swallowed hard. She raised a hand in protest, but the Ghost ignored her.

"The musician's name was Victor, and he had a cat named Sebastian. He would flick the still moving parts of the crickets to Sebastian, who snapped them up in midair. The cat's crunching would send shivers of delight up Victor's spine."

The Ghost spread his long arms wide. "The audacity of crickets is without measure," he would shout as the cat licked its lips. "To think they hope to imitate me. Me!" Victor would crunch another cricket between his thumbs and Sebastian would catch it in midair."

One of the kids giggled, and then they all laughed. Kiran looked around to find them huddled together, entranced. The story of a musician who fed crickets to his cat held no horror for them. They'd seen far worse.

The Ghost proceeded to tell the entire story of the mad musician and his battle against his rival composer, Roman Lavanomov. He described how the musician descended into the pits of Hell itself to write a composition so

CHAPTER 17

powerful that merely hearing it would destroy his enemy. The children leaned in as the Ghost raised both hands above his head, conducting an imaginary orchestra.

"Drums rolled from the depths of time and those who heard the music were swept away, remembering times in caves long forgotten, where their ancestors first found fire. Violins sang and the audience swayed to their command. The bass sounded and women held their hearts, feeling the pressure, the desire for escape from this cold world to a world of passion and fire. Finally, cymbals clashed, and the sky filled with a storm of crickets. The insects formed an angry tornado and descended like a storm upon Roman Lavanomov."

Kiran squeezed her eyes shut as the Ghost proceeded to describe the triumphant and gory death of the rival musician, destroyed by insects. She could think of no worse story. There was no moral, no redemption; it was rivalry, vengeance, and murder all disguised in a symphony. A pure torture for kids who had endured so much already.

She looked around to find the children asleep, two leaning against her, two others with their heads pillowed on the Ghost's bag. The Ghost's story had entranced them, had quieted the fears they'd known for too long. To them, he was a Halloween hero who told funny stories about cats who ate crickets.

Only one of the kids was still awake.

Juan ran his fingers down the Ghost's coat, fingering the buttons. "I like your costume. I'm going to ask my mom to make me this same one for next Halloween." He rested his pie crumb covered face against the Ghost's arm and closed his eyes.

Kiran fell asleep wondering who this monster could have been in a life centuries ago. Who was history's greatest betrayer? Someone the rulers of Hell feared and despised? Someone who told strange stories that bought the trust of children? She closed her eyes and dreamed of being lost on an angry ocean with no hope of ever finding her way home.

* * *

THE TOOLS OF THE GHOST

Krol marched forward through a land of shadows and shadows followed him at every turn. Shadows stretched high along the walls of the dark caverns he traversed, shadows peered down amidst giant stalactites high above, shadows passed over the black basalt floor, shadows lurked, waiting for him to falter.

In this place, the shadows fed on wandering souls and grew ever larger, adding to the darkness with the life of their victims. But Krol paid them no heed. He had died once and spent too long plotting revenge to fear any shadow, however dark it might be. His plans went beyond what anyone had thought possible, even the masters of Hell. Krol had impressed them enough to set him free and supply him with all he required. He was not going to waste this chance. He stomped on past columns of shattered stone and the shadows kept well out of his way. They understood instinctively when a mission had been ordained by the true powers of Hell and knew better than to delay their servant. Krol was on his way to meet someone even the shadows feared.

Krol reached a silver lake that reflected the darkness and stretched as far across the cavern as the eye could see. He stepped into the liquid mercury, wading up to his chest, thrusting forward as the silver metal ran over his shoulders and pressed about him with enough force to shatter bone. But the new body Krol inhabited could not be easily harmed. He drove himself forward with single mindedness, toward the dark spire in the center of the lake, then climbed out and shook himself like a great dog, shedding liquid metal. Krol took two steps forward then went down on one knee.

A figure dressed in white stepped down from the spire and gazed down on Krol. The figure wore royal robes and underneath shone the unbreakable mail of a sovereign ready for war. The eyes examining Krol belonged to a ruler of worlds who would rule again and know no master. Krol lowered his gaze and said a silent prayer for protection, wondering if any god in the universe heard his prayers any longer.

"You have the blessings of all the Lords of Hell, my King. We need only one more to ensure your dominion."

At that moment, light—never before seen in the realm of shadows—shattered the ever-obscuring clouds. Krol shielded his eyes from the blaze and made out a shimmering form descending into the great cavern. It was shaped

CHAPTER 17

like a man, made of light, with eyes of pearl. As Krol watched, the figure spread its wings and circled above them, shedding light in its wake like rain.

The impossible had happened.

The fierce joy of revenge burned bright in Krol's heart, and he smiled. Everything he had set forth had fallen into place. The trap was set. The last blessing had arrived.

In the cavern of shadows, where the creatures of Hell ruled, not a shadow remained, for what creature of the abyss could stand and face that light? The light grew ever brighter as the Archangel descended. Krol kept his eyelids open and let his eyes burn. His grin stretched until his teeth ached and he loved every moment of it.

Chapter 18

When Kiran opened her eyes, the Ghost was gone.

Her panic transformed into puzzlement as she took in her surroundings. A slowly dying flashlight beam illuminated a section of the damp floor and a kid fast asleep on her chest. The rest of the children were piled up against the Ghost's gray sack like a giant beanbag sleepover party from Hell. They'd sheltered on the side opposite the cold wind blowing up from the tunnel. Despite his bag's presence, the Ghost was nowhere to be found.

Reese lay on his back, staring up into the darkness. Gonzales was slumped against a wall with his eyes closed, but she sensed he wasn't sleeping. His eyebrows were furrowed, and his chin rested against his chest. She looked past his closed eyelids and felt his mind turning over their time in the tunnels, reliving his encounter with the dragon, trying to reach back to the other lives he would never remember. She wondered if she could look deeper and find those lives herself, unlock the secrets that he could not unravel. Then the mark on her arm seethed and swirled and she realized what she was doing. She dragged herself out of Gonzales' mind and fled back to her own, breathing hard.

Gonzales' eyes snapped open. He stared at her before she looked away. She hadn't intended to, but somehow, she'd crept into his thoughts.

Reese broke the silence before she had to explain why she was trespassing in other people's heads. "The Ghost said you'd know where he was." Reese kept his voice low so as not to wake the kids. "He asked the two of us for permission before he left. Can you believe that, Kiran? I think he didn't want to wake you up. The guy who told us he'd remove our intestines wanted to

CHAPTER 18

let you sleep in. You snore worse than Gonzo, by the way. He said you could feel him out, would know where he was, if you'd only try."

She didn't need to try. The Ghost was somewhere above them, climbing the shaft of the tunnel like a spider. The mark had already transformed her awareness. The Ghost shone in the back of her mind like a dingy silver beacon in the darkness.

"What's he doing up there?" she asked.

"He said he could sense the moon trying to break through to us and the sadness of the sky. Asked if he could try to find a way out. Gonzo and I thought it was a good idea."

"He left his bag behind?" Kiran imagined the Ghost would sooner leave behind an arm.

Gonzales cleared his throat. "He said it was the first time in over a thousand years. The kids are sleeping on it, and he didn't want to move them. Told us if we touched one zipper, he'd stuff us both inside and forget about us for a century."

She couldn't pretend she hadn't crept into Gonzales' mind uninvited any longer. "I didn't mean to do it, Enrique. I was half awake." Kiran lifted her arm. "This thing is changing me."

Gonzales waved a hand at her, as if brushing away her worry. "I know you didn't. I felt you drifting into my thoughts like in a dream, but you seemed as surprised as me that you were there. I was as worried for you as I was surprised. Then you were running away scared."

"What are you two talking about?" Reese asked. "You reading our minds, Kiran? The Ghost told us you could. Told us you might become more dangerous than he was, if you let yourself be."

The entire idea was preposterous. "When did the hammer, the bludgeon, the crusher of bones and whatever tell you that?" she asked. And what the hell did the Grouchy Reaper mean? The Ghost was danger personified. She was the one being dragged along for the ride, trying to survive.

"Between your snores," Gonzales said.

"He got talkative after all the cake," Reese explained. "Told us that Lucifer and the Archangel Michael had a hand in the making of that mark and that you weren't using its powers to its fullest. That you could slip into our minds and take us over like zombies if you wanted, but it would leave you no better than Krol. You could extend your reach throughout these tunnels and find whatever you were looking for, but you would probably never find your way back to your body and would go insane. He said you weren't a complete idiot to use it as little as possible and not turn into a monster."

Kiran gazed up into the darkness, tracking the Ghost's progress in her mind's eye. He'd almost reached the top of the shaft. "Not a complete idiot is almost like a letter of recommendation from that jerk."

Reese laughed. "It's how he'd address his Valentines' cards in school. Dear Lucy, you're not a complete idiot. Dear Dave, you're not half as dumb as you look, Happy Valentine's Day."

"Word," Gonzales confirmed.

"Do either of you two have an old man in your head trying to get your attention?" Kiran asked. She knew saying it would make her look like she'd already lost her mind, but she had a suspicion.

Reese gave her a weird look. "A white guy who looks like King Arthur and says the Ghost will betray us? That we should leave him behind while we can?"

"That he'll kill us all?" Gonzales added.

"Yeah, that guy," Kiran said. "I thought he might be able to break into your heads too. Either of you have any idea who he is?"

"Someone who I want to stay very far away from." Reese shivered. "Let's get these kids out of here while we can. And don't go using that mark to do anything more than you have to, Kiran. We don't need you trapped outside your body or turning into some demon."

"Padre nuestro, protect us. I think the white king set the dragon upon me. He was the one who placed that demon on the throne. Reese is right. Don't use those powers unless you have to. That mark was meant to call the Ghost. The rest is Hell's work."

"The wish he granted you might be straight out of Hell too, Enrique, but you're not turning that power down, are you? We've got to use every trick we have to get these kids home. I already have the biggest jerk of all trying to

CHAPTER 18

boss me around. I don't need you two telling me what to do."

Moonlight broke through the ceiling above them. The Ghost had slid aside a manhole cover and found a way out. Not that it would do much good if they had to climb the walls like spiders with the children on their backs.

"He's coming down already," Kiran said.

"I hope he's got an elevator in that bag of his," Reese said. "I mean he's supposed to have everything he could ever need, right?"

"The Tools of the Ghost are without number," Kiran whispered the words of Anatol's psalm. She watched the children sleep, piled against the Ghost's bag and shuddered. What weapons and evil devices were they resting their heads on?

"I think whoever opens that bag dies," Gonzales said. "It's like the infinity symbol."

Reese raised both eyebrows. "What?"

Gonzales spread out both his hands. "He's got to have space for tools without number, right? It's like one of those bags of holding that has space for everything and sucks you inside like a black hole. Endless."

Reese shook his head. "I bet it's just a load of shit he's stolen over the centuries. That, and a whole lot of things that can tear your spine out."

"Bones and skulls of all the people he's killed over the years. And their weapons too," Gonzales said.

"Skulls are bones, Gonzo."

"Ay, por Dios."

Kiran considered the implications. "You mean we ate pie and cake that was brushing up against dead bones? Gross."

The Ghost was halfway down already and moving faster, like he was running down the sides of the shaft. The moonlight struck him as he descended, lighting him like a silver statue floating above them all. He leaped the final twenty feet with his coat flying about him, landing ten feet away, quiet as a cat.

He held his hat in his hand. "What are you looking at, woman? Have you forgotten the monster you summoned? Have nightmares sapped your resolve? Has the darkness seeped into your soul?"

THE TOOLS OF THE GHOST

The child asleep on her chest woke and startled. Kiran narrowed her eyes at the Ghost and got to her feet.

"Stop frightening the children. What have you found?"

The Ghost looked around at the kids just waking up. He lowered his voice to the usual rasp of bone on bone.

"A way out. Beyond the manhole cover, there's a short tunnel leading to stairs and the world above." He waved at the wall of the shaft. "There's a path cut into the stone which winds its way up. It is shattered in places, but not impossible. Either that or pursue this path which goes deeper into what I do not know."

Kiran considered the tunnel below them. She could hear water lapping against stone. A fresh gust of air carried the smell of dead fish and the sea. They might find a way out in that direction or be lost ever deeper in the strange world beneath the city. Something told her that if they continued down, there would be no coming back.

"Show me the path up." She followed the Ghost to the north wall of the shaft to find a narrow stairway, cut into the shaft, slick and treacherous, but winding toward freedom.

"Hold this and you will not fall," the Ghost offered her the end of his iron rod.

Kiran examined it for bits of demon skull or blood, but it looked as clean as if it had been taken out of the forge yesterday. She still wasn't going to touch it unless she had to. "Let's just get started."

"A fall will be a quick death." The Ghost shrugged his bag over his shoulder and started up.

A treacherous winding stairway up through a manhole would be a wonderful way to pin them all and drop them to their deaths. She couldn't risk the children unless she was sure it was safe.

The Ghost started up the miserable stairway and she followed several paces behind, knowing he could not touch her, but not wanting to tempt fate. The stone stairs were cracked and slick with black mold. She had to flatten herself against the wall to make sure of her footing. They circled upward in an endless spiral around the chamber. She felt like a mountaineer without a

CHAPTER 18

rope, sure of plummeting to her death at any moment. The slice of moonlight breaking through the manhole seemed impossibly far.

Halfway up, Kiran stretched as far as she could to make it over a broken section of slippery stair. She realized how futile it would be for the rest. "How the hell did you hope to get the kids up here?" She took another treacherous step.

The Ghost turned his baleful stare on her and ascended the next stair without even looking. "Tie them together and I will drag them up. Bind them to my back and I will be your donkey. They will survive, probably. But you are wasting yourself and your weapon by bringing them at all."

Kiran stopped and tried to find the words. "You asshole. You'd just leave them here? Leave Juan to die down there in the dark after you fed him cake and told him your story? What are you?"

The Ghost didn't hesitate. "I am your weapon, Wand Bearer. The tool you are supposed to be using to crush Krol, to hunt him, not to flee from him like mice from a cat. I am a killer, nothing more."

Kiran closed her eyes as wave of dizziness hit her. She leaned back against the wall to brace herself. Being down here in the dark underground for so long had taken a toll. "If you would betray those children after all that, you haven't learned shit all this time you've been in that body. Whatever you are, you've stayed incredibly stupid."

"I cannot betray them!" the Ghost roared at her. "We have no pact, no promises were made, nothing was written in blood. I know what I am here for."

Kiran had had enough. "I have a pact with them greater than any of yours. That supersedes your contracts and blood covenants and any other legal document bullshit you've got in that bag." She held up her arm, displaying the swirls of the black mark. "It supersedes this too. You carried them in your arms when they were scared. They believe in you. You are bound to them as much as you are to me, and you're not going to give up on them no matter what. I want Krol more than you do. I want to smash his face into this wall and watch him fall to the stone for what he did to Anatol. For what he did to the children. But we get them home first. They're all that matters." She wished she could slap the Ghost hard enough that he would wake the hell up for once. Fire burned behind her eyes, but unfortunately, fire was not easy to see through.

She missed the next gap in the stairwell and fell.

Her foot stretched out into emptiness and her weight shifted upon it, and she knew she was gone. Her back foot slid off the stair and she felt the world rushing up at her. In that miserable second her only profound thought was, *Shit*.

Then something hit Kiran in the chest hard enough to break a rib, and she exhaled, "Oof." She swung out into space, and found herself clasping onto the Ghost's iron rod. He'd swung it out and smacked her as she fell, throwing her a lifeline and managing to knock the wind out of her at the same time.

"Holy shit." She clung to the iron rod, hanging forty feet over the shaft.

"Your anger will be your downfall," the Ghost said.

"Hilarious. Goddamn hilarious," was all Kiran could come up with while her feet were kicking in space.

"The rules state that I am not allowed to touch you or harm you while you wear that chain. I have not broken them. You are the one who ran into my weapon." He swung her back against the wall and she scrambled to get her feet planted against the stone. "I will leave the rod here behind me. You may hold it if you like."

Kiran kept hold of the rod like a desperate lifeline. "Alright, but just to make you happy."

The Ghost's teeth gleamed in the darkness in what Kiran imagined was a smile. "Thank you for considering my happiness. I don't think anyone else has ever done that."

"It's just an expression," Kiran said.

"Doing ok up there?" Reese yelled from below. "You know we can hear everything you say."

"Swears too," a child's voice chimed in. A giggle followed.

"That was Juan," Kiran said. "It's your damn fault he had to hear all that."

The Ghost shrugged.

The remainder of the ascent was bereft of near falling-to-your-death

CHAPTER 18

episodes. She tried to keep her thoughts straight, but almost being flattened against the stones kept her from concentrating on anything but her next step. Throughout the climb, the Ghost was better than a mountain goat. He looked like he could do it blind. If they could find a way to secure the children, they might manage to get out of here. Or he could just carry them two at a time.

They reached the manhole without speaking another word. The Ghost disappeared through the hole in the ceiling, and she followed, heaving herself over the edge on her elbows. She lay on her back for a moment and closed her eyes. She never wanted to do anything like that again. The room she opened her eyes to was a disaster. Discarded soda bottles, fast food bags, and cigarette butts littered the floor of a small chamber that was nothing more than an alcove with a staircase. But it was beyond beautiful. Cracked concrete stairs stretched up to a steel-framed arch with the full moon shining through, illuminating everything in metallic silver. It was the real world, and its beauty left her speechless.

Until her mind began to work as it always did.

"This would be a terrible place to be trapped," she said. "If I were Krol, I would have waited, until we struggled up here and then finished us. We'd have to fight or fall back down to our deaths. Let's get them up here and out before anything happens."

The Ghost raised an eyebrow. He took off his hat and slapped it against his pants knocking off a cloud of dust that sparkled in the light. "I am starting to rue your pessimistic predictions." He turned to the stairs as the light of the moon was obscured in shadow.

Unfortunately, she recognized the giant figure on the stairs above them, blotting out the light. She was still on her back and figured she should be terribly afraid, but all she wanted was to watch Krol die. This time, hopefully for good.

Krol, unfortunately, was clearly not planning on dying any time soon.

"My dear Ghost." Krol's confidence gave her chills. "I have been waiting so very long for the pleasure of ending your existence. I would say killing you, but you've been dead for an awful long time already, haven't you?"

The Ghost tapped his iron rod on the floor and rolled his shoulders. "Not as dead as you're going to be."

Chapter 19

Krol threaded the fingers of his giant hands together and cracked his knuckles like a grotesque prizefighter. He sat down on the stairs and stretched back, resting his elbows on the concrete. "I was not smart enough all those years ago, my friend."

The Ghost cracked his neck. "People don't get smarter than they were. Someone told me that just recently." He shifted to put himself between Kiran and Krol.

Krol ignored him. "I'd made a pact with a major devil who promised me I would be safe from everything I could imagine. He allowed me to name all the creatures who could never harm me. He knew you would be the one coming for me in the end."

"I come for everyone in the end," the Ghost said.

"And now I've come for you. This time, they promised me I would have my revenge."

"Then you really have stayed dumb. Believing in the promises of devils is worse than faith in a used car salesman." The Ghost touched a finger to his ear. "I can't even remember how many other assholes have told me they were going to murder me before I smashed them." He let the end of his rod strike the floor and the alcove rang like the bell that sounds before the death of souls. "Round one."

Kiran slid back, avoiding the hole in the floor, and drew her gun, pretty sure it wasn't going to do a damn thing. Her mind started to spin, and the action went into slow motion. She considered four different plans and rejected them all before Krol spoke again.

"Time and Death could not stop my return, Fisherman. You sent me to Hell once with cold and bitter iron, long before my time had come. God would have forgiven me. There was still time to confess my sins. You had no right to break my deal."

The Ghost pointed to his ear. "I already turned on the music. I tend to skip the bullshit soliloquies."

Krol's mouth twisted, displaying a disaster of teeth. His muscles tensed for an inevitable charge.

But if she were Krol and had faced the Ghost before, if she had been sent back to the mortal world knowing she would face him again, she wouldn't just throw herself at him. The Ghost was indestructible and had already killed Krol once. Krol was a super genius. Krol was here either 1) to sacrifice himself—and he didn't seem the type—or 2) because he knew of some way to destroy the Ghost or 3) to create a disaster of a distraction.

And if it were a distraction, there was only one thing to distract them from.

She shouted down the hole. "Reese, Gonzales, watch out! Something is coming from that tunnel."

"The girl is far smarter than you are." Krol drew two steel spikes from his coat and launched himself down the last few stairs like a giant bull intent on trampling his enemy.

The Ghost was tapping his feet and humming whatever music was in his ears.

Kiran fired once, heard the expected click, and threw the gun straight into Krol's face. This was the monster who had sent Anatol to his grave and cursed her with this burden.

Krol flinched for the briefest moment as the barrel of the gun bounced off his forehead.

At that, the Ghost finally moved as if released from a spell. He extended himself and shifted almost too fast for her eyes to follow. His coat flew open like the wings of a great shadowy eagle. His iron rod flashed in the moonlight, connecting with the side of Krol's head with a crack like lightning striking a redwood. Krol careened into the wall and bricks exploded, shooting past Kiran like missiles. She squeezed tight into the remaining space as Krol

CHAPTER 19

rebounded off the ruined wall and erupted forward, his arms spread wide. He flailed at the Ghost with an iron spike in each hand.

The clash of metal on metal filled the room and sparks flew. The scene transfixed her as the Ghost blocked each slash of Krol's spiked fists, using his rod like an iron quarterstaff as they circled.

Before they clashed again, a child cried out below. Then Gonzales yelled. "Kiran, get him down here. We need you!"

Gonzales' voice must have penetrated whatever music the Ghost was listening to. He turned and made the mistake of trying to steal a glance below.

Krol leaped at the opening. He accepted the crack of the rod upon his shoulders, vaulting over the hole in the floor and enveloping the Ghost with his larger bulk. He slammed the Ghost into the wall then smashed his forehead into his skull, crushing him against the brick. The iron rod flew into the air, spinning in a great arc.

"Please," was the only thing that passed Kiran's lips. She felt her heart drop into her stomach as she willed him to rise, to fight for the children. For all of them. He was their only hope to survive.

The Ghost came off the wall like the wrath of an unholy god, seized Krol's head in his hands, and kneed him in the neck.

Krol clutched at his throat and stumbled back. The Ghost seized him and heaved his body over his head. He launched him into the stairwell and the concrete cracked. The Ghost leaped over Krol's prostrate form to retrieve his weapon. Kiran was certain the Ghost had finally gotten the upper hand, that it would be over. But Krol's laugh, echoing in the small space and through her bones, banished her hope.

Krol rolled onto his back and held up a hand the size of her head, displayed one of the Ghost's earpieces between his fingers. "The music is over, Ghost. You'll hear my song now. You'll hear me laugh as you finally die. You'll hear the sound of your own blood as it hits the floor." Krol spit out a tooth. "Look at yourself, Faithless One. Feel your death close, oh so close, and know you have been betrayed as badly as you deserve."

"You messed up my playlist. I hate that." His voice was cold as dry ice.

THE TOOLS OF THE GHOST

The Ghost picked up the rod and raised it to deliver a final blow. Then he stepped back and put a hand to his face. Dark blood dripped from his nose. He touched a finger to his mouth. "Blood," he rasped. "The dead do not bleed."

Krol got to his feet, still laughing. "Look around. Where are your crows? What were you summoned here to do?"

The sound of screaming children reached them from below, punctuated by the blast of Anatol's gun.

"Kiran!" Gonzales screamed again.

"We have to get down there," she pleaded and never felt more helpless.

The Ghost turned to the hole in the floor, his brow furrowed as he heard what was happening. "I was sent here to kill you, Krol. I've listened to your lies for too long. Time to get it over with."

Krol turned a hand palm up. "What's your rush? Why do you care what happens below when you were sent here to destroy me?" Krol snorted before looking Kiran in the eye. "You see, Bearer, he's just realized he's got a bigger problem than me. His crows are not here. Someone has turned the tables on our poor Ghost." Krol sighed. In a blur of movement, he slammed into the Ghost, lifting one of his gray arms high. "Payback time, Betrayer. Hope it hurts." He slammed an iron spike through the Ghost's palm, straight into the wall.

The Ghost cried out, a long guttural scream, as his weapon clattered to the floor.

Krol punched the Ghost's face, and Kiran heard bone cracking. "You've played by the same playbook for too many centuries. You have no idea what's happening, no idea who's arrived, do you?" He waved in Kiran's direction. "The girl never told you she has a voice in her head, did she?"

In response the Ghost drove the thumb of his free hand straight into Krol's eye. "I never bother with the other team's plans."

Krol bellowed, but he didn't let go. He drove his remaining spike right through the Ghost's other hand, forcing it away from his own face until he buried the spike into the brick. His eye came with it.

The Ghost lay splayed against the wall like a scarecrow pinned in a field.

Krol's chest heaved. "They are tired of you, Faithless One. Tired of

CHAPTER 19

everything you've done. You screwed over both sides. Ruined their plans. You've no allies left. No time remaining. The King is already here."

The Ghost's chest heaved. He spat blood in Krol's face. "Whatever demon you summoned, Krol, he's bound to eat you in the end. You know that don't you?"

Krol scraped off the Ghost's blood with a finger, then plunged it into his mouth. "Ahhh. The sweetest taste in the world." He punched the Ghost once again for good measure. "I summoned no demon, Ghost. Herod, the white king, is here, sent back from the dead to redeem himself and rule. He has the blessing of both sides."

The Ghost gave a deep rattling cough that made Kiran shudder. "The Child Slayer? Hell would never let him out. You lie, Krol."

Kiran gauged the distance. She could make it in time to pick up the iron rod, hit Krol once. And then what? The brute would barely notice. The mark on her arm pulsed, heat racing through her muscles, into her bones. She spread her fingers wide. It was now or never, but never seemed the better idea.

Krol put a finger on the Ghost's chest. "You heard right. King Herod is here, already in his tower, gazing down upon his kingdom. Hell has freed him. The Archangel Michael has blessed him. They have ordained that nothing in this world shall kill him, be it angel, demon, mortal, not even you, Ghost. All the children will be his once more. The plans you delayed will come to fruition." Krol peeled his eyeball off the wall and pushed it back into his head. He blinked a few times, and it rotated in its socket once more. "They were sure Herod would be the one needed to finish the job. But I'm the one who won the prize. You're no longer the fearsome monster you once were."

The Ghost slumped against the wall. "And you were never more than a twisted priest, Krol. You suck at soliloquies."

Krol laughed. "You still have the button Anatol gave you when he betrayed me. I paid him back for that. I'll keep it as a memento of the time I killed you."

Kiran took a deep breath. As Krol reached forward, all his attention on the Ghost, Kiran opened herself to the power of the mark, let all its demon-wrought power in, and thrust herself into Krol's mind.

She fell to her knees as Krol's hate filled her, tearing through her like acid. Krol's mad desire to destroy the Ghost had smoldered for decades in a mind already twisted beyond anything she had ever imagined. Now it overwhelmed her. She felt every one of Krol's craven desires, to kill, to devour, to dominate anyone weaker than him. Most terrible, she felt Krol's certainty that his God would forgive him of all his crimes if he simply confessed in the end. If he acknowledged his belief in his creator and begged for forgiveness, he could not be denied the keys to heaven. She retched as she fell to the floor. But she had learned what she needed to know. Before she passed out, she managed to scream the one message inside Krol's skull that she knew could hurt him.

"Your God won't forgive you, asshole. It's a pipe dream, nothing more. Look hard. See the truth. You've forever lost your chance at forgiveness. There's nothing left but your own personal hell." Then she fell on her hands and finished vomiting.

Krol stumbled, covering his ears as her words echoed in his mind. He crashed to the floor in a heap and rolled over onto his stomach. His face was covered in sweat, his disastrous teeth bared like an animal, in his hand a wicked knife caught the light.

He crawled toward Kiran, snarling. "You lie! He has to forgive me when I confess. Endless mercy was promised." He scraped along the floor with his knife as he screamed and crawled toward her. "I will pierce your heart for your lies. I will mount it on the wall to punish your blasphemy."

Kiran tried to rise, but a rush of dizziness sent her to her knees. She slumped against a wall as Krol crept closer. "You're kidding yourself, Krol. You're living a fantasy." She couldn't take her eyes off the knife in Krol's hand, getting closer every second. She reached into her pocket and pepper sprayed the hell out of him.

Krol opened his mouth and drank it in. Evidently, he liked pepper spray. He blinked only once and crept closer. "I longed to kill you back in the church. How it would have made Anatol suffer? But I knew you'd be perfect for my plan. Now I can finally end you." He raised the knife.

In that moment, the Ghost wrenched one of his hands from the wall and slammed it, spike and all, into the side of Krol's head. "That part wasn't in

CHAPTER 19

your plan, I bet. And the white button is mine."

Krol jerked to his feet and fell back down again, the spike still embedded in his skull. He slapped Kiran once with the back of his hand, sending her rolling across the floor. He tried to dislodge the spike but couldn't remove it. He braced himself against the wall, knife still in hand. "You would die for a button, Ghost? You care about all the wrong things."

The Ghost pulled at the other spike still lodged in the wall but couldn't free his hand. "That button was a gift."

"Keep it in Hell." Krol flipped the long knife in the air. "I'm going to find your soul with this and pin it to the wall."

She knew the Ghost wouldn't survive another blow. They would be at Krol's mercy and that couldn't happen. She grabbed the iron rod and struggled to her feet.

"This is your champion, Ghost?" Krol pointed his chin at her, clearly amused. This girl is all you have to defend you? She can barely lift your sad excuse of a weapon."

She lifted the rod high and took aim.

Krol yawned. "He could not hurt me with that, foolish girl. What do you hope for?"

Kiran brought the rod down. She managed to hit the spike in the wall without smacking the Ghost in the head. The spike broke free, spinning in the air.

The Ghost caught it, surged to his feet, and swung it straight through the other side of Krol's head.

It frightened Kiran how much she appreciated Krol's scream. "I hope you enjoy Hell," she said.

The Ghost twisted one hundred and eighty degrees with a satisfying crack and Krol's head was suddenly facing the wrong direction. Krol mouthed something without sound then the Ghost shoved his body through the manhole, and he tumbled headfirst through the floor.

Kiran watched Krol growing ever smaller until he struck the ground in a flash of fire. She turned back to the Ghost who looked worse than dead.

"Krol was right." The Ghost's voice cracked as he took in rattled breath.

"The crows never came." His head struck the wall and he fell onto his face.

Chapter 20

Kiran tried to get up and the room spun. Half of her felt like she was still inside Krol's sick mind. She reminded herself never to do that again. Gonzales' shouting jolted her back to reality.

"Kiran, they've taken the kids. They're all gone."

"Shit." She felt like she was the one with a spike through her skull. She wanted to lie on the floor and scream, but whoever took those kids was *not* going to keep them. She shook her head, and her vision came back into focus.

The Ghost had rolled onto his back but wasn't moving. Blood flowed freely from a gash across his chest.

Her eyes blurred with sudden tears before panic seized her. "Enrique, get up here if you can before whatever came out of that hole comes back and finishes you. I need help. I think the Ghost is dying."

"Ya voy. Reese needs a hospital." Gonzales sounded panicked.

Kiran felt the last of her composure vanish as she freaked out. They had to get help. She braced herself against the wall and managed to make it to the Ghost without falling.

"Don't make me feel sorry for you." She dropped next to the Ghost and watched his chest rise and fall.

Both his hands were torn through with silver bone shards and strings of tendon sticking out. Kiran felt acid rising in her throat and fought it back down. She had to stop his bleeding. He wasn't allowed to die here.

"Shit. Shit. Shit."

She pulled off her jacket and tore off her shirt. She ripped the shirt and leaned forward to press the makeshift bandage to the Ghost's chest. Anatol's pendant went cold against her breast, and she froze. She wouldn't be able to touch him, wouldn't be able to stop him from dying.

"Never, and I mean never, take the necklace off or he will kill you. Don't trust him for a second." Anatol's words were impossible to forget.

Well, screw that. Anatol always said she didn't listen. Kiran slipped the necklace over her head and held it in her hand. The Ghost didn't move. He wasn't in any condition to kill anyone.

Kiran held pressure against the wound until the bleeding slowed. She wrapped the remainder of her shirt around each of his hands. She said a prayer to Ganesha that it would be enough.

Her body went cold when she realized his chest was no longer moving.

She slammed her hands on his sternum, one over the other, and started compressions, fast and hard. He had to have a heart in there somewhere. "Come on, you monster. You are not supposed to die. You're the bludgeon, the hammer, remember? Hammers don't die."

Reese moaned somewhere below as Gonzales encouraged him to climb. She was not going to get help anytime soon.

She pumped harder. "I don't care what you did. Those kids need you now. I need you. I can't do it alone."

The Ghost took in a long rattling breath, and she felt her own heart start to beat once more. His arm swept across his chest, knocking her away. She scrambled backwards, pulled the pendant out of her pocket, and dropped it over her head.

Gonzales pushed Reese through the manhole and crawled up after him. Gonzales had a deep gash on his forehead and his lower lip was split in two. Reese's arm hung limp at his side, bent at an entirely wrong angle with a shard of white bone sticking out.

Gonzales looked at the Ghost, then at her. She was covered in blood. "You touched him, and he didn't kill you?"

The Ghost held up his bandaged hands. "I'll do better when I'm not in pieces." He closed his eyes and passed out again.

Gonzales helped Reese to a spot where he could lean against the wall. Reese looked in almost as bad shape as the Ghost.

CHAPTER 20

"They came from the tunnel. Dozens of the damned cultists with spears and clubs," Gonzales said. "We took a bunch down before one of them broke Reese's arm, but there were too many. By the time we realized what had happened, the kids were gone."

Reese shook with a long cough. "It was a shitshow." He dropped Anatol's gun on the ground. The brass barrel was bent in a ninety-degree disaster. "I'm not going to be much use to you without that gun." He pointed his chin at the Ghost. "He looks worse than the gun."

"Oh, Reese. Your arm. We're gonna get you out of here." Both the SPD detectives looked like they needed to get to a hospital and stay there for a long while.

"Was that Krol who blew up down there?" Gonzales asked.

"Spikes through his head and a lot of twisting seemed to work. But the Ghost said it was all wrong. Something about the crows not being here." She remembered the vision of the white king that had plagued them all. "Before Krol died, he said Herod was here to claim all the children. He claimed Herod couldn't be killed by anything."

"King Herod from the Bible? Just our luck." Reese squeezed his temples. "Wasn't he the one who commanded that every child born on the night of Jesus's birth be killed? Damn. He's the damned white king who's been creeping around in our heads? That bastard has won the game. We've got nothing left."

"We're all still alive. We're not letting them keep those kids." Her mind went into high gear. They needed something to save them.

Gonzales picked an earbud off the floor and put it to his ear. "That's a sick beat. I can see why he fights to that." He handed the earbud to Kiran, and she held it to her own ear.

She recognized the song and fought down the sudden lump in her throat. "It's the words. He's looking for someone to save him as much as those kids are." She straightened her shoulders. "I'm opening his bag. He's supposed to have everything in there, right? Every tool we could ever need? We need something. Something that could fix him. Fix all of us."

"That bag will suck you in and you'll be gone," Gonzales said. "There's a

195

blackhole in there, I'm sure."

"Then hold onto me, and don't let go." The Ghost looked like he might die again any moment. "He needs whatever is in there. Whatever terrible thing he did before, he's stuck with us. He could have let us die plenty of times. He may be an ass, but he's our ass."

Gonzales nodded. He lay on the floor and held Kiran's ankle with both hands. Reese grabbed her other ankle with his good arm.

Kiran ran a hand over the gravestone-colored bag. The main zipper was a three-inch-long piece of mottled brass. She pulled it open, expecting the crack of doom to appear or an interdimensional vortex to suck her inside. This bag was the temple of history's greatest villain. Did it hide a warehouse full of weapons of torture? Morbid battle trophies? A door to Hell itself?

Gonzales and Reese squeezed the circulation out of her ankles, ready to pull her back or be dragged inside with her.

The zipper opened without a sound. Kiran lurched back as the contents spilled out in a torrent of rust and iron. The SPD detectives dragged her away as the bag emptied itself.

"Madre de Dios," said Gonzales.

Chains, great iron links that looked strong enough to bind an elephant, poured out of the bag as if there was no end. The links of the chain writhed as if it was alive, seething like the black snake of Eden. They coiled themselves in a great pile, no bag could ever contain, and still more crept behind them. The chains gave a final swish, and the bag emptied its last contents; a steel thermos from the all-night diner, a crust of pie, a cake tin, and the blue electric guitar the Ghost had stolen. Nothing more.

"Chains! All he has is chains and bakery?" Reese asked.

"And a thermos he lifted from that diner," Gonzales added.

"I stole nothing." The Ghost raised his head like a corpse rising from its grave. "I paid in silver." He reached out and lifted a handful of chains in his ruined hand as if weighing each link.

"I thought you had everything in the world in there?" Gonzales threw up his hands. "You were supposed to have anything we needed for this fight. You've got nothing but weight to carry."

CHAPTER 20

And then it came to her. Eleven children kidnapped. The note said when the twelfth is taken all will be complete, but they had never meant a twelfth child. She picked up a silver coin that had spilled out of the Ghost's pouch and felt its weight. Heavy Roman silver. The suit of Coins. She knew who he was.

"You have twenty-nine more of these in that pouch, don't you? Thirty pieces that you can never spend no matter how much you give away." The names of the children—Petra, Andrea, Juan, Thaddeus, Felipe, Bar, Mateo, Thomas, Jamie, Simon, and Paul—made sense to her now. They were the names of the apostles in disguise. All but one. All but the twelfth.

The Ghost tried to sit straight, but only managed to lean against the wall. He bared his teeth but said nothing.

Kiran let out a long breath that felt like it had been held inside her for centuries. She had found the betrayer, the betrayer of God. "You're Judas, the one who betrayed Jesus, aren't you?"

The Ghost held his head with his bloodied hands. "They cannot be exhausted. I cannot give them away. Two thousand years ago, there were thirty coins and every time I count them there are still thirty. They cannot be spent, and I cannot be forgiven."

Gonzales stepped back as far from the Ghost as he could. "Judas Iscariot. Dios mío. You killed him. You betrayed the son of God and they murdered him."

The Ghost stared Gonzales in the eyes. "Yes, I betrayed the Son of God. Yes, I caused his death and took coin in payment. Yes, I committed the crime that can never be forgiven. And I have rotted in limbo alone in my cage ever since, carrying that bag of chains everywhere across space and time. Heaven barred me. Hell would not take me in. They came together to forge that chain and bind me like they did to no other soul in all eternity. I am doomed to be a slave at the end of those unbreakable chains. I tied them to the Colossus of Rhodes and dragged it down. I tied them to the hounds of hell, and they would not shatter. I will carry them forever until time itself ends."

Gonzales raised a fist and Kiran barely recognized him. "We can't work with the Betrayer of God."

Kiran swallowed hard. She had no idea what would possess someone to betray someone who they knew as the Son of God, who they loved and who loved them back. She also couldn't imagine such loneliness, carrying those chains for more than two thousand years.

"He was the Son of God," the Ghost's voice was barely audible. "Can you imagine what it was like to walk with the Son of God? What did he ever need? What did he ever desire? What pain did he feel? He asked us to turn the other cheek, to love our enemies, to do unto others what we would have them do unto us." His breath rattled in his chest before he continued. "Did he ever see a son of his starve? Did he ever need money or know how much it could change in the world for someone who had no bread? I could have changed everything for my family with that money, and he had everything. Loaves and fish appeared from the sky for him. I loved him, but I could not forgive his perfection or fix my soul. I loved him and failed him. And I wish I could rip my heart from my chest and change it every day. But I know my wishing makes no difference to anyone."

Reese closed his eyes tight. "Shit. The Betrayer of God. I mean, that's messed up."

"Whatever, Reese," Kiran said. "We knew he wasn't Mr. Rogers. I'm not going to cast the first stone or whatever you Christians say."

Reese raised his good hand. "I'm Muslim. The Quran says, 'Let them pardon and forgive, Do you not love that Allah should forgive you and Allah is forgiving and most merciful'."

The Ghost slumped further down the wall. "There's a quote for every side in all religions. A new one for anything we need to believe each day."

"Whatever," Kiran continued, "I'm not here to forgive. I don't know what deserves forgiveness. Some things sure don't. Can you forgive a man for abandoning his family? Can you forgive his family for not knowing how to help him, how to bring him back?" She ran a hand through her hair and left it there, holding back the tangles. "The only thing that matters now is those children and stopping whatever this Herod guy wants to do." She turned to the Ghost. "Look, I don't know why you were a supreme asshole back then, but it was a long time ago."

CHAPTER 20

The Ghost didn't lift his head. "Time changes nothing. It was a crime that can never be forgiven."

Reese shook his head in disbelief. "And there's nothing in the damn bag. You have no weapons for us, nothing at all?" He threw his ruined gun down the manhole. "Why are we even called the Cup and the Sword?"

The Ghost closed his obsidian eyes, looking into the past. "You used to have a sword like no other. The edge of the blade was bathed in the dust of stars. The sapphire upon the pommel held a piece of the true sky. When it struck another sword, it made music like no other weapon. Few dared to stand against it."

"Well, where is it?" Reese asked. "Why isn't it in that bag?"

"We lost it long ago in a fight on a boat. It was a beautiful fight. One of our absolute best. Toward the end you slid across the deck with a spear through your chest and dropped the sword over the railing. You would have risked the world to reclaim your weapon from the spirit that haunted the lake, but it was not easy when you were dead. It seemed fitting to let the weapon lie with your bones and the fish at the bottom of the lake."

Reese swallowed hard. "I died, like an old version of me? I've lived other lives?"

The Ghost shrugged. "I don't bother with the theory. I've had enough of philosophers and prophets."

"And what about me?" Gonzales looked lost. "Where's my weapon to fight all these creatures?"

The Ghost sighed. "You received the raw end of the bargain. All you got was a golden cup, most of it shoddy brass really, though it was always advertised as gold. You tended to bash people with it and pour holy water on them. Completely ridiculous as a weapon. Got lost in the end of course. Knights and all sorts of fools wasted centuries looking for it like some kind of holy symbol."

"Damn. So, we've got nothing." Reese shook his head. "Other than stories and a broken Ghost. Well, shit. It's going to have to be enough. Those cultists aren't keeping the kids as long as I live."

"Probably not a lot longer." The Ghost was unhelpful. At least, he was back to being his asshole self.

"We've got to get back down there." Gonzales peered down the manhole. "Sounds like we don't have much time before Herod uses them to bring on whatever apocalypse he's meant to rain down upon us."

Kiran looked down the manhole and into the darkness the children had disappeared into. "It'll be some kind of trap, I'm sure." She considered the broken stairs leading to the world outside. If they got Reese to a hospital, maybe the rest of them could go on. She knew Anatol would tell her she was wrong, that the trinity must stay together to control the Ghost, or all their purpose would be lost. They were screwed.

The Ghost got to his feet and shoved the chains back into his bag. Moonlight shone from above, lighting his wounded face in silver. He picked up the coffee thermos from the diner with his bloody hands and handed it to Gonzales. "A poor substitute for the Grail, but at least it's coffee."

Gonzales took the thermos and tried to avoid the places where the Ghost's blood had stained the steel black. He unscrewed the lid and steam covered his face in the cold, subterranean air. "This coffee smells like the finca back home when my grandmother ground the beans early in the morning."

Gonzales poured himself a lid full of the coffee. "And it's still hot."

The Ghost reached into his sack and pulled out the blue electric guitar he'd liberated from the music store and handed it to Reese. "This might work for a cane to lean on. It's no Excalibur, but we're not the A team anymore."

Reese picked up the V-shaped guitar with his good hand. He stood and braced himself against it and tried walking around the room. "Shit, we're not even the C team. We're the dregs, the ones they send in when they've already given up. Speaking of dregs, I could use some coffee, Gonzo."

Gonzales handed Reese a lid-full of coffee. "The stuff is strong. At least, the C team will be awake."

Reese drained the cup and handed it back. Kiran got the next cup.

She had never needed coffee so badly. It burned its way down and she felt her brain cells soaking in caffeine. She drank every drop and returned the lid.

Gonzales poured a third time and held the cup out to the Ghost. "There's a

CHAPTER 20

little left. I can hold it for you if—"

"If I need a nurse," the Ghost finished. He grimaced as he stretched out the fingers of his ruined hand. "No, Gonzales. You will find no nurse in this world for me." He bent his fingers around the cup and swallowed. Half the hot coffee dripped over his chest before he dropped the lid to the floor. He laughed a sad laugh. "Who knew I would die by coffee burns or that drinking diner filth could be so hard?" He looked at Kiran and held her gaze. "I would not fail Little Juan if I had a choice, would not be the Betrayer again. He deserved much better, but I am undone."

Then she understood. They'd tricked the Ghost into finally caring about someone. The crown of thorns, the baptism, the crucifixes on the wall, had all been there for a reason. They forced him to remember, forced him to realize the children mattered. The change had broken his untouchable shell, released the blood from his dry veins. Now, when they needed the unstoppable Ghost more than ever, he had to go and develop a heart that could be ripped open.

Reese stomped around the room, testing the guitar as a cane. "This thing works. I feel a little better. Let's get down there. They aren't taking those kids away and getting away with it."

Kiran squeezed her hands together. Reese was ready to throw himself back into the fire with a bone sticking out of his arm. There had to be a way.

The Ghost pulled himself off the floor. "You don't understand. Heaven and Hell have conspired against me. They've sent King Herod, the Lord of the Lake of Shadows, the Sorcerer King. The books say Herod died long before I betrayed anyone, but that's all lies. He lived on, plaguing the world with his desire to rule over everything. Hell rewarded him by making him one of the kings of the Abyss. Krol wasn't lying. They've sent a monster beyond my power." He held up his ruined hands. "Even if I still had power."

Kiran spun at the sound of Reese's scream. He was trembling against his will like he was having a grand mal seizure. He swung the guitar in a wild arc, smashing it against the wall before he collapsed to the floor. There was a loud crack and Reese cried out again.

Don't let them swallow their tongue or hit their head. She tried to remember what she was supposed to do in case of seizure. Call an ambulance? Yeah, right.

Gonzales dropped first and cradled Reese's head. "What's happening? Is it poison?"

Kiran held Reese's legs, praying it wasn't because of some brain injury or hidden tumor that had chosen to reveal itself because it was exactly what they needed on top of everything. She squeezed Reese's arms as hard as she could to try and hold him down. She needed Reese. She needed Gonzales. They were supposed to be there for her through this whole nightmare. The shaking ended before she could do anything else.

Reese took in a long breath. "Holy shit." He grabbed his head in both hands. "I thought I was going to explode."

"Your arm," Kiran said. "How can you…"

Reese's eyes went wide as he stretched his right arm over his head. The shard of bone had retreated under his skin. A fine scar decorated his biceps where before bone had protruded. He pushed Gonzales away and got to his feet. He walked to the wall and ran his hand along the brick. A clean slice had seared through the wall where he'd struck it with the guitar, as if it had been hit with a laser. "What kind of coffee did you give me, Gonzo?"

Gonzales picked up the blood-stained thermos. "I think it was French Roast." The gash on his forehead had closed completely.

The Ghost roared and thrust out his hands. They watched as bones snapped into place, tendons slid over them, and the skin closed. He screamed again and stretched out his new fingers. He bared his teeth and formed his healed hands into fists. Then he smiled a smile more wicked than the fires of Hell.

"It was coffee from the Cup, Gonzales. After all these centuries you've found it. All those damned knights were looking in the wrong place. You've found the Grail."

Gonzales looked into the thermos. "I mean, I can see why it would be hard to find. That diner was terrible. Who would ever look there? But if I'd known, I would have saved some. There's maybe one sip left."

"You didn't find anything." Kiran examined the blood-stained thermos and realized the truth. "That demon thing said the pieces of Reese's sword were decorating the walls of some fortress in Hell. The spirits told us that the Cup

CHAPTER 20

and Sword were destroyed and would never be found. They said they would never grace the earth again until they were remade with blood that had never been spilled." She pointed to the thermos and guitar. "They've got Ghost blood all over them. You didn't find anything. You made them again."

The Ghost braced his hand against the wall and rose to his feet. He picked up his iron rod and stretched his arms wide. "Then my blood is useful for the first time ever. The blood of the Betrayer has done one good thing. That one drink may be all we need until the Grail is found again in another century. You can never save the fruit of the Grail. You have to spend it all." The Ghost ran his finger over the wall where the unmarred guitar had sliced a deep line into it. He picked up the guitar and handed it back to Reese. "It's more of an axe than a sword this time, but it will do. Even King Gilgamesh would be satisfied."

Reese examined the guitar. "There's not a scratch on it." He slung the strap over his shoulder. "Now we get those kids. The A team is back."

The Ghost made a fist. "It will not be enough. Heaven and Hell have betrayed me. King Herod is back. Nothing on this earth, be it an angel or demon, living or dead, will stop him. Krol was not lying. No tool of God in this world shall harm him."

Kiran felt the heat behind her eyes again. The wheels inside her head had gone into overdrive. "Bullshit," she said. "Those are your gods, not mine."

Chapter 21

The coffee from Gonzales' stainless-steel grail had sent a jolt of lightning through her. She led them at a run for half a mile through the tunnel below. The cold wind picked up as they descended, bringing with it the scent of the ocean and of blood.

At the end of the tunnel the Ghost stopped and picked something off the wet stones. He held up a child's shoe. "Juan will be needing this."

"We're going to take them to the best shoe store we can find and get some fancy sneakers," Reese said. "I'm going to have money I need to spend."

The tunnel opened into a stalagmite covered cavern studded with sewer pipes leading out to Puget Sound. A concrete shaft descended through the center of the cavern. Steel freight elevator doors shone dully at its base. They'd found a way out.

"Convenient," said Gonzales.

Kiran ran her hand over the gray steel. "Maybe a little too much." The mark on her arm throbbed as she touched the door. She made sure not to extend herself too far. There was something waiting for her, hoping she would make that mistake. "I'm going to push this button and they're going to send down a welcoming party to kill us all."

"Customary." The Ghost turned to Reese. "Your weapon will slice through their defenses." He nodded to Gonzales. "Yours will protect you both, I hope."

"What about me?" Kiran asked. "These two get all the powerful magic and I get nothing?" Gonzales' coffee had done wonders. She felt like she had slept twelve hours and could run a track meet and win. But why the hell did they get all the cool stuff? She could have used an enchanted scimitar that ate

CHAPTER 21

demons or a bow and arrow or something.

The Ghost spread out empty palms. "Traditionally, you wish for some great weapon or a power to equalize both sides, like lightning that shoots from your eyes or at least invisibility, that's always fun. Sometimes you extend yourself too far with the power of the mark and go mad and try to kill us all with whatever magic you possess. You tear the necklace from your chest and vow to destroy everything in your path. It makes things interesting, but I usually have to kill you. You, however, wished for the dog to go to your mom's house."

Kiran sighed. "Oh yeah, that's right." She pushed the button. The elevator dinged.

The Ghost stepped in front of the door and leaned on his iron rod. "It appears we've finally found our way out of this dungeon."

The light over the door showed the elevator descending from ground level.

Kiran shook her head at him. "Step back. I said they will be coming for us."

The Ghost didn't move. He slid Juan's shoe into a coat pocket. "I am ready to welcome them."

Kiran waved him away from the door. "No. You can't do it that way any longer. You're not the same man you were. They can hurt you now, and we can't afford to lose you again."

The Ghost stayed put. "I'm not a man of any kind. I am a monster, an apparition, a ghost."

"Whatever. You're still a person. A big stupid boastful person, all caught up in yourself and your self-pity. And now you can die. So, get back."

The elevator dinged another floor down.

Kiran pointed. "You're going to have to fight differently, change everything. To be careful because those kids are depending on you. We have to do this whole thing differently. Beat them at their own game. And you have to stop feeling sorry for yourself."

The amulet went cold against her chest. The Ghost looked like he was going to smash her. "We still have no idea how to take Herod down."

"Leave that to me. I'm the one who solves the mysteries, right? Just destroy whatever comes out of this elevator and don't get hurt – any of you. They took Anatol. They took those kids. I'm not letting them take any of you. We're the ones coming for them."

The Ghost glared at her, but he stepped out of the way. Gonzales and Reese had already retreated. They didn't need to be told twice.

Kiran looked around the room as ideas spun through her head. "Damn, I wish we had something we could drop on top of them. Or just blow the whole elevator up. How am I supposed to do this without equipment?"

With a final ding, the doors opened, and a sea of fire that would have incinerated them all erupted into the room. Two demons that looked like huge black toads with mouths aflame stepped out.

The Ghost slammed the first one with his iron rod and it tumbled across the chamber. He leaped after it. The second turned and belched out another stream of flame straight at Reese.

Gonzales stepped in front of him and held out the steel thermos. The fire broke, spreading around him in a red-hot umbrella of plasma. When it died out, Gonzales' hair was singed and he was shaking, but they were both still there.

"Hell yes!" Reese shouted. He jumped out from behind Gonzales and swung the electric guitar at the rather surprised-looking demon. It held up an arm to block the ridiculous weapon and promptly lost it.

Kiran pulled out her gun, fired, and was not surprised to find it useless. She was surprised to find the Ghost having similar problems.

The iron rod was bouncing off the Ghost's demon and apparently doing no damage at all. These monsters seemed to be made of rubber, and the most the Ghost could manage was to knock one around. On the other hand, it seemed quite capable of frying him to a cinder. He couldn't dodge forever.

"The chain. Use the chain," she shouted.

For once, the Ghost listened. He threw the rod a final time which bounced off the demon and slowed it long enough for him to whip a length of chain out of his bag. He dodged a gout of flame and then swung the chain over his head like a lasso. He let the length go and caught the demon's arms in links of unbreakable iron. The demon did not like this. It charged the Ghost with a mouthful of teeth. This proved to be a poor decision as he just wound the

CHAPTER 21

chain tight and pulled it off its feet.

A downward swipe of Reese's guitar removed the demon's head from its shoulders. Kiran turned to see the other demon lying in two similar pieces.

"I think we're getting the hang of this," Reese said.

Kiran pointed to the elevator. "Good. We don't have time for a learning curve."

The elevator brought them to a street level disaster. Two hundred yards in front of them, the Space Needle soared into the sky, lit up red like a monument to Hell. Of all the immense buildings and shiny new structures in the city, it was the Space Needle, that monumental tower that remained the symbolic center of Seattle, around which the entire city revolved. It was completely different, a concrete spire capped with an immense disc and spike that drew together all that was modern and all that was old.

Kiran pointed to the top of the tower. The mark told her the right direction. "Herod is up there with the kids."

"The wall of fire and the crows circling the spire are kind of a giveaway," Gonzales said.

A thirty-foot-high circle of fire stretched around the outside of the Space Needle. A host of military vehicles were scattered across the street in various states of complete destruction. An assault tank was flipped upside down and on fire. The attack on the tower had been a bust.

Kiran counted at least four of the toad-like demons already starting in their direction. "We could barely handle two of those. We can't afford to fight our way inside."

Reese scanned the wall of fire. "Think of something fast. They don't look happy to see us."

"Then let's get out of their way." Kiran scanned the cars parked on the curb for the oldest vehicle she could find. She spotted an old red Mustang parked tantalizingly close. Some kid had tricked it out for racing. They were a joke to steal. "This time I drive. Come on."

"Shotgun." The Ghost smashed the driver's window and ripped open the door. He slid across the front seat and pulled out a long length of chain.

Kiran bent under the steering wheel and gave thanks for the hours she's spent as a child, pondering getaways from banks, daydreaming about hotwiring cars.

"Why am I not surprised you know how to do this?" Reese asked.

"Standard FBI training," she lied. The engine turned over as she finished connecting the wires. "Hold on tight."

She shot out from the curb and her skull pressed against the headrest. The first demon in their way opened its mouth to bathe them in fire. She hit it as it inhaled, and it sailed high into the air until it splatted into a lamp post.

Three more monsters stepped out from the wall of fire.

Kiran squeezed the steering wheel. She managed to avoid hitting the burning tank, swerved around a Humvee, and pressed down on the gas. "That thermos of yours better protect us all, Enrique." They rocketed forward.

"Better if we get them all at once." The Ghost stuck his head out the window and swung his chain over his head.

"What are you doing?" Kiran screamed. The problem was, she knew exactly what he was doing. The last stretch of road was slick with black rain. She could feel the tires slipping.

The Ghost whipped the chain out high. It wrapped itself around a concrete streetlight like a living thing. He braced his feet against the door. "Hold on. This'll be fun." The car swerved then skidded sideways at full speed screaming like a ride at a deadly amusement park.

"Ay, Dios mío." Gonzales braced an arm against the car door. "We're going straight into it." He held his stainless-steel grail high.

The car hit all three demons broadside and went airborne into the wall of fire.

Chapter 22

Kiran closed her eyes as the inferno pressed about them. Flying through fire, they crashed into something, rolled up a set of stairs, and flipped back onto the car's wheels. Then the airbag hit her face.

The next thing she knew, Reese was pulling her out of the destroyed window. "Come on, K. Let's not wait for those things to come back."

"That's what I was doing, Reese. Waiting around here to shoot the shit with demons."

The car had flown through the fire and crashed sideways on the stairs leading to the tower. All its paint had burned off, leaving it a smoking shiny silver. There wasn't a demon in sight.

The Ghost threw a handful of silver coins in the front seat of the Mustang and slammed the door closed. "Not bad driving."

Kiran decided the Ghost might not be as horrible as she thought.

They ran through the lobby doors and found splattered demon covering the walls.

"Shit, how did this happen?" Reese asked. "Oh no."

Two legs they recognized were sticking out from behind the front desk.

They found Director Jefferson leaning against the wall with both hands pressed hard against her abdomen. Garner lay next to her on the floor, no longer breathing.

"I got your message, Patel. You were right about everything. Krol set us up. Picked us off like fools."

Kiran knelt next to Jefferson and held her. "Don't talk, Director. We've got to get you out of here."

THE TOOLS OF THE GHOST

"I'm not going anywhere except the afterlife, Patel. You've got to get up there and save those kids.

"Don't die so fast, Director." Gonzales opened his steel thermos. "I've got one drop of this left. I was saving it for a big dramatic moment, and this qualifies. You can never save a drop from the Grail. Gotta use it all when you can." He held out the thermos.

"Gonzales, I don't want your damned coffee," Jefferson could barely get out the words. "Listen to me—"

Gonzales pressed the thermos to her lips and tipped it. Jefferson gagged, then coughed as the final sip went down the wrong pipe. She took in a coffee-gurgling breath and her eyes closed. Kiran held her tight as Jefferson shook and her wounds knit together. Finally, her breathing steadied. Reese pulled Jefferson to her feet, and she surprised herself by staying upright.

"That's God's coffee." Jefferson ran her hands over the wound that had already closed over in amazement. "With enough of that you have a chance."

Gonzales held the thermos upside down. Not a drop came out. "Let's just all plan on not getting torn to pieces anymore."

Jefferson picked her gun up off the floor. "We're going to need a lot more help. It was never about Krol. There's some other monster he's brought into this. I've seen it. Those demon things follow its orders. The damn tank did nothing to it."

Kiran met Jefferson's panicked gaze. "Director, we need your help to get out of here, not with more fighting."

"You're not getting rid of me that fast, Patel. I fought my way through this. I was the only one who survived. I know what I'm getting into. And I've seen the kids. They've taken all eleven of them to the top. That monster is with them. They don't have any more time."

"Then I need you to get an extraction team to get those kids out of here if it all goes wrong. Get the fire department. Get any other assets we have on the ground. We're going to need everything. This place will be surrounded by demons and cultists soon. Get out and get help before it's too late."

Reese raised his guitar and sliced the whole front desk in half. "She's right, Director. We've got weapons of our own. We don't need you to die again

CHAPTER 22

here tonight. We need backup."

Jefferson looked at the front desk and then at the Ghost, whose hat was still smoldering, "Alright. But I'm bringing back everything I can find. Go get that bastard for Anatol's sake. Bring them home, Patel."

Kiran fought down the lump in her throat. "For Anatol."

The Ghost hurled half the desk through a glass panel in the back of the tower and Jefferson ran out into the night. He rolled his shoulders. "I may bleed now, but I feel stronger than I ever have." The Ghost gestured to the glass elevator that traveled up the side of the tower. "We're going to go up in style. I am going to enjoy breaking Herod into little pieces."

Reese balanced the guitar over his shoulder. "Oh, you're not the only one, my gray friend. Gonzo and I may beat you to it."

"Don't get cocky." Kiran hit the button for the elevator and the doors slid open. Reese and Gonzales stepped in, but the Ghost hesitated. He looked completely lost. "What is it?" Kiran asked.

"No one has named me a friend in a very long time."

Gonzales waved him inside the elevator. "It's mostly a figure of speech, if it makes you feel better."

The Ghost visibly relaxed. He stepped in, and the doors closed. "It does. It really does. I have no idea what friend means anymore."

Kiran examined the Ghost. He reminded for the first time of a lost kid. Terrifying and brutal, true, but lost. "It means you don't do everything alone anymore," she said.

"Word." Gonzales held out a hand for a fist bump and the Ghost stared at it suspiciously.

Reese shook his head. He reached out and fist bumped Gonzales. "Not hard at all."

The Ghost still seemed confused. "Harder than you think."

Chapter 23

As the glass elevator rose, they looked down on a swarm of demons and cultists rushing toward the base of the tower.

"They couldn't give us a ten-minute break, could they?" Reese asked.

Gonzales wiped the sweat from his forehead. "Good news is, they'll have to take the stairs."

"We'll never be able to fight that many," she said. Just when she'd hoped they had a chance, every path of escape was shut down. She clenched her jaw so hard it hurt. When would they ever have any kind of luck?

The Ghost reached into a pocket and handed her a pack of clove gum. "Got it at the drug store on the way."

Kiran took the pack of gum and her heart cracked more than a little. Only one other person in the world had ever remembered her favorite flavor. She had no idea how the Ghost knew, but it mattered more than she could express. "Thanks," she stammered. She shoved three pieces in her mouth at once. The familiar flavor brought a feeling of coming full circle back to where she began. She was about to enter that church again and lose all that was dear to her. She chewed harder and the fear eased off. This time it would be different. She wasn't going to let any of them die. She rubbed her eyes and kept looking down at the crowd streaming into the Space Needle so the others wouldn't see.

"Traditionally, all we have to do is kill Herod," the Ghost explained. "Once he goes down, the demons who follow him will be banished and the cultists will lose their purpose and go back to whatever video games they were playing before all this."

CHAPTER 23

Kiran looked up at him. "What are those, Dungeons and Dragons rules?"

The Ghost shrugged. "Where do you think they got that game from?"

"Something still bothers me," Reese said. "What about Gonzo and me? Who were we, really? How did we get wrapped up in all this?"

The Ghost looked up at the numbers flashing by. Still fifty floors to go. "The Sword and the Cup forever reborn. Gilgamesh and Enkidu were heroes of ancient Sumer. They were the greatest of friends and fought the most terrible enemies together, long before my time. They were brought back endlessly, as kings and knights of the Round Table, brothers seeking justice against Ravana, warriors trying to free a queen in Troy, but always as heroes searching for who they once were. Whether you are them reborn after a thousand lives or whether you are Reese and Gonzales, nothing more, is not for me to say. I always believed there was a little of them in many of you mortals, like a grain of sand I needed to seek out, forever reborn." He nodded toward Kiran. "Reincarnation is more of a Hindu thing. You should ask her. But I promise you this: I could have picked you both out amongst a thousand others with my eyes closed."

Gonzales looked worried. "Kiran, what would you say?"

"If you asked my mother, she'd tell you that of course you were born before. She'd invite you over for dinner and explain the Bhagavad Gita to you until you were sick of it."

The Ghost seemed to consider her words. "And if I die here a final time? What does your faith say will happen? How will I return if I am never forgiven for my deeds?"

"Probably as a fly or something," Gonzales said. "I mean, isn't that how it works?"

"I'm not sure it matters." Kiran squeezed her hands together. "We're all so caught up in our salvation or our redemption or all that shit. That's all religions ever care about. Look, you did something unforgiveable thousands of years ago and you've hated yourself ever since. Hated everyone. Stopped caring about anything. What you did was horrible. I can't wrap my head around it. There's no redemption for something like that in my book. That man you were was no good and that man died. But you've lived a thousand

THE TOOLS OF THE GHOST

lives since then. Maybe you're another man now. Maybe you were given a gift, a chance to be something else. You can only do the best you can. We've got to get those kids and send Herod home. The kids are what matters. Whatever gods are out there have brought you back to help them. They've brought you back to be Justice and unholy Vengeance. Those kids can't fight for themselves."

"Unholy Vengeance." The Ghost banged his iron rod on the floor and the elevator shook. "I like it. And Justice too." He let out a breath and his shoulders relaxed. "Whatever happens, if I die, I will no longer be forced to return to the emptiness, to my own world where there is nothing." He turned his black eyes on Kiran. "If I live, do not send me back. Let me live here and die as any man would. Promise me I will not suffer the void again."

Kiran bit her lip and nodded. "No more voids. Voids suck." Whatever happened, he would not have to return to that emptiness.

"Great, we've got a happy ending either way." Reese shook his head. "Immediate miserable death, or death sometime in the near future. So cheery."

They passed the seventieth floor and the question burning inside her could wait no longer. "What about me?" Kiran asked. "What is all this about the Wand, really?" Part of her was not sure she wanted to know the truth.

The Ghost avoided her eyes. "You are a strange one. The Wand is the spirit, the fire, the passion to do what is right. You were ever born to find us and lead us, to unravel the mysteries and find out why we are here. Your lives have been lonely and misunderstood. The life of the seeker is ever hard." The Ghost pointed to the black mark spiraling up her arm. "Long ago, you had a hand in the making of that."

"What? How?" Kiran stammered.

The elevator dinged before she could get an answer.

"We're stopping on eighty, ten floors too soon. It'll be a trap." She didn't need the mark for this.

They didn't need her to explain. They rolled to the sides. The doors opened and a storm of foot-long spines blasted past. The glass in back of the elevator shattered, spilling out into the night.

Reese pointed to the Ghost, who nodded. They rolled out and the next

CHAPTER 23

thing Kiran heard was a ghastly scream that didn't come out of any human mouth.

She and Gonzales stepped into the corridor to find two demons on the floor in several pieces. Their tails were covered in the spines they had just fired into the elevator. One of them started to get up despite having its legs removed, and Gonzales hit it with the thermos. It didn't move again.

A final crack and crash of glass behind them made clear that the ruined elevator was no longer an option. "We'll have to take the stairs," Kiran said.

The Ghost hung his head. "I hate stairs."

They pushed open the door to the stairwell and heard a thousand boots or claws racing toward them. Kiran glanced down the stairwell and felt her heart drop.

Creatures with horns, claws, and far too many tentacles were swinging their way up the stairs, followed by what seemed like an army of cultists. One of them opened a mouthful of teeth and lightning burst forth.

Gonzales held out his steel Grail and a translucent shield appeared in front of them. The blast of electricity struck the barrier and vanished. Kiran breathed again.

Reese patted Gonzales on the back. "This looks as good a place as any for a last stand, eh, Gonzo?"

"Vámonos," Gonzales said. "The stairwell is narrow. Two can hold off an army of demons here. It'll be like old times, though I don't have any idea what old times were like back in Sumer."

Kiran looked at the two cops through suddenly clouded vision. She wiped her eyes before she yelled at them. "You two are not dying here in some great sacrificial moment just to be cool. That's so stupid. Ghost, drop the stairs."

The Ghost smiled. "Those two always have a big moment like that where they try to get themselves killed. Usually, you let them die. This time you're full of surprises." He swung his iron rod and a huge section of concrete broke loose and tumbled down the stairs. "This won't take long. Reese, take out the I-beam. We'll drop a thousand tons of rubble on them."

Reese's guitar sliced through the steel while Gonzales protected them from blasts of lightning and fire. They had half the stairs down in minutes. The cultists below started to scream and run the other way, trampling whoever was below them. The demons just came on faster.

The Ghost raised his rod for a final blow. "This should do it." He struck the ceiling and the entire stairway started to crumble, including the flight going up.

They threw themselves back down the hallway while the ceiling broke to pieces and a rain of concrete tumbled down the stairs.

"You were supposed to leave the part that's going up." Kiran gave the Ghost her best glare.

The Ghost shrugged. "I destroy things."

"Yeah, right." Her hair flew into her face with a sudden gust of wind. A chunk of the tower lay open to the night sky, and a storm was coming. She prayed that no innocent people were hurt by the falling rubble. "How do we get up there now?"

The Ghost reached into his bag and pulled out of a length of the black chain. "Tie yourself to me and we will travel together."

Gonzales looked down at the eighty-story fall. "No, no, no!"

Chapter 24

Kiran braced her feet against the side of the tower and held tight to the chain wound about her waist. The wind buffeted her as she focused her gaze straight at the Ghost's back and made sure not to look down. Gonzales and Reese hung ten feet to either side, suspended by lengths of chain wrapped around the Ghost as he scaled the outside of the tower. She'd never realized how unlike a regular skyscraper the Space Needle was. They were climbing up a concrete and steel beam that bent up and out toward a UFO shaped saucer deck looming above.

"Damn. This is the dumbest idea yet," Reese shouted into the wind. He stumbled and fell flat against the building, swinging in space, both hands clutched around the chain.

Gonzales jumped across the chain holding Kiran in place and righted Reese. He made the mistake of looking down. "Mierda. It would have been better to fight the demons in the stairwell."

Kiran had a hard time arguing with either of them. Safety was not optimal at the moment. Clouds hid the stars as the Ghost climbed and the wind howled. On cue, the first raindrop hit the middle of her forehead and squeezed the chain tighter. They were about to get soaked out here.

The Ghost had scaled five stories already with his bare hands finding a grip on the edge of the concrete beams and never slowing. She wasn't sure how much trouble the rain was going to give him, but they were about to find out.

Thunder growled above them, and the rain let loose, plastering her hair to her face. A flash of lightning illuminated the Ghost above them, struggling on through it all. They'd tied themselves to him as their last hope. He could drop them into space any moment and they couldn't do a damned thing. But in that moment, despite the deluge, she had more faith in the monster than in anyone else in the world. He was Justice and Vengeance, and he was taking them to get the kids back. No amount of rain was going to stop him.

The Ghost's hat fluttered in the wind, then blew up and away in a great arc. He stretched out a hand to catch it and slipped.

Kiran screamed, "Don't!" as she felt the drop in her stomach.

The Ghost grabbed the edge of the building again, slid down ten feet, then caught himself.

The hat spun and dropped straight down. Reese snatched it out of the air. "Got you, my man."

The Ghost hesitated. "Thank you," came out in a whisper.

"My man is just a saying," Reese shouted over the wind.

The Ghost sighed and started climbing again. "Good. I am not used to being anyone's man."

Three stories to go and Kiran's hope rekindled. This was going to work. The Space Needle's disc stretched wide just above them. They might be able to snatch the kids before anyone noticed and get away.

A horned head on a yard-long neck peered down at them from an open window on the saucer deck that shouldn't exist this high and Kiran's hope died. Three other demons, looking much the same, stepped out of the tower window, and their damned clawed feet clung to the wall like they were lounging on the rocks of Hell. Of course, they had clubs in their hands and ran straight for them. The Ghost held tight to the wall and succeeded in glaring at them uselessly.

"They're going to knock him right off the building," Reese said. "He can't do a damned thing."

"Reese, destroy one of these windows, get inside and anchor us. I'll take care of the demons."

"You'll what?" Reese asked. But he took the guitar off his back and sliced through a pane of glass.

Choices were limited before imminent death. It had worked for Anatol, but he had only brought down two cultists. A demon's brain was another

CHAPTER 24

thing entirely. Kiran opened herself to the mark and threw her mind at the oncoming trio.

In the next instant she found herself looking out of the demon's multifaceted eyes bathed in the not-so-welcoming fires of Hell. She screamed and heard gurgles come out of her throat. She tried to run away from herself, lifted both clawed feet and felt nothing but air as the demons slipped off the tower and started a long deadly fall. In desperation she jumped away into another demon's mind and screamed again as the alien thoughts overwhelmed her. She swept out her demon arms, hit one of the other demons, and closed her eyes. When she opened them, she made out Reese raising his guitar over her and knew if she didn't make it back to her own body, she was going to be sliced in two. The guitar came down and she jumped away, hoping she could find her way back into her own mind.

The next thing she remembered was being dragged through a window and laid on the floor.

"Gracias a Dios, she's awake. Kiran, we made it. What did you do?" Gonzales knelt on the floor next to her.

"Like a fool, she saved us." The Ghost was leaning over her with is rod in his hands looking menacing. "She took over the minds of those demons to save us and tossed them off the building. She will be drooling and having a seizure within moments. Her mind is forever ruined."

"*Armarghat decaras baralacan!*" she yelled in protest. Various gurglings followed. The words seemed to come straight out of her gut and skipped her vocal cords entirely.

Reese bent over her, cradling her head. "Damn. What the hell did she say?"

"Exactly," the Ghost said. "It was the language of Hell. She said, 'I am Kiran, Queen Mother of the Sixth plane of the Abyss. Kneel before me and grovel.'" The Ghost sighed. "I'll have to kill her soon or she'll try and possess us all."

Gonzales crossed himself. "Dios mío. She really said that?"

"She also said something about her mother needing to go into therapy and swore to never take a standardized test again, but I couldn't make it out. Her Hellish is terrible."

"You're an asshole and I don't like you," Kiran managed in actual English.

The Ghost's eyebrows shot up. "She shouldn't be able to speak her own tongue ever again. Her mind is stronger than I thought. Maybe I won't have to kill her."

Kiran pushed Reese away, tried to stand, and promptly fell on her butt. "No trying to kill me until we get the kids back." Lying on her side, she got her first look at the ninety-first floor.

They'd broken into a circular penthouse overlooking the city. Before them was a giant conveyor belt draped in black velvet. The belt fed into a massive steel press that had no place being on top of the Space Needle.

"What is that machine for?" Kiran asked. Words in a demonic language had tried to sneak out of her throat, but she beat them away.

"Gaudy. Looks like it's for crushing people," the Ghost said. "Some kind of sacrifice thing."

A door to another room opened and two ceremonially robed cultists entered, leading all eleven children between them.

The lead cultist seemed sincerely shocked to find them there. "Where are the guardians of this room?"

"Dead," the Ghost answered.

Kiran counted them again and couldn't believe it. Eleven children, they'd found them all.

"Ghosty!" Juan tried to run forward with his hands tied behind him and faceplanted.

An inhuman growl escaped from the Ghost's throat and the cultists cringed. He leaped over the mechanical contraption with his coat spread around him like the wings of an avenging angel. He seized a cultist in each hand and lifted their feet off the floor.

"Small people, close your eyes now," he ordered.

The Ghost waited for the children to close their eyes. "Juan, yours are still open." As soon as Juan complied, the Ghost spun and tossed the cultists out the window. He wiped his hands against each other. "Magic trick over. Open your eyes." He snatched Juan off the floor and sat him in the crook of his arm before he turned to Kiran. "Better?"

"Better," she agreed. At least, he had asked them to close their eyes. She ran

CHAPTER 24

forward to seize as many of the kids as she could fit in her arms.

Reese and Gonzales herded together the rest of the children not already piled on Kiran. With a touch of Reese's guitar, their bonds fell away. She started to consider how they were going to get them out of here. Jefferson must have found a way by now, helicopters or something.

Juan held tight to the Ghost's arm. "I knew you would come back. I even told the others."

The Ghost pulled Juan's shoe out of his pocket. "Keep better track of your shoes."

Juan grinned from ear to ear. "Thanks."

"I knew he would come as well." The voice was regal and majestic and made Kiran want to jump out the window to get away.

Herod stepped through a doorway at the far side of the room, revealed in all his sickening splendor. A head taller than the Ghost, he was robed in white with steel mail underneath, a gold-hilted sword at his hip, and a golden crown upon his head. His beard was tinged with white, but he looked anything but old. An aura of menace radiated from him that felt like flame against her skin. He raised his hands and every object in the room trembled. Kiran felt herself falling away, looking for any path out of the room. Any way to run from disaster. Behind Herod streamed in at least thirty cultists, half held crossbows which they promptly aimed at them, the other half hefted wicked spears.

Kiran sensed the cloud of despair spread across the room with Herod at its center crushing hope and spirit in its wake. She struggled to control her thoughts.

"Shit," said Reese. He took a step back. "This is not worth the paycheck."

Gonzales had frozen completely. He looked as if he had shrunken inside his own skin. "Now, we die."

Lightning tore the sky and the cloud unleashed sheets of rain because Seattle, and therefore weather.

Herod lowered his arms and drew his sword. "Correct on both counts." He pointed the weapon at Reese and Gonzales and a cyclone erupted. The two detectives were knocked off their feet, picked up, and smashed into the far wall. Herod swept his sword in an arc and the whirlwind continued to drag Reese and Gonzales across the room, mashing them into every column and piece of furniture in its path. As a final punctuation, Herod slashed the weapon across the floor. Reese and Gonzales dropped in a bloody heap and lay far too still.

Kiran felt her heart drop away all the way to the base of the tower. The two of them had been her only friend in this nightmare, the best ones she could remember. Her legs were no longer willing to support her. She had no idea how she was standing.

Herod pointed the sword at the Ghost. "I am the only one here for you. These others never measured up. They are but remnants of what they once were, just as you are now." A shadow swept across the room, darkening everything.

The Ghost stood by himself as the darkness fell. His silver skin caught the remaining light and held it as it faded. Kiran knew he was lost; they were all lost.

The Ghost lifted his iron rod as if it were the heaviest thing in the world. "I never needed anyone's forgiveness, Herod. I never needed anyone's help. I never needed anything." He spoke the lie in a weak rasp. "Let's do this for the last time. At least this time the end will be different."

Herod gestured and half of the back wall fell away. Two hulking demons stepped forward so covered in horns and spikes that Kiran could barely make out their red skin. The cultists leveled their spears and crossbows at the Ghost.

Herod smiled a smile that burned away the last bits of hope. "How fitting that at the end of your story you find yourself quite alone." Herod let the quiet of the inevitable fill the room.

The Ghost's shoulders slumped awaiting the demon's charge.

"That's a lie," Kiran said, and her voice carried and echoed across the room. Anatol had died before she could do something. That shit wasn't going to happen again. She opened herself to the mark and let her feelings rage. Let the black threads of magic reach out like tendrils of destruction. She seized every mind she could find and struck out.

CHAPTER 24

The cultists fell to the floor en masse, writhing in pain, then went silent. She'd dropped them all into unconsciousness. Sweat dripped into her eyes and she fell to her knees. She reached out again, this time for the demons' minds, and hesitated, knowing it would be the last thing she ever did.

A voice so quiet that it barely registered in the back of Kiran's head broke the silence.

"It is a lie. Wherever he finds himself; be it Hell or worse, he will not be alone." Gonzales stepped out of the shadows with blood streaming across his face. He reached down with both hands and straightened his left knee with the resounding crack of gunfire.

Reese stumbled out from behind a column and adjusted his leather jacket. He shook his head and spat out a tooth. "Damn right, my brother." He winced as he dragged the guitar off his back. "No more hiding in the back. I'm tired of being on the outside looking in." Tears filled his eyes. "We're coming straight out of Oaxaca and Detroit." He smiled a smile that even with a tooth missing was the most goddam beautiful smile Kiran had ever seen. He winked at her. "With lots of love."

Gonzales stretched his arms out wide, and Kiran felt the tectonic plates of the world shift. "Word."

Reese swung the guitar in a lazy arc of destruction, ripping through the floor and up a wall. He straightened his shoulders and turned to Kiran and the Ghost. "You two have done your share. Take a break. We got this."

The Ghost held out a fist in a vaguely threatening angle like he wasn't sure what to do with it.

Reese reached out and tapped the Ghost's fist with his own. "That's the way, my man." He nodded to Gonzales.

Gonzales sprang forward like the lost hero of Sumer he apparently was, the Grail held high. With each step he took, his shadow shifted, growing huge behind him, like the figure of the wild man of Uruk, accustomed to wrestling lions before breakfast. He held his steel thermos high, and it transformed into a silver rod topped with a golden cup that drew in the weak fluorescent light and cast it back as the pure rays of a raging sun. The stink of sulfur the demons had brought with them was dispelled, replaced with the scent of the mountain wind.

Reese was a step behind and looked furious. His black leather jacket shone like obsidian armor. He raised the guitar and it wavered in front of him, its edges bending until it became something else altogether. Reese held before him the legendary silver blade, whose sapphire pommel contained the sky, whose edge held the dust of stars.

Lightning flashed and the two detectives' shadows danced across the walls. Kiran glimpsed the two Sumerian heroes before it flashed again, and the shadows shifted. Now they were Achilles and Agamemnon. Another flash and the shapes of Rama and Lakshmana with bows in hand took their place. With a final flash of lightning, they became once again the shapes of the two detectives.

"Damn," Reese said. He nodded to Gonzales. "Sometimes in life, you finally figure out what you're supposed to do, and it feels good. Let's end this, G."

Gonzales raised both fists and shook the hair out of his eyes. "It feels very good. Vámonos."

The demons threw themselves at the two detectives like four tons of spiked disaster.

Gonzales met the first one with his fist against its skull. The demon sat back on its haunches stunned. Gonzales roared the roar of a freed tiger and struck it once with his rod whereupon it dissolved into mist. Reese simply dodged the other demon's every strike and divided it in two with a single swipe of his blade.

"We need our own soundtrack," Reese said. Sweat shone on his forehead. He swung his weapon in a graceful arc.

Gonzales smiled like a berserker let loose upon the world. He looked like the primordial man, returned to life.

Herod raised an eyebrow and two tentacles, dripping clear slime, whipped out of his back, thick as tree trunks, faster than a snake's strike, swirling at the detectives with suckers and spines. Reese sliced through the first and the severed piece shot across the room, just over Kiran's head. The second struck Gonzales who took it in two hands and tore it straight down the middle.

Herod narrowed his eyes. "You two are nothing but trouble." He snapped a finger and a dozen more sucker-covered tentacles seethed out of his back straight at the two detectives. Reese and Gonzales wove between the purple tentacles, slicing, tearing, smashing their way toward Herod, as he unleashed ever more octopus arms at them. The Ghost leaned on his rod and didn't move a muscle.

"Aren't we going to help them?" Kiran screamed.

The Ghost adjusted his hat. "They work better on their own. You will find no greater souls in all creation." The Ghost turned back to her as if he'd made a great mistake. "Don't tell them I said that. They were ever the most conceited of fools."

And he was right. Reese and Gonzales were like twins who'd lived together all their lives. They anticipated each other's moves, stepped in when the other was in danger, let nothing hinder them in their path of absolute demolition as if they had fought this battle a thousand times. Herod's tentacles were fast disappearing as Reese and Gonzales came on like a thunderstorm unleashed. The two heroes had arrived.

"Sometimes, they finish the job without me, and I can kind of kick back," the Ghost explained. He scratched behind his ear. "They fought the Bull of Heaven alone, they fought Humbaba the Terrible alone. They probably won't need help. Too many cooks in the kitchen sort of thing." He turned to look her in the eye. "You saw their shadows on the wall. Did you see your own?"

Kiran had but she hadn't wanted to think about it. A woman riding a lion had raised a trident in her hand and another woman with snakes as hair had flashed upon the wall. She'd tried not to look at the rest. She was Kiran, not some legend from the past, and that's who she wanted to be. She was here to finish this and bring the children home, that's what mattered.

Then a giant tentacle slapped Reese in the chest, and he stumbled. A second tentacle swept Gonzales off his feet, and he slid across the room on his face. Suckers dragged their weapons out of their hands while more tentacles entwined them, jerked them off the ground, and slammed them high against a wall. Both heroes stuck fast, limbs flailing, covered in ooze. In a moment it was over, and the SPD detectives' onslaught abruptly ended. The tentacles retracted, and Herod appeared nothing more than a very angry sorcerer king once again.

The Ghost adjusted his bag on his shoulder and sighed. "Maybe this time they could have used the help."

"You think?" Kiran asked.

Herod raised both hands in a grand gesture. "The Two Heroes. Glorious. You've caused so much difficulty over the years. I believe I'll preserve you half-alive to decorate my hall for the next few centuries." He stroked his chin. "Or perhaps you'll become mounted trophies for some prince of Hell I particularly admire. So many possibilities."

Reese tried to say something, but with ooze over his mouth all that came out was, "Gllecht."

Herod sighed. "Now I must finish things."

The Ghost stepped in front of the children. He dropped his sack to the floor and held his iron rod before him like the last line of defense of Sparta. He seemed utterly unconcerned. Like Death come to a party. No creature in any universe had fought more battles or terrible enemies. Herod was supposedly indestructible, but in that moment, Kiran wouldn't want to be any monster or deity who would have to face their champion.

The Ghost leaned on his iron rod. "Herod, I don't usually take time to listen to speeches, but I'll give you one chance. Whatever foul plan you have for this world, let it go. Leave the children in peace, leave this world in peace, and I will let you return to whatever Hell you choose. Or stay here. I'll grant you an entire diner to hang out at. I know a truly lousy one. Your other choice is I rip you to a thousand pieces that can never be put back together again and chew each one of them with my tea."

Kiran thought she saw a flicker of fear pass over Herod's face, but it was gone before she could be sure.

"I thought you were the one who hated soliloquies, Ghost. Now I've had to listen to yours. But you've misunderstood this game. It was never about the children or this world. *When the 12th is taken, the King will once again sit on his throne.* The fools thought it meant a child, but the twelfth victim was always you. Heaven and Hell want you to die forever and never bother them again. They want your soul extinguished. You betrayed the son of God. You

CHAPTER 24

set up the one mortal the angels loved, and they hate you. But you managed to make him into a martyr and ruined Hell's plans as well, so they hate you more. Hell is full of little "I Hate the Ghost" clubs and "The Ghost killed me" support groups. The one thing Heaven and Hell ever managed to do together was forge the amulet that binds you. They will never forgive you. And now they've had enough."

The Ghost shrugged. "Screw all of them."

"It's the other way around this time, my dear Ghost. It was the Archangel Michael who joined with the masters of Hell to let me return to this world and earn my redemption. My only task is to destroy you once and for all, then I ascend to my place in Heaven where I have been sorely missed. You made the mistake of caring for this crew of mortals after two thousand years. The girl made it all too easy. She is equally blinded by the heart. Love makes you vulnerable. It is a mistake I will never make."

Kiran saw it all. The Ghost had become like all of them.

The Ghost raised a fist. "Then let them go. Take me, Herod. Go find your place in Heaven and sit on a cold throne."

Herod shook his head. "I appreciate your offer, but I will need their souls to perish to complete the ceremony and finally destroy your own. Hell made that part of the plan clear. Oh, I will find my place. The sun rises on the just and unjust and the rain falls on both alike. Weren't those his words?"

The Ghost slammed his iron rod on the floor and tiles cracked. "The rain does not fall on us all alike, Herod. Every drop of it falls on me like vengeance, every drop for two thousand years like terrible justice. I don't care what he said. It's time for you to feel it too." The Ghost sighed. "Why can't the fools ever deviate from the script and take the diner offer?" He pulled his hat down tight. "I'm not big on forgiveness either. I've been looking forward to smashing your brains in for two thousand years. It's what I do." The Ghost leaped across the room. One foot touched the conveyer belt and he spun in the air, coat swirling about him like the Holy Spirit come to life in the form of Death.

Great tentacles as thick as a man's chest shot out at the Ghost faster than Kiran could follow, but none of them found him. He wove between them and came on faster than Herod could strike. Herod had been gifted the strength of Heaven and Hell, but the Ghost was a warrior with two thousand years of experience, fighting everything Hell could dish out. The great warriors of the past had studied under masters, learned the art of the sword, meditated on the ways of war, and became one with the blade. The Ghost had learned through trial and error with a dented metal stick against creatures no one else dared look at. Once he was an apostle, but now he was their worst nightmare. She'd never seen him move like this. He was liquid silver with a fist of lightning. The tentacles couldn't reach him.

Herod lifted his arms. "You shall not touch me, Betrayer." A new storm of tentacles tipped with claws of bone shot out at the Ghost in a swarm. Kiran knew he was doomed.

The Ghost, apparently, knew no such thing. He took off his hat in one motion and threw it in the air. Half the tentacles shot after it. Then he twisted sideways until he seemed to disappear, slipping between the knives of bone, sliding down one great slimy tentacle straight toward Herod.

The mass of tentacles smashed into the ceiling, sending plaster showering around the two combatants, then disappeared into Herod's back as the King drew his sword. In a heartbeat the Ghost reached him and brought his iron rod down. The two weapons flashed back and forth in a torrent of steel and iron.

Kiran wished she could watch the fight on TV. She knew a proper battle enthusiast would have choreographed the entire thing and called out the moves they each made as they danced around the room destroying everything. All she could tell was that Herod wasn't dead yet despite the Ghost unleashing a hurricane of iron upon him. He wasn't going to be able to do this alone. She took a deep breath. She was still reeling from being inside the demons' brains. Herod's mind would be far worse. Entering it would be the last thing she did. She reached out with the mark, searching for a way to distract the bastard long enough for the Ghost to finish him off. Before she got close, an impenetrable wall of spirit slapped her back into her body so hard that blood shot out her nose and her head snapped back against the floor.

She spat out a mouthful of blood. Well shit, that wasn't going to work. She

CHAPTER 24

tried to ignore the ache and possible skull fracture and pressed her nostrils together to slow the copious nosebleed. Hopefully, it wasn't blood from her brain or spinal fluid, if that was even possible. Whatever, time for plan B. As the Ghost and Herod crashed through the room, she pulled the children to her and told them what to do. They didn't argue with the woman with blood all over her face. She gave them the little hope she could find, and they ran, doing what she told them they must do to survive. She offered up a prayer to Ganesha to protect them and she ran.

She turned to find Herod raising his sword high to plunge it into the Ghost's heart. What was left of her aorta started to leak again.

But that particular sword move did not seem to impress The Ghost. He kicked the Jerk King in the chest. Herod's sword flew out of his hands as he crashed through a glass wall and straight out of the tower. He dropped away a thousand feet below as the wind rushed in with a gust of rain. A host of aged crows rode the wind and flapped into the tower, their wings casting black shadows that danced and swirled. There were eleven crows, the same number each time, and this time Kiran counted. The black birds cried out and perched about the room, clacking their beaks, and preening their feathers.

"You were a little late, weren't you, birdbrains?" the Ghost screamed at the crows. "I mean, how can you be late with wings? I thought you'd let me down this time."

One of the crows cawed at him.

"Ok, I let you down too. I know, I know. Rub it in. We're all stuck like this. But at least Herod's gone. Can we go now?"

"If only it was so easy, Judas Iscariot."

The Ghost turned to the window. There, floating in midair, was Herod. He drifted down through the broken window, reached out, and his fallen sword flew back into his hand. "Round two."

This time the Ghost hit him with the rod before Herod could even raise his sword. He struck him a dozen times, every blow enough to send a prince of Hell to the emergency room. Herod didn't bother to block a single blow. The Ghost stepped away panting. Herod was untouched.

Kiran ran to the wall and grabbed Reese's sword out of his hands. She pulled with all her strength, but the damned thing was stuck fast with tentacle glue. She braced a foot against the wall and heaved.

"Nothing in this world can harm me, be it demon, angel, or the Ghost himself. Nothing is easy to interpret and hard to get around."

She fell on the floor with the sword in her hands and rolled to her feet. "Here, Ghost!" She tossed Reese's sword high into the air.

The Ghost caught the ancient weapon and swung it with the strength of justice and the anger of a couple of millennia.

Doubt entered Herod's eyes. He raised his sword to block, and Reese's blade tore through it like it wasn't there. The blade struck Herod above the collarbone before he realized what had happened.

Unfortunately, it bounced off, accomplishing exactly nothing. In one quick move Herod punched the Ghost in the face and snatched the enchanted blade from him.

Herod swung the blade, testing it. "Basic grammar and definitions seem to escape you, Betrayer. Nothing can harm me." He dropped the sword and in the next moment a tentacle entwined around the Ghost's waist and jerked him off the floor. Another tentacle wrenched the iron rod from his grip, while a third lifted the massive steel press's jaws. Herod lowered the Ghost between the machine's teeth and let it crash across his legs.

The Ghost threw back his head in a silent scream of pain.

"And it ends, far too easily, just as Michael and Satan promised." Herod turned to the crows. "Why are none of you fools applauding? He betrayed all of you. Cost you everything. Every one of you died horrible deaths and it was all because of him. You, Peter, were crucified upside down. Upside down. That couldn't have been nice. You, Matthias, were burned to death. Slowly. Are you all so quick to forget? Which one of you did the lions eat? You each should join me in celebration as we rip his soul to shreds."

Kiran tore the pendant off her neck and ran. The Ghost was a complete asshole, true, but he was their Ghost. She grabbed him under the arms and braced herself against the press.

The Ghost looked her in the eyes as strained. "I've failed the children. What will happen to them now?"

CHAPTER 24

"Nobody's failed yet." Herod was not going to touch those kids. He wasn't going to get to have the Ghost either. She pulled for all she was worth. He didn't move a damn inch.

The Ghost's black eyes dimmed. "At least this time I will die and receive the punishment I deserve. I will not return to the void, though for the first time, I wish there were another way."

"Shut up." Kiran tried to think of some other way to save them all. Before she could summon another idea, a tentacle grabbed her by the waist and pressed her down to the floor with the force of the Kraken. Herod strolled up to her and placed a finger against her chest as the tentacle unwound itself.

"I can hold you with one finger, girl. You should have listened long ago and delivered him to me. I would have saved you. Would have told you what happened to your father. Would have united you with him. But instead, you find yourself at game's end. Your bishops are on my wall, your knight is crushed, and now I have the queen. You must surrender."

Kiran ran her tongue over her teeth. So dry, the air was suddenly so dry. And she needed more time.

"They taught computers to beat chess grandmasters long ago. But they couldn't teach them the true lessons the game plants deep in our souls. The lessons it wrings out of us when we've lost for the thousandth time. You never learned those lessons, Herod, did you?"

"What lessons? Friendship? Fidelity? Belief in some higher purpose? All false idols, nothing more. The game is won by those who destroy their enemy, who sacrifice their pieces and crush those before them to survive and conquer. Justice and Vengeance die beneath Power and Violence. There is no other lesson. There is only one."

Kiran grasped her necklace, held the silver fishhook before her. "Lucifer and Michael made this, but it is no longer theirs. It belongs to all the ones who need protection. Belongs to the ones who call on the Ghost."

Herod raised an eyebrow. "Who killed the Ghost, Kiran? You did. You tricked him into caring, delivered him on a plate, made him into something he was never meant to be. When we fail to follow our true nature, we become twisted shadows, nothing more. You did what no monster has ever been able

THE TOOLS OF THE GHOST

to do. You solved the unsolvable riddle, opened the unbreakable lock. You reduced an implacable warrior to a weak puppet. What good has caring done him? What good has it done any of you?" Herod sighed. "Krol planned it all. He really was a genius. Hell may send him forth again as his reward. You see, caring for the children was only part of it, the Ghost made the mistake of caring for you as well. Krol looked into your soul in the very beginning and let you live. He knew Anatol had chosen wrong." Herod waved a hand in the direction of Reese and Gonzales, still plastered to the wall. "The Ghost cared too much for those fools as well. All through the centuries as arrogant heroes and only in this incarnation as blunderers, does he appreciate them." Herod shook his head. "How Krol figured it all out, is still a mystery, but he did. I will return the necklace to Michael. I will tell him the Ghost fell just as it was foreseen."

Kiran tried not to let her gaze wander around the room and see what the children were doing. See if they had followed her instructions. She kept her eyes on Herod and kept his attention on her. "You never understood, Herod, caring about the pawns is what matters. They're the most important pieces. They all become queens. And you forgot your psalms. I'm not even Christian and I remember."

Herod raised an eyebrow. "What psalm is that, fool girl?"

"Though the weapons of Hell be vast, the Tools of the Ghost are without number." She raised the necklace. "Go home, my Ghost, that's the last order, go home and know you are loved." She hoped the kids had done what they needed to. She'd sent her pawns to the last squares. Plan C was all she had left. She had to sacrifice one piece to save them all. Kiran ducked.

Herod's eyes went wide as chains flew across the room. The children had laid them out just as she'd explained. The chains rose like living things, flying toward the Ghost like an endless stream of infinity symbols returning home. They entwined Herod in a storm of steel.

Herod fought to break free of the thick links wrapped around him. "Nothing in this world shall harm me. Lucifer promised it. The Archangel Michael promised it. I cannot die here."

The chains pulled tight, slamming Herod into a wall. They rose into the

CHAPTER 24

air, lifting the King and the Ghost's iron rod. They snaked into the Ghost's bag, and it flew onto his shoulder.

Finally, the ends of the chain wrapped themselves around the Ghost's hands, and he pulled them tight. "The chains come back home with me, Herod. We're like old friends that stick together. Nothing in this world can kill you. The rules will be different in mine."

Eleven crows flapped their ragged wings and the wind roared. They rode the gusts, circling above Herod, beating down the winds of fate.

Kiran pulled herself off the floor. Two of the girls ran to her to try and help. She squeezed them with one arm and with the other reached out to the one person she could not save.

The Ghost smiled at her, and her heart broke into a million pieces. A space opened behind him, blacker than a nightmare, the one place he had asked her not to send him, and he vanished within it. His chains whipped about him, dragging a screaming Herod into the infinite night. The iron rod spun through the hole, the bag followed, and lastly, a single white button.

The hole closed, and they were gone with nothing but old crow's feathers, drifting down to the floor, to mark their passage.

Kiran held the children tight. "Let's take you home. Your families have waited long enough."

Juan ran to the steel press, searching inside its jaws. "What about, the Ghost?" He turned back to her; his eyes wet.

Kiran tried not to collapse. "He'll meet up with us at Halloween. You just wait and see."

Juan picked something off the floor. "He left his ear pods and his phone too. He's not gonna be able to listen to his music."

"We'll mail them," she lied, but the words came out all choked.

"Before you hit the post office, get us down from here," Reese said. "Let's hope all those demons play by the D&D rules and went home on their own."

"Word," said Gonzales.

She got to her feet with the children all around. She let her awareness stretch outside the tower and sensed no demons, no danger. "Let's get everyone out of here. I need to get more gum."

Chapter 25

11 months later

Special Agent Kiran Patel surveyed a desk covered with teetering piles of paper. She stopped herself from chewing a pencil and laid it back down. Her urge to organize the heaps by to-do date competed with her growing passion to set them on fire. Instead, she opened a drawer, and slid all but one of the piles inside. Tomorrow, she silently promised the papers, and knew she was lying. Her promotion had come with more forms to fill out than ever. Left to their own devices in a dark drawer, she had no doubt the papers would conspire against her and have little paper babies to further waste her time.

A note on top of the one stack she'd allowed to remain read, "I knew you could do it, Cutie!" Her mother hadn't minded seeing her picture in the paper or any of the awards the mayor or the FBI had given her. The recognition had worked better than any medical school acceptance letter. She'd also loved having Reese and Gonzales over for dinner and watching them devour everything placed in front of them. Her mother even missed having Spartacus at her place and made Kiran bring him along whenever she stopped by. The living rug got to sleep on Mom's sofa whenever an investigation took Kiran out of town.

Le pulled up a chair and offered a paper cup of coffee. "This is the Kona that Jefferson sent us. We're supposed to celebrate, though to tell the truth, I'd rather forget it all."

Kiran took a sip. "Same."

The two of them sat quietly, turning over memories. The Bureau had lost

CHAPTER 25

agents, the SPD had lost officers. The survivors wanted simultaneously to remember the fallen forever and scrape the horror of the whole experience from their brains. If only Le knew how much he, and the rest of the department, had already forgotten.

Kiran set the fancy coffee down. The Kona was okay, but nothing like drinking from Gonzales' stainless-steel thermos. Late at night, when everything was quiet, she still felt the tingle of the Grail's magic in her bones and wondered if it was the only thing keeping her sane.

Her dreams of missing children had stopped, but the nightmares that replaced them were no better. When she closed her eyes and finally drifted off, she was often lost in a demon's mind, lounging on a fiery chair in the Abyss. At times, she woke with a start, speaking a language spoken only in Hell. She considered seeing a therapist, but they would consider her beyond delusional, and who could blame them? At least if she ever *did* visit Hell, she would understand the lingo. She rubbed at her forehead. The Grail might have saved her, but it hadn't prevented the scars.

Le put down his coffee. "You're even more distracted than usual, Kiran. Hard to forget going up against those cultists with just Reese and Gonzales, hey? You don't have to talk about it, but I was here for all of it. I get it."

Kiran did *not* say, "No, you don't, Henry. You've forgotten every damn thing that matters." But she thought it for the thousandth time. Everyone believed that a rookie FBI agent and two SPD detectives took down the cult and rescued the kids alone. It wasn't a cover up; they'd somehow forgotten the monster with the tattered coat and the iron rod. Krol, Herod, a slew of demons coughing fire, all of it had faded from their memories like a bad dream.

"Thanks, Henry. I know you're always there to listen," were the words that came out instead. "Sometimes I just remember a hard moment, and wonder, you know?" What she wondered about was the Ghost. What was he doing in a world full of nothing, all alone? She fingered the silver fishhook hanging around her neck.

"Anatol used to do that same thing, whenever he was worried. The two of you were not so different."

"Anatol was a grouch."

"Case in point." The phone rang and Le answered it. He sighed and raised both eyebrows. He held his hand over the receiver before he spoke. "You've got a problem."

Kiran opened a pack of clove gum. "What kind of problem?"

Le handed her the phone. "Reese. See if you can understand him."

Kiran put the receiver to her ear. "Reese, I told you I don't want to go to that lousy diner again. I get flashbacks and it's a blatantly cheap date."

"Kiran." She imagined Reese running his zipper up and down on his leather jacket. "I'm worried about Gonzo."

Kiran held her breath and waited. In the last few months strange things had been happening to Enrique and Reese. Someone had been calling Reese repeatedly and hanging up, and they hadn't been able to trace the call. Thieves had ransacked Gonzales' apartment and taken only his keepsakes from Mexico. Gonzales hadn't been himself ever since.

"He's been wandering around the city. Says he's not sure what he's looking for. He'll tell me when he finds it." There was a long pause. "I'm not sure where he is."

"He used that many words?"

"Of course, not." She heard Reese thinking on the other end. "We're the only ones left who remember, Kiran. It's like it never happened. Gonzo tried to tell the Chief about it, and they made him take a psych eval. If I hadn't made him lie, they'd have hospitalized him. He wonders if he's the one who's lost it. He carries around that thermos, fills it with soup and whatnot, but it stays soup or whatever. Look, maybe we should have stayed with the SPD. Going private with Enrique was a dream, but he's lost his focus. Maybe you could talk to him?"

Kiran started on two more pieces of gum. "Tell him my mother wants him over for dinner tomorrow. He won't miss a meal at her house. I'll be there."

"I'd tell him if I could find him. He's left his phone behind. I've looked everywhere. When I can't find him, it's a problem."

Now she was worried. "I'll take a look."

"Thanks, K-Dog." Reese sucked at coming up with nicknames.

CHAPTER 25

She handed the phone back to Le. "I'm leaving early. There's something I have to do."

Le held up a hand. "But we've got the Remembrance Thing. Jefferson will be here. The mayor is supposed to stop by."

"Then goddamn represent me, Henry. Please."

"Represent? But..." Le let out a big breath. "You got it. I'll represent the hell out of you. Do what you've got to do, K-Dog." Henry Le didn't ask questions because he was the best of agents and the best of people.

"Don't ever repeat one of Reese's dumb nicknames again or I'll tell my mother."

Henry's look of fear was all the evidence she needed that the evil nickname K-Dog would not be heard in the office again.

Kiran grabbed her coat. On the way out she passed a three-foot long framed picture of Seattle's mayor, grasping her sweaty hand. Reese and Gonzales stood at her side dressed in full regalia. Reese was holding Little Juan in his arms. The kid was stretching out his arm to shake the mayor's hand next while the families of the other kids waited in the background. She hated that picture. It forced her to remember who wasn't there and, in her mind, she filled him in every time. He'd have that immense bag over his shoulder with the "This is a total waste of time" look on his face. Or possibly the "If anyone speaks to me, I'm going to totally murder them" look, which were hard to differentiate unless you were used to him. The FBI had found a reasonable explanation for the whole nightmare. It wasn't hard to do, there were plenty of cultists to blame. With Krol's influence over them gone, the cultists were utterly confused about what happened. It wasn't hard to get them to agree to take the blame for reduced sentences.

And despite the promotion, things at the department were not going smoothly. In the past month there had been three inquiries from Washington asking for details about her activities. The higher ups were watching and that only happened if they were upset about something or looking for someone to blame. She'd have to find out what was going on before everything went to hell, but she'd worry about all that after she found Gonzales.

Kiran stepped into the rain, letting her feet take her where they would, while she chewed her way through another pack of gum. She ran her fingers over the mark on her forearm. Reese would never have asked her if he wasn't beyond worried, and if Reese couldn't find Enrique, there was only one way. Finding Gonzales shouldn't be hard for her now. Magic had faded in the months since she sent the Ghost back and Herod with him. The other members of the trinity were almost all that was left of magic in the city. She knew it shouldn't be hard, but ... She reached for the power.

And the world flashed dull silver, sharp outlines painted with mercury and moon. The mark pulsed on her skin, a living thing, thirsty to be alive. She calmed her breathing and sent the power out like fine black threads across the city searching for anything touched with enchantment. The mark beat against her skin like a pulse, begging her to draw deeper, to search people's minds, to stretch into other worlds where it promised to show her all that she desired. Demonic words fought a battle for command of her tongue as the magic awakened. Nausea hit her and the ground spun.

But she'd found who she wanted. She beat back the garbled speech threatening to escape her lips and let the power go. Most of the dizziness passed as she rubbed at her temple and kept walking. Damn. That shouldn't have been hard, but the Ghost had been right, throwing herself into a demon's mind was a death sentence she'd barely escaped. Now, the mark seemed to be waiting for her to make her next mistake.

She walked across half of downtown and picked up a hot sandwich before she arrived at her destination. A sign with a bright red triangle over a blue circle read, 'The One and Only Underground Tour – Tickets Here.' She walked past the line to the narrow metal steps recently installed.

A yellow-hatted ticket seller called out to her, "Ma'am, line's over here for tickets. You've gotta pay to go down." He pointed at the sign, then smiled, and gestured at the ticket booth.

Kiran flashed her badge and shot him a look. It wasn't as good as one of the Ghost's glares of doom, but it got the message across. He returned to pointing at the sign and selling tickets. She clanked down the stairs before the first tour group of the day descended and found herself back in a world full of low wattage yellow lights and red brick interspaced with wooden beams

CHAPTER 25

and darkness. She felt it close about her like the grave. Sweat was already running down the back of her neck.

She traversed a set of low wooden stairs, a narrow ramp across a section of the tunnels clearly marked, 'Do Not Enter.' She turned an unlit corner into darkness.

"Thought you might like lunch." Kiran held out the sandwich she'd picked up on the way.

Gonzales was sitting on the floor with his back against the wall at a dead-end section of the tunnel. He was wearing a new maroon shirt a shade darker than his usual. He looked up and took the sandwich. He could never resist a Reuben.

She sent a text off to Reese then slid down next to Gonzales. The brick wall felt cool against her back.

"These tunnels used to extend much farther." Gonzales took a bite of the sandwich. "Now it's all dead ends. There can't be more than a few hundred yards in any direction, then the ceiling comes down. Didn't we walk for hours? Or was it days down here?"

"It was a long-ass time," Kiran said. "Could I have the pickle?"

Gonzales handed her the giant dill pickle. He unscrewed his thermos and took a drink. "Just water this time. Didn't feel like trying coffee again."

Kiran accepted the thermos and took a sip. Water alright. Rather stale too.

"Why are we the only ones who remember, Kiran? I mean was it some weird drug trip we were on, or what?"

Kiran held up her forearm and the mark shone blacker than any darkness the tunnels could muster. "I don't remember ever getting a tattoo. This cursed thing jumped from Anatol to me. I stare at it every day as proof that it wasn't all a dream." She let her sleeve cover the black mark again. "How did you get down here? Hustled down those stairs so fast the ticket guy didn't notice? Leaped over that planking back there and never felt one click in your knee? The speed wasn't there before, Enrique."

Gonzales fingered his rosary beads. "I see visions of past lives and wonder if I'm losing it. I never told you this, but before we left the force, some punk pulled a gun on Reese and me. Said he would shoot us if we didn't back off.

Before I could think I stepped in and grabbed his arm. Squeezed so hard he dropped the gun."

"And..."

"That's not the training. That was Enkidu, charging in to protect his best friend. You know, the legend says he was shaped out of clay by the god Anu. He was a wild man. It was hell to civilize him enough to enter society. He fought like a maniac at Gilgamesh's side. That's not me, Kiran. I know I look big and rough, but I'm not. You know I'm not."

"You're a damned stuffed penguin, Enrique."

Gonzales laughed. "A Mexican penguin, if they've got those."

Kiran took a bite of the pickle. "Well, my mother didn't believe anything I tried to tell her about the Ghost either. I think she's even forgotten I mentioned it. But she wouldn't bat an eye at your story. She'd say you have a lot more lives that you've forgotten about and will have a lot more to come. It's that reincarnation thing. No big deal. You know, you're invited over to her house for dinner tomorrow? We're all coming."

Gonzales finished his first half of the sandwich and wrapped up the rest. "Excelente." The look of worry on his face had eased off. He still looked exhausted, but it was an improvement.

A creaking on the stairs caught their attention. The footsteps were headed in their direction.

"First tour of the day. They'll break up our lunch."

"No. I bet we'll get a buffet out of it." This close she didn't need to reach out to the power of the mark. She could tell who it was simply by closing her eyes.

Reese walked into the tunnel and shook his head in mock disappointment. He had his black jacket zipped up and the blue guitar on his back. He tapped his chest. "This hurts, my people. Pickles and sandwiches and I wasn't invited?" He held out a cardboard container and plastic forks. "Chicken biryani from the best truck in town. This is *the* stuff."

Gonzales grabbed a fork. "Word." Reese slid to the ground on the other side of the tunnel. Gonzales handed him the other half of his Reuben.

Kiran grabbed a fork. "I don't think you want what's left of this pickle." She

CHAPTER 25

popped the last bit in her mouth.

Reese smiled. "Nah, I'm straight." He kicked out his legs and his shoes pressed against theirs. He took a bite of the sandwich and smiled. "I'm happy with what I've got."

* * *

Later that night, Kiran unlocked the front door of her house and let Spartacus in through the big red door. Three thousand square feet, four bedrooms, in a quiet Seattle neighborhood, and all hers. It was hard to believe. Anatol had left it to her in his will along with everything that came with it, including Spartacus. She supposed it was a fair trade for having to deal with the Ghost and demon's voices in her head for the rest of her life. She looked around the house: high-beamed ceilings and endless nooks to curl up and read in. Maybe she got the better part of the deal, even with demon's voices.

Spartacus finished his food and began snoring, which was her signal. As she got up, his lip curled back, and his paws began running through the air. She wondered whether he was reliving his fight with the demon or imagining other dangers he felt it was his duty to protect her from. Kiran rubbed his head until he calmed down then headed down a long hallway that ended in a glass-paneled door. She didn't remember leaving the door open.

She poked her head around the corner, and, of course, the library was empty. She took a deep breath and let it go. Maybe she should see that therapist. This place, thank God, was a therapy of its own.

Three walls of books from floor to ceiling, thick carpet, and the most comfortable recliner she'd ever imagined made this the best place in the house. She eased into the recliner and felt her muscles relax. She reached over to an oak reading table and gently lifted her old copy of *The Collected Stories of Sherlock Holmes*. A neat bullet hole graced the front cover, and a ragged exit wound marred the back, but she'd found most of the pages and glued them in. The pages were ragged and uneven; fiction wounded by the events of reality. That was the price of becoming a weapon thrown at a demon.

Reading around the holes in the stories wasn't hard, she had most of them memorized already. Her father would probably find Reese's bullet wound fitting. Holmes was always in the midst of danger. She ran her hand over the cover then set the book back down and examined the shelves.

Anatol had never shown her this place while he was alive, and she understood why. Not just because it was the best place in the world to be alone and who would want to be bothered here, but because of what it contained. Amongst the first edition bound volumes she'd found Conan Doyle, Twain, and Agatha Christie. Every major religious book was here, most of them filled with Anatol's notes and thoughts about how a particular line might relate to the Ghost. She'd poured over his journals, detailing the three times he'd called on the Ghost over the last twenty years and his search for who the Ghost might be. She'd cried when she'd read of the deaths of the other two members of the trinity who'd helped Anatol and felt his torment, worrying what he would do if the need rose to call the Ghost again.

Amongst the pages of Anatol's journal she'd found a letter written in a woman's hand by someone she could only assume had been one of the two of them. A few lines had stayed with her.

What if we had it all wrong, Anatol? What if the psalm referred to the Holy Spirit, after all, and not the monster we so fear? Are we all tools of justice in the end, imperfect and wounded, unforgiven and unredeemable? Are we three soldiers, dragged along for this painful purpose, the true Tools of the Ghost? Or is every human striving for justice one of the tools without number, all of us implements of the Ghost in the end?

She'd stayed up many nights wondering if the woman who wrote those lines ever came to a conclusion about what it all meant. What was Kiran's role in all this meant to be?

But none of that was why she was here tonight. Who the Ghost was in some past life was no longer a mystery. She rose from the chair and pulled a book down from the shelf, its crumbling brown spine familiar to her touch. She flipped it open and started reading. Where the hell he was and how she might get him out was her problem now. We might forge the chains we wear in our lives, might build the locks that keep us confined, but if we did, we

CHAPTER 25

could damn well forge a set of keys to break out too. And somewhere in here there had to be a clue on where she could find her father.

She read until the streetlamps went out, putting back one volume and reaching for another, until the moon had passed through much of the sky. She worked her way through three packs of clove gum and had almost decided to sleep for the night when she noticed a book on one of the high shelves she had never noticed. She needed to use the ladder to take it down. An hour later and she knew she'd found something special. She had no idea how she could have missed this volume. There on the last torn page was written, "I am the door of the sheep, knock and the door shall be opened, pass through and never return the same way." A script followed, written in no language she'd ever seen before, yet somehow, she understood. It was a language of magic, of demons, and angels, rakshasas, and gods who had nothing better to do than mess around with reality.

Kiran ran a hand through her hair, half asleep already, and mouthed the words, with no idea what they meant or what might happen.

Books tumbled from the shelves, and she jumped out of the chair. The temperature dropped and she shivered. She swore under her breath, knowing she wasn't ready for whatever was happening.

When she turned, she found a wooden door standing in the middle of the room where no door had a right to be, and she hated it already. The last thing she needed was some stupid door to another dimension where she'd end up in Narnia with witches offering her Turkish Delight. Turkish Delight got stuck in her teeth, and she sure as hell didn't need to end up in Oz or down some rabbit hole. Doors were always bad.

Unless this one led to the Ghost. Or her father. She sent a text to Reese, and another to Gonzales. They'd need to come and get Spartacus. It was time to make some keys.

* * *

Ripples ran across the silver lake in the Realm of Shadows, where Herod no longer ruled, and the shadows were left to their own dark devices. The shadows took notice of the disturbance for nothing could live within the lake that was filled with the tears of endless nightmares, tears that pressed upon any intruder with the weight of a mountain.

The ripples widened and from below the surface a bearded figure emerged. Silver tears ran across its shoulders as it rose from the waters, ran down its broad chest and over its hunchbacked form as it defied the weight of nightmares and survived. The figure stood upon the waters of the lake as only the King of the Land of Shadows had a right to do and shook itself like a dog, shedding droplets into the darkness.

The hunched giant trod across the surface of the lake until he reached the shore where the black spire soared into the darkness and endless clouds that covered the lake. He took up the white robe and golden scepter that had fallen upon its shores. He lowered the robe onto his shoulders and lifted the scepter high. The shadows took notice and bowed before their new lord and the black spire, the castle of the Lord of Shadows, shone in the darkness.

The new king entered his home and candles blazed to life as he passed, throwing his long shadow upon the lake. The Lords of Hell had been well pleased with the new king and had given him his reward. No champion of theirs had truly harmed the Ghost in over two thousand years and there was no one else in the universe they wished to be harmed more. Everything Krol had promised had come to pass and his new promises had entranced even the Lords of Hell, who were in the business of making promises to enchant and entrap.

Much to Krol's delight, Herod's domain was now his and with it came the power to do all that was necessary. Krol smiled until his face hurt with delicious pain and readied himself for what was to come.

* * *

The Archangel Michael leaned over the edge of a high cliff with his chin resting in his right hand, overlooking an endless night sea. The stars shone down on him, wondering what thoughts ran through his mind while the

CHAPTER 25

crescent moon looked on with a worried expression.

Angels feel no emotion, have no desires, no doubts, no fears. Theirs is a realm of transcendence and service to a purpose that mortal minds cannot fathom. Frustration, revenge, anger—all these are lesser emotions that plague only lesser beings.

Michael's eyes were mother of pearl, his wings were pure light gifted from the moon herself when she was born. He was the highest of Archangels in the host of angels. A thousand angels across the worlds waited on his every command. This had been his honor for all time. But he gave no orders, provided no direction.

In his right hand he held a gray stone he had ripped from the ledge. He held it before him and closed his hand over it as he thought the thoughts only an immortal could fathom. The Archangel was beyond emotion, beyond sadness, beyond desire. There could be no doubt.

Yet, as he gazed across the night sea, the Archangel Michael's eyes burned pearlescent white and the stone in his hand that had withstood an eon crumbled as if it were nothing. A tremor coursed through the mountain and the stars dimmed in the sky above. The Archangel raised his head to the moon and the moon hid herself behind a curtain of clouds. Michael raised his hand and from between his fingers ran fine grains of black sand that fell as a river of dust to the sea.

The End

Wait, don't forget your free stuff!

After you read this, be sure to download your free copy of the thrilling prequel **The Fist of the Ghost** at hemantnayak.com as well as the short story **The Tale of the Ghost.** Join my newsletter, and tell me what you liked and want to see more of! Get updates on new releases and other fun stuff. (and if you loved TOOLS, please leave a review! Thanks! Word.)

Printed in Great Britain
by Amazon